BAD NEWS

"I thought you were dead, Trace," the insurance executive named Marks said. "I didn't hear from you and I didn't get any obscene mail and no one was calling my secretaries perverts. I didn't have any weirdos calling on my private line with disgusting propositions. No strip-a-gram belly dancers at the office. My life has just been peaceful and quiet. Naturally, I thought you were dead. It was logical, right? Jesus, I wish you were dead."

Trace settled back in the chair where Marks had finally found him. Trace knew what was coming next. Marks was going to offer him a job. And the only kind of job Marks would offer him would be one too nasty for anyone else to handle.

That wasn't the worst part, though.

The worst part was that Trace knew he would take it. . . .

TRACE

Ø

The Best in Fiction from SIGNET

TRACE

WARREN MURPHY

A SIGNET BOOK
NEW AMERICAN LIBRARY
TIMES MIRROR

PUBLISHED BY
THE NEW AMERICAN LIBRARY
OF CANADA LIMITED

PUBLISHER'S NOTE

This novel is a work of fiction. Names, characters, places, and incidents either are the product of the author's imagination or are used fictitiously, and any resemblance to actual persons, living or dead, events, or locales is entirely coincidental.

NAL BOOKS ARE AVAILABLE AT QUANTITY DISCOUNTS
WHEN USED TO PROMOTE PRODUCTS OR SERVICES.
FOR INFORMATION PLEASE WRITE TO PREMIUM MARKETING DIVISION,
THE NEW AMERICAN LIBRARY, INC., 1633 BROADWAY,
NEW YORK, NEW YORK 10019.

Copyright © 1983 by Warren B. Murphy

FIRST PRINTING, OCTOBER, 1983

2 3 4 5 6 7 8 9

SIGNET TRADEMARK REG. U.S. PAT. OFF. AND FOREIGN COUNTRIES
REGISTERED TRADEMARK - MARCA REGISTRADA
HECHO EN WINNIPEG, CANADA

SIGNET, SIGNET CLASSIC, MENTOR, PLUME, MERIDIAN and NAL BOOKS are published in Canada by The New American Library of Canada, Limited, Scarborough, Ontario

PRINTED IN CANADA
COVER PRINTED IN U.S.A.

With love, for P. S.,
only happy endings.

Frederick Plesser, 67, of 4254½ Sellers St., Harmon Hills, died yesterday at Meadow Vista Sanatorium, after a long illness. Cause of death was given as a heart ailment.

Mr. Plesser, a longtime auto-assembly worker, is survived by his wife, Gertrude (née Koople), and a daughter, Jasmine.

Funeral arrangements will be made today.

1

Walter Marks, the vice-president for claims of the Garrison Fidelity Insurance Company, was wearing a charcoal-gray pinstripe suit and a fedora. His jacket and trousers were so neatly pressed that it looked as if the creases had been sewn into them. The snap-brim hat was also sharply pressed, its peak sort of resembling the prow of an ocean liner.

If Marks wore the hat in the hope that it made him seem taller, he had failed, because it managed only to make him look like a five-foot-tall man in a hat too big for him.

He stopped just inside the door of the cocktail lounge, his ears bombarded by the din, and looked around, the distaste obvious in his scowling face. Then he worked his way toward the crowded bar and waited for the bartender to come to him. He waited three minutes before waving to get the young man's attention.

When the bartender came, Marks asked him something, but because he leaned back, away from the bartender when talking to him, the young man did not hear him clearly and said, "Who?"

Marks repeated the name. "Devlin Tracy."

"Oh. Trace. Back there." The bartender pointed toward a cluster of small tables in the rear of the room and turned back to his customers.

Marks rudely pushed his way through the press of customers at the bar and walked to the table where he saw

Trace, a very tall, blond man, sitting at a table writing something on a cocktail napkin with a red Flair pen.

Marks put his hat on an empty seat, smoothed down his oiled hair, then sat at the table opposite Tracy.

"Shhh, ' Trace said without looking up.

Marks looked but could discern nothing very impressive on the cocktail napkin. Just a few letters. He waited a moment, then cleared his throat.

"Shhhhh," Trace said again. He still had not looked up.

"I thought you were dead," Marks said. "I didn't hear from you and I didn't get any obscene mail and no one was calling my secretaries perverts. I didn't have any fags calling me on my private line with disgusting propositions. No Strip-O-Gram belly dancers at the office. My life has just been peaceful and quiet. Naturally, I thought you were dead. Why shouldn't I think you were dead? It was logical, right? Jesus, I wish you were dead."

Trace, a once-in-a-while investigator of claims for Garrison Fidelity, still did not look up as he answered. "Yeah, dead," he said. "Right. Wish I was dead. When I'm rich and famous, you won't wish that. You'll be telling people you knew me when. You'll say, 'Oh, yes, Devlin Tracy. Why, sure, he's a friend of mine. 'Course, now that he's rich and famous, he doesn't call me much anymore. Busy, I guess. But we couldn't be closer.' " He still hadn't looked up and he was mumbling.

"What the hell is it you're scribbling there?" Marks asked.

Tracy pushed the cocktail napkin across the table. On it was neatly printed, in large block letters:

O T U A

Marks looked at it, then at the tall blond man, whose face showed his invincible self-satisfaction.

"Okay, Trace, I surrender. Please tell me. What the hell is O-T-U-A?"

"Hah," Trace said triumphantly. "You know, Groucho, it's a mark of little minds that even when the light of discovery is shining right on them, they can't see it."

"I can see it, I can see it. I see O-T-U-A. What the hell is it?"

"This is only the first step," Trace said. "From here we conquer India. Like a mighty ocean, rolling across the world, country by country falling before our power. Kill. Kill. Kill. Kill. Kill for the love of Kali."

"Trace, you're yelling." Marks looked around nervously, but no one seemed to notice. At the bar, men were still talking to women and women were talking to one another.

"I'm sorry. I always get that way whenever I see *Gunga Din* on television. It's my favorite movie. It's why I stay up late. It's always on at four in the morning. I'll tell you what, Groucho. I'll sell you half-interest in what's on that napkin. For, say, twenty thousand dollars, you can get in on the ground floor. That'd be best for you actually, since you're so small. Trying to get in on the second floor might be difficult."

"Cut the wise-ass and don't call me Groucho anymore. What is O-T-U-A?"

"You ever drive a car down the street and you're minding your business and then an ambulance drives up behind you?" Trace asked.

"I suppose so," Marks said suspiciously.

"You know how they have a sign on the front that says Ambulance?"

"Yeah, sure. What the hell are you talking about?"

"Well, the only reason you can read that sign on the ambulance is because it's lettered backwards, and when you see it in your mirror, it's frontwards."

"I don't believe I'm doing this," Marks said. "I fly three thousand miles to find you in this sink and we're talking about signs on ambulances."

"And then whoever's driving sees the ambulance sign and they pull over," Trace said.

Walters Marks shrugged.

"Well, I think everybody ought to have one. This is the first one. A prototype. Imagine it, Groucho, you're in on the design of the prototype. Favored inside position. You'll make millions. It's the wave of the future."

"How do I make millions?"

"See, you think that napkin you're holding says O-T-U-A. But it doesn't. It says auto backwards. If you mount that on the front of your car, then you sneak up on some other car and he sees you in the mirror, and you're going to have this big auto sign on your car and he'll pull right over. We can make them for everybody. I tried R-A-C first for car, but those letters won't reverse in a mirror without special printing, so O-T-U-A works just perfect. When you give me some development money, we can make them up, all kinds of them. Pizza for pizza trucks. Drunk Driver. I like a sign that says Drunk Driver backwards. You know how you kind of get out of the way when you see one of those cars with the big billboard, Student Driver. Or when you see M.D. plates, 'cause doctors are all nuts. Imagine how people will move when you come roaring up at them from behind and you've got Drunk Driver written backwards on your grille. I tell you, Groucho, this can make us. The possibilities are endless. We can use magnetic signs that just stick on front. Change the signs to fit your mood. Drunk Driver. Auto-out-of-Control. Get-the-Fuck-out-of-My-Way. That would really be a good one. I-Can't-Drive. That would work too. People will be sitting on the side of the road, idling their engines, wasting gas, and you'll be zipping by at seventy nine miles an hour. Everybody'll be afraid of you. Why should ambulance drivers have all the luck? Maybe we can get you one that says Small-but-Powerful. Would you like that? Maybe Insurance-Man? Or

V-I-P? This is a wonderful idea and all I need is twenty thousand dollars from you."

"So I can write auto backwards on my car? I think I'll pass," Marks said.

Trace looked stunned by the rejection. "You sure?"

"I'm sure."

"All right but you're missing out," Trace said. "I hope you're a big-enough man to come to me someday and admit you were wrong."

"Somehow, I don't think it'll be one of my pressing worries for years to come," Marks said. "And speaking of pressing worries—"

"You're going to talk business, aren't you?" Trace said. "I'm in the middle of the most intensely creative few minutes of my life and you're going to want to talk about some freaking insurance policy. Groucho, you will always be a philistine. I ask only one thing from you."

"What's that?"

"Don't breathe a word of this to anybody. Not until I get all the patent and copyright protections. There's sharks out there in the world."

"You have my word," Marks said. "I'll never repeat this to anyone. Now we will talk business."

Marks pushed the table napkin across the table to Trace, who folded it neatly, sighed, and put it into the breast pocket of his tan cashmere jacket. He waved to the waiter and circled his finger, indicating another round of drinks.

"All right," he said. "You have my undivided attention."

"Read this." Marks handed him a small newspaper clipping and Trace skimmed it quickly.

"I didn't know this Frederick Plesser," he said. "How'd the family take it?"

"Trace, dammit, I don't know how the family took it and I know you didn't know him and I don't give a shit. Will you just listen?"

"Speak."

13

"This Plesser was insured by us. A hundred-thousand-dollar company policy. When it came time to pay up, we found out that just before he died, he changed his beneficiary. It used to be his wife. Instead, he made his beneficiary somebody . . ." Marks pulled a sheet of paper from his inside pocket. "He left his money to Dr. George Matteson. He's the director of this Meadow Vista Sanatorium. So, naturally, Plesser's family is going nuts, but we have to pay the beneficiary, right?"

"Good for you. Do your duty. What's the paper?" Trace asked.

"It's a letter he wrote us changing his beneficiary."

Trace took it from Marks and read it. In a tight, pinched handwriting, it read: "I am Frederick Plesser and your company has an insurance policy on me for a hundred thousand dollars. I want to change my beneficiary from my wife, Gertrude, to Dr. George Matteson, director of the Meadow Vista Sanatorium. Make this effective immediately."

The letter was signed by Plesser and on two lines under his name were the names of two witnesses, Barbara Darling, M.D., and Thelma Simons, R.N.

Trace looked up and Marks said, "Now, here's where you come in. Mr. Swenson has a friend named Mitchell Carey who lives in Harmon Hills. That's where this Plesser lived."

"Time out," Trace said sharply. "Here comes the waiter. I don't want him to overhear any of this important stuff. And don't mention my signs for cars."

The waiter set a glass of vodka in front of Trace. He looked at Marks questioningly, but the small man waved him off.

After the waiter left, Marks said, "Mr. Swenson has a friend, Mitchell Carey. Anyway, he had a stroke and now he's in Meadow Vista."

Trace crossed himself when he heard the name of Rob-

14

ert Swenson, the president of the Garrison Fidelity Insurance Company. Marks ignored him.

"Anyway, the Carey family got wind of this Plesser thing, about leaving his money to the sanatorium, and now they're worried that maybe somehow this Dr. Matteson can get Carey to leave all his money to the sanatorium, if he dies."

"Has this Carey got money?" Trace asked.

"Yeah. He's very rich."

"Think he'd want to give me twenty thousand for these car signs?" Trace asked.

"Ask him. So Mr. Swenson wants you to look into it."

"Look into what?"

"This whole thing. Why Plesser left the sanatorium the money. You know we're going to wind up in court over that. And make sure nobody's brainwashing this Mr. Carey to get his money. Stuff like that."

"You say that this Carey is Bob Swenson's friend?"

"Yeah. That's the way I get it," Marks said.

"So this is more personal than business."

"I suppose so."

"Why didn't Bob call me himself?" Trace asked.

"I knew you were going to ask that," Marks said. "He tried to. He called you for three days. All he kept getting was your tape machine. You're some hell of an investigator. Don't you ever answer your calls?"

"I was getting around to it. Anyway, I'm not really an investigator. I'm more of a free spirit, soaring mightily over the workaday world."

"You're drunk enough most of the time to soar," Marks said. "Anyway, Mr. Swenson had to go to Europe for a convention, so he told me to get you. That's why I came here, all this way to sit in this degenerate bar and watch you doodle."

Trace shook his head. "I don't want to go to New Jersey."

15

"Why not?"

"My ex-wife lives in New Jersey. There's a price on my head in that state. If she finds out that I'm there . . . or even worse, if What's-his-name and the girl find out I'm there, my life's not worth a plugged nickel."

"Mr. Swenson said this was very important to him," Marks said smugly. "Should I tell him you turned it down because you're afraid of your ex-wife and kids?"

"Why didn't you send one of your other people? You've got all those people who work for you. Some of them aren't wanted in New Jersey. They could go right in and right out, just like it was part of the United States and nobody would even mind. Why didn't you send one of them?"

"I suggested that to Mr. Swenson, but it seems he has this inflated idea of your ability. He wanted you to go."

"It's tough on me, being Bob Swenson's friend," Trace said, sighing.

"It's tougher on me," Marks said.

"I could go to Israel, you know," Trace said brightly. "My mother's Jewish. I'm allowed in Israel."

"Go to New Jersey," Marks said.

The luxury condominium on the Las Vegas Strip was empty when Trace returned there, and he thought how nice it would be to spend a quiet evening alone.

He spent a great deal of time looking through his phonograph records, selecting the discs for the evening program. He narrowed the choices down to a half-dozen and put them all on the phonograph spindle, then dimmed the lights and poured himself a water tumbler of vodka from the bottle of Finlandia he kept in the refrigerator's freezer compartment.

He kicked off his loafers and was about to start the phonograph when he noticed he had only a few cigarettes left. He called the doorman to bring him up three packs.

Trace gave him six dollars, which both he and the doorman thought was a good deal because Trace was always running out of cigarettes and the doorman bought them by the carton and kept them under the desk inside the front door. The doorman made a profit on the sale, and by not being forced to go out, when he would probably spend the night expensively in a bar, Trace figured he saved money, too. It was a good world, he decided, when one hand washed the other and both hands got clean.

Trace started the stereo and sat on the couch, sipping from his drink, puffing a cigarette. He felt very civilized.

Pavarotti sang the "Ingemisco" from Verdi's *Requiem*.

Yes, very civilized. Then Pavarotti sang "O Mes Amis" from Donizetti's *Daughter of the Regiment*. He hit nine high Cs, which Trace assured himself was wonderful because most people, himself included, couldn't hit even one without first having their private parts caught in a dresser drawer.

Very, very pleasant. A civilized evening at home.

Then two records dropped at once, one under the phonograph stylus and the other atop the tone arm, and the phonograph began to screech.

Trace ran over and pressed the stereo's reject button, but it didn't work and he remembered he had been planning to have it fixed. By the time he got the top record back into place, the lower record had been scarred beyond recognition.

As long as he was up, he decided he would freshen his drink. He did and sat back down on the couch, but his cigarette lighter ran dry. He couldn't find a match anywhere in the apartment so he lit the cigarette from a burner on the gas stove.

He didn't mind doing this since he had perfected the technique of approaching the burner from a low level with head turned to the side. This protected hair and eyebrows. The only problem with using the stove was that he couldn't take it into the bedroom with him. What would he do later when he wanted to smoke in bed? He couldn't very well get up every time and go to the gas stove to light his cigarette.

In a kitchen cabinet, he found one of the Yahrzeit candles that his mother kept hiding in the apartment on her visits to Las Vegas. In some forlorn effort to reinstill religious zeal in him, she kept leaving behind religious artifacts, so many of them that he felt sometimes as if he were living in an archaeological dig. The last trip, she had hidden a beaded yarmulke in his dresser drawer. He thought that he had everything he needed to sit Shiva except a corpse. His father had retaliated by hiding a crucifix in the bread drawer.

Trace lit the little squat religious candle and put it on the coffee table in the living room. Then, cigarette lit, full glass of vodka in hand, feet up on the table, stereo humming along impeccably with the Weavers singing their greatest hits, he sat back to enjoy a civilized evening at home.

Two minutes later, during "My Darling Clementine," he snuffed out his cigarette. During "Fili-me-oo-ree-ay," he put down his empty glass. Another minute and he was sleeping soundly.

He slept until 2 A.M., when he got up, undressed, and got into bed.

He woke up two hours later when Chico came into the room. In the brittle illumination from the bathroom light Trace could see she was wearing a powder-blue evening gown. In silhouette, her long shiny black hair framed her face like an Egyptian queen's headdress.

Trace hissed, "Climb right in here. The bitch is out tonight."

"Oh, you're awake."

"Of course I'm awake. I couldn't sleep a wink all night, worrying about you. I thought you might be dead, lying drowned somewhere in a water bed that cracked under the strain."

"I had business," the young Oriental woman said. She still stood in the doorway, backlighted.

"You've had business every night this week," Trace said.

"It's that season," she said blandly.

"Yeah. Open season."

"Go to sleep. I want to take my makeup off."

"You don't wear makeup," he said.

"This guy liked makeup, so I wore makeup." She walked into the bathroom and closed the door.

Trace went into the kitchen, lit another cigarette, and brought it into the bedroom. He was smoking a cigarette when she came out of the bathroom, naked, ten minutes later and slid under the covers on the other side of the bed.

"You know, I've about had it with you," she said.

"And with everybody else," Trace said sourly.

She rolled over on her stomach and propped herself up on her elbows. With both hands, she grabbed his right forearm and squeezed.

"Listen to me," she snapped. "I am a part-time hooker. What do you want from me? You want to marry me? Go ahead. Propose. Trace, what the hell *do* you want from me?"

"I want you home when the stereo breaks and I don't know how to fix it," he said.

She sighed, released his arm, and rolled back onto her own side of the bed.

"Go to sleep," she said.

2

When Trace woke up, he heard Chico in the kitchen cooking breakfast. He waited in the bathroom for a few minutes, trying to decide whether or not to throw up. He didn't, and when he came into the kitchen, Chico had just set the table and was portioning out the food. Onto Trace's plate went one sausage link and one pancake. There was a giant mug of black coffee next to his plate.

On Chico's plate went seven pancakes and the remainder of the pound of sausage. She also had a twelve-ounce tumbler filled with fresh-squeezed orange juice. And toast. And coffee.

Trace sat down and said, "I can't eat all this."

"Try to eat something. You have to replace all that you throw up every morning."

"I have to go to New Jersey," he said. He lit a cigarette.

"What for?"

"I don't know. Some asylum is making nuts leave them their money. Something like that. Marks was in town last night."

Chico's mouth was full of food and she nodded and mumbled thickly, "Ummmm-hummmmm."

"I'm kind of afraid of going to New Jersey," he said. "If the ex-wife finds out I'm there, I'm a dead man."

Chico said, "Ummmm-hummmm. "Hmmoww fmarhr msh mt mooo Mmmmmmphz?"

"You Oriental Sicilians are disgusting, Mangini. Please

20

dispose of that package in your mouth before you talk. Didn't you learn anything in college?''

Chico swallowed. It took three attempts to empty her mouth.

"Okay. When are you going to New Jersey?''

"I don't know. Tonight, tomorrow. I don't know,'' Trace said.

"Do you know how long it takes to get to Memphis?'' she asked.

"Memphis, Egypt, or Memphis, Tennessee?''

"Memphis, Tennessee, you asshole. Who the hell goes to Memphis, Egypt?''

"I might ask you the same thing about Memphis, Tennessee,'' Trace said. "What do you want to know?''

"How long does it take to get to Memphis?''

"From New York?''

"Yeah. Try from New York.''

"Two hours and twenty-eight minutes by air from Kennedy Airport,'' Trace said.

"I don't believe you told me that,'' Chico said.

"Why not?''

"Because people don't answer questions that way,'' she said. "You ask people how long it takes to get to Memphis and they don't tell you two hours and twenty-eight minutes. They tell you, like, oh, three hours or so, or like that. They don't say two hours and twenty-eight minutes.'' She hesitated. "You made it up, didn't you? You don't know how long it takes to get to Memphis.''

"I know,'' Trace said stubbornly. "It takes two hours and twenty-eight minutes. There's a Delta flight that leaves JFK at nine A.M. and gets into Memphis at ten-twenty-eight A.M. There's an hour time difference to Memphis. That's Memphis, Tennessee. Memphis, Egypt, I think there's a fourteen-day time difference.''

"I know I'll regret this,'' she said, "but I've really got to know how you know it's two-twenty-eight to Memphis.''

The cigarette had calmed Trace's stomach and he thought he might be able to dare a little breakfast. So he sipped his coffee and was pleased when it stayed down.

When he looked up again, Chico was staring at him. Her eyes, even without makeup, were long-lashed and darkly outlined. There was a healthy glow on the skin just above her high cheekbones and her long hair shone almost blue in the sunlight that flooded the room. She was a tiny woman, small-boned, but she had the trim conditioned body of a dancer, and Trace thought he had never seen anyone so beautiful.

"There was this woman once," he said, "and I was really in love with her. This was before you."

"You were never in love with me," Chico said. "We're roommates 'cause you don't like to sleep alone. It was me or a night-light."

"I don't like to argue during breakfast," he said, "so I'll let that pass. Anyway, this was after my divorce. Before I met you, there was this woman and I really loved her."

"What was she like?" Chico asked.

"She was as fat as a hippopotamus and she had thick hairy legs and inky dirt under her fingernails. What do you mean, what was she like? She was beautiful. She was redheaded and beautiful and funny and smart and sexy and kindhearted, and she didn't know how far it was to Memphis either. We were talking once about going to Memphis on a vacation and I said I'd drive and she said it was too far to drive and I said it wasn't and she said it had to be because it was a four-hour flight and I said it couldn't be a four-hour flight because it was less than that to Miami and Memphis wasn't as far away as Miami."

"Sounds logical so far," Chico said.

"Right," Trace said. He decided it was probably still too early for breakfast so he put his coffee cup down. "So she said I was stupid because Memphis was in a different direction than Miami and she called two airlines and those dips told her it was four hours to Memphis and she said, 'See?' So I called an airline and it was Delta and they told me two hours and twenty-eight minutes and they gave me the times and I told her and *I* said, 'See?' Well, it turned out that two airlines she called gave her the time with a stop in Atlanta, and I said if she wanted to make the flight really long, I could make it twelve hours by giving her a layover in San Diego and she didn't think that was funny and she called me an opinionated moron and left me flat. She said I had the wrong attitude."

"That's a sad story," Chico said.

"I know. I really loved her."

"Did you ever see her again?" Chico asked.

"No. I've got this vision of her flying endlessly, connecting flight after connecting flight, and never getting on a plane that stops in Memphis, Tennessee."

"I've got to go to Memphis," Chico said. "I thought maybe I'd fly east with you and then hop a plane to Memphis."

"It's two hours and twenty-eight minutes," Trace said. "Why do you want to go to Memphis, Tennessee?"

"My sister's there visiting relatives. I thought I'd go hang out with her for a while. I'm due a few days off."

"Oh," Trace said. "I didn't know you had relatives in Memphis, Tennessee."

"Will you stop saying Memphis, Tennessee, like there's a non-Tennessee alternative?" Chico snapped. "We've got relatives all over. It's a Japanese plot to conquer America from within."

"Okay," Trace said. "Why don't you book us on a plane to New York?"

Chico nodded and went back to her breakfast. Trace finished another cigarette, sipped his coffee again, stood up, and said, "Thank you for breakfast," then went inside to throw up.

When he came out of the bathroom, she was on the telephone with an airline and Trace yelled out, "Don't forget to leave yourself two hours and twenty-eight minutes to get to Memphis, Tennessee."

It was just before midnight and Trace was standing near the entrance to the Araby Casino watching Chico work. Along with all the other women blackjack dealers, she wore a harem costume with billowing gauzy pantaloons and a low-cut sequined top. She was working at a twenty-five-dollar table, and to ease the strain on her back from leaning over the table, she stood on a six-inch-high platform.

Three men were playing at her table and Trace knew immediately that they were losing, because Chico was chattering away, smiling a lot, and dealing very quickly. The rules for dealers were pretty standard from casino to casino: when the players are losing, deal fast and chatter; when they're winning, slow down the game and get them drunk.

A fat little floorman, whose ill-cut tuxedo made him look like a hungover penguin, stood alongside Chico as she dealt. Trace saw him talk to the players at the table and Chico's face flushed. She stopped talking while the floorman joked with the players, and a moment later, when her relief dealer arrived, she quickly clapped her hands together so that the overhead cameras could see that she had not stolen any chips, and walked briskly away from the table.

She had not seen Trace, but he followed her down an escalator, then pushed his way through a door that said No Admittance into the casino employees' lounge, where Chico was standing by a window overlooking the parking lot, smoking a cigarette.

She turned when she heard the door open, saw him, tried to smile, and said, "Hi, Trace."

"What's the matter?"

"That bastard."

"Around here, you'll have to be more specific," Trace said. "Which bastard?"

"That fat freak of a floorman. Ernie."

"What'd he do?" Trace asked.

"I told you about him. He's been playing grab-ass with me all week, ever since he got this job."

"Hell, you're used to that from these guys."

"I can deal with that, Trace. I told him nice, thanks but no thanks, but he just won't let up. So just now I'm dealing to those three bombthrowers and he comes over and tells them he's going to auction me off, that I put out for the highest bidder. I don't need this crap."

"What'd you say?" Trace asked.

She shrugged. "Nothing. My relief came and I got the hell out of there. He wouldn't be doing that if I'd sleep with him. I think I'm going to go back and tell him to take his job and shove it."

Trace said, "This is your last shift. You're going to go back and keep dealing like nothing happened."

"You're a big help, roomie," she said in disgust. She turned and stabbed out her cigarette, and when she looked back, Trace had gone.

Upstairs, Trace took five thousand dollars in cash from the safety-deposit box he kept at the casino cashier's. He stuffed the money into his pants pocket, then went to the cigarette shop in the hotel lobby, where he bought a pair of teardrop-shaped sunglasses. He put on the glasses, and in the men's room he wet his hair, combed it straight back, and parted it in the middle. When he arrived at Chico's table, no one was playing and the young woman stood behind the table, the four decks of cards spread out in front of her, faceup, so that potential players could see they were all there.

He sat at the seat to her far right, and when she saw

him, she said, "What the hell are you made up for? You look like Alfalfa."

"Shut up," he said softly. "You don't know me. Deal."

She shuffled the cards and Trace pulled out his big stack of hundreds and put them in front of him.

"Chips, mister?" she asked.

"No," Trace roared. "Money plays." He put a hundred-dollar bill on the table in front of him.

"Money plays, a hundred," Chico said, just loud enough to be heard by Ernie, the floorman, who walked over and stood by her side as she dealt out the first hand. Trace got a blackjack and she paid him $150 in chips as his winnings.

"Yahoo," he said thickly. "Now I got you suckers. Let it all ride." He glanced at the pudgy floorman. "Got you guys for five thousand already tonight. I'm gonna buy the casino."

"How long you been playing?" Ernie asked.

"All night. I won here and I won at the Trop and Caesar's and now I'm back and I'm gonna punish you guys good." He pulled down his teardrop-shaped sunglasses and winked at Ernie. "Unless something else comes up."

Chico dealt Trace a pair of tens, and he split them into two hands, doubling his $250 bet. He drew two more tens, stayed on those cards, and won both hands. Chico counted out five hundred more dollars in chips and put them in front of him.

"Let's keep rolling here, tootsie," Trace said. He pushed his thousand dollars in cash and chips up into the betting circle, and Chico dealt him another blackjack.

"Yahoo. Sweetie, I'll give you a dollar if you keep letting me win."

"Sorry," Chico said. "The casino gives me two if I make you lose."

"I'll give you three dollars to go home with me," Trace said.

"Did the entire regiment take up a collection to send you to town?" she asked.

"No, it's all my own. I'm a zillionaire."

Ernie was watching and Trace could tell that he was calculating that this hick in sunglasses had just won $2,500 of casino money. A big winner on Ernie's shift wouldn't look good for the new floorman.

Trace reached under his jacket, behind him, and pressed a button, as Ernie leaned over him.

"Listen," Ernie said. "The lady here's available."

Trace raised his eyebrows and slicked down his wet hair. He leaned close to Ernie.

"You mean to do the dirty thing?"

"She'll do any dirty thing you want," Ernie said. "Won't you?"

Chico just stared stonily ahead.

"You can arrange this for me?" Trace said, slurring his words to sound drunk.

"Casino policy. It'd be my pleasure for a good bettor like you." Ernie smiled. His teeth were yellow.

"Would I take care of you?" Trace asked. "Does the casino allow that?"

"Well, what they don't know won't hurt them," Ernie said.

Trace stood up. He jammed his money and his chips into his pocket and said to Ernie, "Come on down here and talk for a minute."

He walked down to a cluster of empty tables and sat down. As Ernie approached, Trace reached under his shirt and removed a small tape recorder that had been taped to his waist.

Ernie looked at the recorder in surprise as Trace took off the silly-looking sunglasses and put them in his jacket pocket.

"What's that?" Ernie said.

"Something for you to listen to, asshole."

Trace pressed a button and Ernie winced as he heard his own voice. "The lady here's available. She'll do any dirty thing you want . . . won't you?"

Ernie reached for the recorder, but Trace clapped his big hand over the fat man's pudgy fingers.

"Does the casino know you're pimping?" Trace asked.

"You're not drunk, are you?"

"No," Trace said. "I think you ought to call the shift boss."

"I'll call security is what I'm going to call," Ernie said. "Have your ass thrown out of here."

"You call them and your next call in this casino is going to cost you a dime. Get the shift boss," Trace said coldly.

Ernie turned and looked toward the island in the center of the ring of tables, but before he could say anything, a tall thin man with a deep suntan got up, walked over to them, brushed by Ernie, and threw his arms around Trace's shoulders.

"How you doing, goombah?" he asked. "What the hell's your hair like that for?"

"I'm in disguise. I'm going to break this joint," Trace said. "On your shift, too. I may just wind up getting you fired."

"If you win, nobody complains," the shift boss said. "You met Ernie?"

"Just now. We were having a nice chat," Trace said.

"Our new man," the boss said. He clapped Ernie on the shoulder. "Listen, Ernie. This is Trace. Whatever he wants in here, he gets."

Ernie gulped and nodded. "I thought he was a card counter," he said. "I was going to heave him."

"Count?" the shift boss said. "He couldn't count the change in his pocket."

"He split a pair of tens," Ernie said.

"That's nothing. I saw him once count a blackjack as

eleven and double down on it. He's the worst blackjack player in the world."

"He's winning," Ernie said.

"He always wins. Leave him alone. Last year we were nipped for a half a mill by two wise guys before Trace figured out how we were being taken. And before that— Well, forget all that. He's the owner's friend. Leave him be."

Ernie nodded and the shift boss turned to Trace, then heard his name called from across the room. "Gotta go, kid. See you later."

"Zei gezunt," Trace said.

"Thanks. Leave some money for the other players." The shift boss walked off and Trace turned back to Ernie.

"Now, Ernie, we're going to get something straight," he said.

"I didn't—"

Trace interrupted him. "I'm going to save this tape, and anytime I need to, I'll march into the owner's office and play it for him. Now you remember that and you remember this too, you cretin. You stay off Chico's case. You mouth off to her again or you embarrass her in front of anybody, and I won't just play this tape. I'll play it and then I'll shove it down your throat. Don't get her mad because that gets me mad."

"I'm . . . I'm sorry," Ernie said.

"Yeah," Trace said as he rose, shoved his tape recorder in his pocket, and walked away.

He stopped at Chico's still-empty table. "I'll wait for you at the bar," he said.

"Everything all right?" she asked.

"Everything's fine. How bad can a night be when I win two thousand dollars?"

"And you didn't tip me anything, you cheap bastard," she said.

"I'll take care of you later," Trace said.

*　　*　　*

Later, the phone in their bedroom rang and Chico snaked an arm over to the end table by the bed and lifted the receiver.

"Hello," she said, then listened for a few moments.

"Actually," she said, "I'm already having that work done." And she hung up.

Trace looked up. "Who was it?"

"An obscene call. Keep going; you've got about eight hundred dollars more to work off."

3

"I'd forgotten how much I hate to fly with you," Chico said as they waited for their bags at New York's Kennedy Airport.

"I was the model of propriety," Trace said. "I don't know what you're talking about."

"Why did you tell that stewardess you were on a strict Muslim diet?"

"Because otherwise you get codfish or chicken and I wanted lamb," Trace said.

"So you had to convince her by spreading a blanket in the aisle and salaaming toward Mecca?" Chico asked.

"I thought it might help my case. I wouldn't have tried it if I wasn't so sure that we were heading east. I just had to pray to the nose of the plane. Actually, I was praying that the pilot was sober. Pilots drink like fish."

"And why did you keep asking for magazines and then sending them back?"

"'Cause they had all those goddamn cards in them," Trace said. "I've got this new rule I live by. I'm not reading any more magazines that have postcards in them. They always fall out in your coffeecup. What's on those cards anyway? I never even look at them. If advertisers are spending money for that crap, they're getting taken."

"I hate to fly with you," Chico said.

"Well, you're not much either. You aren't really a bundle of fun at forty thousand feet."

"Because I didn't want to ball under a blanket?"

"You wouldn't even go into the bathroom with me," Trace said, then made a lunge as their luggage came roaring by on the carousel. He got Chico's three bags but missed his own and had to wait for it to come around again.

Chico called a skycap, gave him her ticket, and he wheeled her bags away.

"I've got to go," she told Trace. "You be careful." She stretched upward to kiss him on the lips. For a moment, he thought about putting his arms about her and hugging her, but instead he just pecked at her mouth.

"Where can I reach you?" he asked her as she turned away.

"I'll call you," she said. And then she was gone.

Trace watched her walk off, neat, trim, exquisitely beautiful. Whenever she left, he always had a sinking feeling that when he saw her again, things would somehow be different between them. His eyes followed her as she walked through the terminal, oblivious to the stares of men passing by, and he thought about the three years they had been together. He had gotten Chico—Michiko Mangini, actually—her first job as a blackjack dealer when she came to Las Vegas. Her added job, helping the casino out by "entertaining" visiting high rollers in town, she had gotten on her own.

It was her decision and he had never been really able to understand it, but at least it had kept things between them simple.

She was a whore and he was a drunk and half a crazy, but at least they were honest with each other about it.

Until now. Until this sudden interest in visiting relatives in Memphis, Tennessee.

Trace turned and missed his bag again as it went by.

4

New Jersey got a bad rap from the world, Trace thought as he left New York and the George Washington Bridge behind him and headed out, in his rented car, toward the New Jersey countryside.

Most people who passed through the state did just that: they passed through, usually along the New Jersey Turnpike, which sliced through the heart of some of the most unredeemedly ugly industrial areas ever devised by man, and so got the idea that that was what the entire state looked like.

Trace, after getting his divorce, had moved from New Jersey to New York City and spent the most dismal three months of his life there. It cost him $31.75 to park his car in a lot on East Forty-eighth Street for five hours. After two days of driving in the city, he realized that the only effective way to get from West Side to East Side was by National Guard airlift. New Yorkers didn't mind that because New Yorkers, he realized, didn't own cars. If they owned them, the city streets would tear out their transmissions and they'd have to own an oil well to be able to afford parking. Restaurants were overpriced, waiters were surly, and cabdrivers were homicidal. He paid $1.79 for a can of tuna fish. His telephone didn't work for three weeks, and when somebody at the phone company told him that if it really upset him, he should start his own telephone company, he moved to Las Vegas. He had never regretted it.

As he drove his car toward the gentle rolling hills ahead of the horizon, Trace thought there were only four things wrong with New Jersey: his ex-wife, his two children, and Richard Nixon.

With luck, he wouldn't be around long enough on this trip to meet any of them. But if he had to pick one, he'd take Nixon.

The town of Harmon Hills was fifty miles from New York, in country so foxy that it might have been in England.

When he pulled through the high brick columns that marked the entrance to the Sylvan Glade Country Club, he was faced with four roads that trailed off in different directions through the trees. There was no sign pointing the way toward the clubhouse, so Trace picked one road at random and drove around aimlessly between fairways, past putting greens and teeing areas, for ten minutes, until he saw the clubhouse as he came over a hill. The clubhouse sat in a glade, down so deep that Trace got the feeling that if someone came out at night onto the porch of the clubhouse and stamped his foot hard, all the golf balls that had been lost on the course during the day would roll down to the pro shop.

Trace parked in front and walked through the large double doors of the main entrance. He had expected a golf-course inn to have some jock in a turtleneck sweater and four-tone plaid pants working as a clerk. But at the reception desk was a man with oiled, slicked-back hair that pressed so tight to his skull that it looked as if it were trying to prevent his head from escaping. He wore a pencil-line mustache and a three-piece suit, and both looked painted on, mustache and suit.

"Do you have a single?"

"Yes, we do." Trace noticed the man looking with open curiosity at his ratty, scarred canvas valise.

"Something wrong?"

"Err, no. Do you have golf clubs, sir?"

"Should be here any day," Trace said. "Actually, I scratched the finish on the shaft of my mashie spoon niblick. It's at the jeweler's being resilvered."

The clerk nodded as if it happened every day, and handed Trace a registration form and a gold-plated pen. It was the only hotel registration form he had ever seen that asked for a lodger's occupation and for work references.

Trace dutifully filled in: "Advance man."

When Trace was done, the clerk took the form back and read it carefully before doing anything else.

"Devlin Tracy. That's Irish, isn't it?"

"Only on my father's side," Trace said. "My mother is Jewish. Sits near the stove and moans most of the day."

The clerk looked pained and bent over the registration form more closely.

"For whom do you advance?" he asked.

"I'm not at liberty to say, er, what is your name?"

"Dexter, sir."

"Well, Dexter, I really can't talk about it, but let's just say that I represent an official of the Vatican who does a great deal of traveling and just may be coming to your great state in the near future. I am here to make arrangements. More than that I can't say."

"Ohhh. The Vatican," Dexter repeated numbly.

"Don't hold it against me. It's a job. Actually, it's a pretty good job. I used to be advance man for a punk-rock band. Farmer Brown and the Cowflops. Ever heard of them?"

"No."

"Well, maybe they were picked up before they got this far. They were awful. Used to eat furniture. Before them, I handled the Electrical Disturbance. Ever hear of them?"

"I'm afraid not, Mr. Tracy."

"Maybe you wouldn't have. They're all in jail for setting fire to a Budget Six motel outside of Tallahassee. It was all affecting my nerves, so I went to work for the Vatican. Haven't had a hotel fire or an act of cannibalism since then. The man I work for is kind of dull." Trace winked at the clerk. "He mostly just likes to sit around and pray."

"Oh."

"He doesn't pray loud, though. He sort of mumbles. In Latin."

"Will he . . . the person you work for . . . will he be coming here?"

"It's kind of on the q.t.," Trace said. "He's a golfer."

"He is?"

"Not much of a long game," Trace said. "But he's miraculous on the greens."

The clerk, looking totally bewildered, pushed forward a room key. "Room Eleven, up the stairs at the end of the hall."

"Thank you. Do you have a restaurant here?"

"Sorry, Mr. Tracy, but it's closed for the night. However, you might get a sandwich in the cocktail lounge."

"How late is the lounge open?" Trace asked as he hoisted his bag and started for the stairs.

"It varies. Sometimes till one A.M.," the clerk said.

"Do they serve sacramental wine?"

Trace unpacked his canvas suitcase and hung his clothes any-which-way in the big room's massive walk-in closet. He took a small leather case out of the bag, then upended the bag and dumped the rest of its contents into a dresser drawer, and when his razor, toothbrush, and deodorant appeared, he snatched them up and put them on top of the dresser.

He sat on the bed and carefully opened the book-sized

black leather case. From it, he took a small portable tape recorder and a bag holding two dozen tapes. From another small bag, he took a long strand of electrical wire and an inch-high medallion of a gold frog with an open mouth.

He put a tape into the recorder, then plugged the long wire into the side of the machine. The other end of the wire fit into a slot on the back of the gold frog.

He pressed the recording button and spoke into the mesh that covered the open mouth of the frog.

"CX-Four to Control Tower. CX-Four to Control Tower. This is Hop Harrigan, coming in."

He rewound the tape and pressed the play button. His voice echoed out through the high-ceilinged room.

"CX-Four to Control Tower. CX-Four to Control Tower. This is Hop Harrigan, coming in."

Trace nodded with satisfaction, then dug in the leather bag until he found a roll of white surgical tape. He tore off two foot-long strips and stuck them to the headboard of the bed. Then he pulled his T-shirt out of his belt, placed the recorder against his lower back, and stuck it in place with the two pieces of surgical tape. He twisted vigorously several times to make sure the recorder was securely fastened to his body, then tucked his shirts back in.

He opened the shirt's front buttons and pulled the wire and the golden frog through the opening just below his sternum, then rebuttoned the shirt.

He separated the golden frog from the wire, placed the frog in front of his tie, then pushed the sharp end of the wire through the back of the tie into the slot on the back of the frog. He pulled his tie tight and looked into the mirror. Satisfied that he was neat, with no wires showing, he reached behind him with his right hand and pressed the tape unit's record button.

"This is Devlin Tracy, folks, broadcasting live from the land of the thousand terrors, New Jersey."

He rewound the tape and pressed the play button, and

when his message was repeated loud and clear, he nodded with satisfaction, turned the recorder off, put on his jacket, and went downstairs to find the bar.

Three men were sitting in a row at the end of the bar nearest the door, and when Trace walked in, they did not even glance at him. He walked past them to the far end of the bar where he sat, saw no bartender, and looked at the three men in the mirror behind the bar.

He guessed their combined age at two centuries. They were dressed for the golf course and were sipping from glasses of some dark amber liquid that he guessed was cream sherry.

They were arguing about a round of golf and from the slurred sound of their voices, they had been drinking since the round ended and it might just have been the final round of the nineteenth century.

"Ed, you left it short because you babied it. You didn't hit it."

"Not hit it, my ass. I hit it, Art. I hit it, but it was uphill and I didn't hit it hard enough."

"It wasn't that it was uphill," the third man said. "It was that you were putting against the grain. You forget that the grass grows toward the water. The water was behind you and so you were putting into the front of the blades of the grass. That's why it didn't reach the hole."

"You're an asshole, Frank," the one called Ed said. "You and your water behind you. The only water behind me was the goddamn fountain on the seventh tee. I putted it that way because the grass grows away from the mountains. I had the mountain behind me, so I was putting with the grain and I had to putt it easy, otherwise it would run away from me."

"You just didn't hit it. Never up, never in," said the man named Art.

"Miss it on the pro side. No pussy putts," said Frank.

"You two don't know shit. You putt away from the

38

water and the nearest water is the Atlantic Ocean. What about the frigging Pacific? That's water too. And you, you're so goddamn worried about mountains that the Rockies spook you."

"Yeah? Well, we didn't miss that putt," said Art.

"Yeah," said Frank.

"Hey, you," the man named Ed yelled at Trace. "You play golf?"

"No," Trace said.

Frank turned to him. "What do you think about a guy who leaves a twelve-footer three feet short and costs us a match?"

Trace sighed and said, "I think it was solar flares. Everybody knows that this is one of the most intense periods of solar eruptions since time began. Back when you were young. When the sun flares like that, it affects every orbital object, all the planets, all kinds of spheres. It's why baseballs don't carry very far this summer. If it affects Jupiter, you don't think it's going to affect your putts? And before you know it, it's going to change our weather. Winter in July. You'll see. It's as bad as all those Russian spaceships."

Frank turned away and said to the other two, "He says maybe it was solar flares."

"Maybe it was. I know I hit it."

"You didn't hit it. It was a pussy putt."

Frank said, "He says maybe we'll have winter in July."

"Good. Then we play winter rules all year round."

"Winter rules ain't gonna help you make a putt that you don't hit."

"Leave me alone," Ed said.

They were still arguing when the bartender came from a small storage room behind the bar. He was a small gnomish man, Trace guessed in his early fifties. His face was freckled and his thinning hair was sandy. He walked with a bowlegged sailor's roll and Trace thought he looked like Popeye. The name tag over his shirt pocket read Hughie.

"Well, Mr. Solar Flares, what can I do for you?" the bartender asked.

"Finlandia rocks. You heard?"

"I've listened to nothing but that missed putt for the last five hours. They'll make you nuts." As he poured the drink, he said, "How do you like it here?"

"Okay so far. I don't think Whozis likes me."

"Whozis?"

"The guy on the desk. The one with the fiberglass underwear."

"Oh, that's Dexter. He likes you fine. He thinks you're going to make the place famous by bringing the Pope here. You tell him that?"

"And I told him not to tell a soul. I told him that because he seemed upset that my name's Irish."

"At least you're not Jewish. That'd kill him. This is Waspland."

"I'm half Jewish," Trace said.

"Don't tell him."

"I already did. Join me?"

"Well, why not? Anything's better than listening to that missed putt. I spent most of the last five hours hiding in the storeroom. They won't go home. You a golfer too?"

"No."

"How come you're here, then?" Hughie said. He poured himself a shot of Scotch, neat. Trace reached under his jacket and pressed the tape machine's record button.

"Ever hear of a place called Meadow Vista Sanatorium?"

"Sure. Hard Artery Village. I keep trying to get these three committed, but they won't go. What's with Meadow Vista?"

"I've got a friend in there. Stopped to visit 'cause I was in this neighborhood. You know him, Mitch Carey?"

"Sure. I know who he is. We don't travel in the same

social circles, but I know who he is. I saw him up here a couple of times playing. He tipped me five dollars both times he was here. He's okay. Runs a computer company or something, doesn't he?''

Trace didn't know if Carey ran a computer company or a hardware store, but he said, "Sure, that's Mitch. He had a stroke and he's in Meadow Vista. My name's Tracy, by the way. Everybody calls me Trace.''

"Hughie," the bartender said. He shook Trace's hand with a muscular, tendony mitt.

"So I came up to visit. What kind of place is Meadow Vista?''

"I don't want to hurt your feelings. Your friend, you know?''

"My feelings are hard to bruise.''

"Okay, Meadow Vista's like a morgue," Hughie said. "People ship their old relatives up there to die. That's what I hear anyway.''

"I heard something like that too. Almost made me think there was funny business going on somehow.''

"Funny business?''

"I don't know," Trace said. "You know, people die all the time, you wonder sometimes if something's going on.''

"Naaah, I think those people up there, they die anyway anywhere. They just die up there so they don't mess up their sheets in their houses.''

He was interrupted by a bellow from the other end of the bar.

"Hughie, you old peckerhead. Three more of these.''

"Just a minute, Trace." He yelled out, "Coming right up.''

Trace turned off the tape recorder until the bartender was back, then turned it on again.

"You were saying about people dying at Meadow Vista.''

"Yeah, I don't know. Maybe they're running that place

41

so people get left alone to die. That's nice, kind of. When I die, I don't want anybody hanging around me and relatives crying. Just put me someplace clean and let God turn the lights out. Maybe that's what Matteson's doing.''

"Matteson? Who's he?"

"Doc Matteson. It's his sanatorium," Hughie said.

"You know him?"

"I see him a lot. You know, this place is like the only joint in town where you can get real lunch or dinner. Zoning. The town council thinks you let in restaurants, you're going to get Mexicans selling tacos out of pushcarts. So everybody comes up here. I see Doc Matteson once in a while. He plays here sometimes too. He's not a member. You got to be a hundred and fifty years old to be a member. He comes for lunch.''

"Business-lunch-like?" Trace said.

"Ladies too. Mostly ladies. Always for lunch, a lady. I think he likes ladies.''

"Is he local, this Matteson? From around here?"

"No. Just been here a couple of years. Nice fella.''

"All those people who die up there? Their families think he's nice too?" Trace said casually.

Hughie hesitated, that split-second hesitation that Trace recognized as the first sign of awareness that a person was being pumped for information.

"Never heard anything bad," Hughie said.

And Trace said, "Ahhh, it doesn't concern me. I just want to stop in and see Mitch and the family and then go home. I'll take another one of these. You too.''

Trace drank his vodka quietly, doodling on a cocktail napkin while Hughie washed glasses behind the bar. The three golfers at the end seemed to have exhausted the debating possibilities inherent in a missed putt, because now they were dissecting a trio of drives on the ninth hole. One of them was a whiff, one was lost in the trees, and the third seemed to have landed in a water fountain sixty yards down the side of the fairway. When they tried to embroil Hughie in their argument, he came back to refill Trace's glass.

"You too," Trace said.

"Don't mind if I do. I can hide out here. If I stay in that little storeroom there, I'll run out of air."

Trace said later, "No, you know, I was talking to Amanda, that's Mitch's wife, and she was saying that somebody was suing Meadow Vista because somebody died and left their money to the hospital. That's what I thought you were talking about before."

"You know the name?"

"Yeah. Presser or Plesser, something like that. That's it. Plesser. Mean anything to you?"

"I think I heard the name before," Hughie said vaguely.

"Yeah, they're suing or something. Like the sanatorium twisted this Plesser's head or something and made him leave them his money."

Hughie thought for a moment. He seemed to be offended at the idea of an out-of-towner knowing something about Harmon Hills that he didn't.

Finally, he said, "Yeah, maybe I heard about that. Something about suing the sanatorium because the guy didn't leave them his money or something."

And Trace knew he had gotten everything there was to get out of Hughie, so he nodded, quietly turned off his tape recorder, said, "Yeah, something like that," and when he finished his drink, he left. He signed the check and left a ten-dollar tip for the bartender.

5

Trace's Log:

All right, it's midnight Monday and here I am at the Doddering Hills Country Club. Tomorrow I have to buy some vodka 'cause all I've got are these two little airline bottles I stole when Chico wasn't looking and that's not even going to last me any time at all.

This is Master Tape Number One, I forgot to say. I don't think I fit into this place. First of all, I'm not eighty years old. Second, I don't own knickers. Why did people used to play golf in knickers anyway? I would think the longer the pants, the better, so you could kick the ball and improve your lie and nobody would notice. I'm surprised that Scotsmen didn't figure that out right away.

Anyway, I'm here and tomorrow I will go and do Bob Swenson's bidding. I will check out the Plessers and find out if there's anything to their complaint about the old guy being twisted into leaving his money to Matteson.

And then I'll look in, maybe, on the Careys, and hopefully this is all going to be done and done in just a day.

And then what am I going to do? I don't know where Chico is and she doesn't know where I am, so there's not much chance of us getting together. Unless she comes up here to go golfing. Somehow I don't think that's part of your usual tour of Memphis, Tennessee. Anyway, I don't believe she's on any kind of usual tour of Memphis, Tennessee.

In the Master File, there's a tape of my conversation tonight with Hughie, the bartender. Sorry, Groucho, don't jump to conclusions. I didn't go there to drink. But when you get to a strange town and you want to find things out fast, always find yourself a bartender. What they don't know, they make up, so you always feel fulfilled.

Hughie doesn't know anything bad about Meadow Vista, except a lot of people die there. Well, they deal in old folks. I bet a lot of people die at Hughie's bar, arguing about solar flares and Russian putts. Problem is, at Hughie's bar nobody notices they're dead.

And Dr. Matteson might be a womanizer. That doesn't mean anything by itself 'cause a lot of people are womanizers. I used to be one, until an hour ago, when I decided to go straight. Stay with me, God, until this passes away.

But womanizers tend to spend money, sometimes money they don't have. I'll keep that in mind.

I always thought that places named sanatoriums were for nuts, not for sick people. I hope not. I don't want to have to go and visit some ha-ha house. It's too dangerous. Who'll come and sign me out when they won't let me go? Not you, Groucho. I know that.

This whole thing better not be complicated. If I stay in Jersey too long, my ex-wife Bruno's going to find out about it and I'm in trouble.

Okay, expenses for this wild-goose chase. Air fare and car and gas on credit card. Room and tonight's restaurant bill on credit card. Five-dollar tip to the skycap at the airport and fifty dollars for drinks and tips at the bar downstairs. Oh, and five-dollar tip to the desk clerk who helped me with my luggage. His name's Dexter and he's a prince of a man, Groucho. You'd really like him.

The bar bill might seem a little high, but I was talking to some Harmon Hills old-timers to find out what makes this place tick. So that's sixty dollars total for the day. That's too low. Let's call it sixty-five 'cause I know there are some things I must have bought and I just forgot them. I'll itemize them later when I remember them.

I think maybe that I resent Bob Swenson getting me involved in this nonsense. Just because he owns an insurance company that sometimes sends me a check, that's no reason to impose on our friendship for personal things. I find being in New Jersey very annoying.

I wonder what Chico is doing right now. No, I don't.

6

At night, as Trace had passed through, Harmon Hills had seemed a sleepy little bucolic town, but now, in daylight, he saw it as a trendy mock village with enough boutiques and specialty shops to be selling every shawl and piece of macrame ever made in Mexico.

He knew he was going to hate Harmon Hills. He hated towns with boutiques. He hated Westport, Connecticut, and East Hampton, New York, and Carmel and La Jolla in California. He liked Toledo, Ohio. He liked Las Vegas, where he lived. He could occasionally find a warm spot in his heart for Hoboken, New Jersey, but he had heard New Yorkers were starting to stream across the Hudson River to buy up Hoboken brownstones, and if New Yorkers came, could overpriced restaurants and boutiques, *très intimes*, be far behind? The city would be inundated with Mexican macrame. Scratch Hoboken.

Trace liked towns with gas stations, not auto service centers.

The man who wears the star told him how to find Sellers Street, and as he got farther away from Harmon Hills' main drag, following the directions, he saw that there was an underbelly to the town.

He moved across some railroad tracks and was in an older section of town. The homes here were not mansions or estates; they were just houses, and most of them would have been helped by a fresh coat of paint. Lawns were frequently uncut and there were too many tricycles next to too many weed-bordered walkways. Tricycles meant toddlers and toddlers used to be infants and only the poor had children in America anymore.

He checked the address on the insurance form Walter Marks had given him. It said 4254½ Sellers Street, and right off he felt uneasy. He didn't like houses with half-numbers. What did they mean anyway? What kind of people lived in a place with half a number?

The house was the last one on the block. An empty lot next to it was overrun with weeds. The house itself had once been white but was now dingeing toward gray. The front of the house was surrounded by a screened-in porch, with holes in the screening, and the screen door had a green frame that reminded Trace of a rent-it-by-the-week Jersey-shore bungalow. The door hung slightly askew on its hinges.

Trace rang the doorbell and hoped nobody would be home. No such luck.

A grotesquerie of a woman rumbled through the inside door and advanced upon the screen door and Trace like a brakeless tractor trailer rumbling down a hill. For an instant, Trace thought about running, but he decided that with her head of steam, the beast could catch him. Maybe if he lay still on the ground and covered his head with his hands, he could survive. He had heard that that worked with polar bears. Maybe this thing was nearsighted too.

"Son of a bitch," the woman bellowed. But then, just when it seemed she would crash through the thin screen on the door and bear Trace to the ground, crushing him under her weight, she managed to slam her bulk into reverse and slowly quivered to a stop just inside the screen door.

"Who are you?" she demanded. "I thought it was those goddamn kids again. They's always ringing the bell and running away."

The woman stood just inside the screen door and Trace

saw her clearly now. She was around sixty and she wore a green and purple housedress that buttoned down the front.

One of the buttons had vanished and another was in the act of fleeing, held on grimly by a thread more noteworthy for tenacity than taste.

The woman had the fat droopy under arms that went with chronic obesity and having a kitchen in your cellar. Her face was garishly made up with mosquito-blood lipstick and sky-blue eye shadow. She had used eyeliner to paint extra lines at the outside corner of each eye, a style Trace thought had died with Cleopatra. Her hair was lifeless, like straw, blotched rather than bleached to a shade that Trace thought could only be described as burnished shit.

"I'm sorry, sir or madam," Trace said. "I'll come back some other time."

"Hold on," the woman snapped. She pushed open the screen door and stared at him. "Who are you?"

"I'm from the Garrison Fidelity Insurance Company. I'm looking for Gertrude Plesser."

"Yeah, me. From the insurance company, hah? You talk to our lawyer?"

"No. I should have. I'll do that right now. Right this minute. I'll see you."

Trace turned but was caught up shortly by the woman's drill-instructor voice. "No. You better come in and talk to me. The insurance company, hah?"

Trace wanted to explain that it wasn't the insurance company's fault, whatever it was, but even if it had been, he wasn't the insurance company, but just a poor hired hand, downtrodden just as she had been all her life by the forces of untrammeled capitalistic greed and big business.

He didn't have a chance to say anything because she grabbed his upper arm in a big paw and jerked him up the stairs.

She led Trace through an inside door, through a living room that featured a mouse fuzz rug as its principal decorating attraction. Then they were heading down a hallway toward a kitchen in the rear. Trace could see its yellow-and-brown flowered wallpaper far off, as in a vision.

As they drew nearer, the sound of acid-rock music pummeled his ears. The house smelled vaguely of sauerkraut, and Trace cautioned himself not to let the exposed skin of his body touch any surface.

Inside the kitchen, at a table with a black-and-white enameled top, chipped at the edges, sat Thing Two.

But for twenty years, it might have been the twin of the vision who had met Trace at the door. Daughter Plesser was just as large, just as over-made-up, and just as fashionably dressed, except that her housedress was black and red. She had an enormous hand curled around a quart bottle of Pepsi-Cola, and she was drinking from the bottle.

"This here guy's from the insurance company," Mother Plesser announced. "What'd you say your name was?"

"Marks," Trace said. "Walter Marks. Remind me to give you my home phone number when I leave."

"Yeah. Move Jasmine, and let Mr. Morris sit down there."

"Marks," Trace said.

The daughter rumbled unwillingly for a few moments, like a volcano trying to make up its mind, then lurched upward out of the kitchen chair, like a bubble rising through thick tar.

Mrs. Plesser sat at one side of the table, and Trace guessed he was supposed to occupy the other seat. When she glared at him, he sat.

"You want something to drink?" the older woman said. "This is my daughter, Jasmine. Jasmine, get the man something to drink. And turn off that radio."

"You want Pepsi-Cola?" the daughter asked Trace sullenly as she switched off the radio atop the refrigerator.

Trace looked at the bottle clutched in her hand, a bright red band of lipstick about its rim, and shook his head no.

"No, just had a Pepsi for breakfast," he lied.

"Like something else? How about some coffee?" Mrs. Plesser said. "Jasmine, make the man some coffee."

"No, thanks, Mrs. Plesser. Actually, I don't really want anything."

"All right," Mrs. Plesser said.

Jasmine looked relieved and Trace thought that she was probably down to her last nine cases of Pepsi and didn't want to share them with anybody. He glanced toward the stove, but there was nothing on it except a layer of grease. So where was the sauerkraut smell coming from?

"I don't mind telling you, we think it was a dirty deal we got from you," Mrs. Plesser said ominously.

"Well, that's why I'm here." Trace tried a smile. "I just want to get all the facts for my company."

"You shoulda gotten all the facts before you said you was going to pay off to those quacks at that hospital. That's why we got us a lawyer," she said proudly.

"That's right," pitched in Jasmine. "We gonna hang your ass, us and our lawyer."

"I can't really help if I don't know what happened," Trace said.

"What happened was that my poor husband, God rest his soul, went up to that fancy sanatorium and they killed him."

"Had he been sick?"

"Of course he was sick." Mrs. Plesser looked at Jasmine as if needing to share with someone the secret of Trace's utter stupidity. "Don't nobody go to no sanatorium without they being sick."

"What was wrong with him?"

"What was wrong was that he wasn't feeling good for a long time. He used to have these head pains and things and his memory wasn't so good no more either. It was getting kind of worse all the time and he wasn't working so good, so he stopped going to work."

"Where'd he work?"

"At the auto plant over in Muckluck," the woman said. "Forty years he was there."

Trace was sure he had heard her say Muckluck.

"What did the doctor say was wrong with him?"

"Doctor said he was just getting old. Jasmine, make me some coffee."

"Yes, Mama."

"That was a laugh 'cause the doctor is older than oak," Mrs. Plesser said. "But Freddie was getting bad and the company was paying for it on the insurance so we sent him up to the sanatorium 'cause he couldn't like dress himself or anything like that. He was, how do you say—"

"He wasn't competent, that's what he wasn't," said Jasmine triumphantly.

"Incompetent. That's what he was. That's why when they got him up there, they just twisted him around they little finger and made him leave them all his company insurance."

"That was how much?"

"It was a hundred-thousand-dollar how much, that's how much," Mrs. Plesser snapped.

"The company paid for that insurance?" Trace asked.

"Yeah. 'Cause he was there a long time. It was all he had, 'cause they don't pay pensions if you die."

"They pay for the sanatorium too?"

"Yeah."

"What do you think happened to Mr. Plesser at the sanatorium?"

"He wasn't getting none better, but he wasn't getting no worse neither. He just lay around there, but they wouldn't let him come home. I asked him, 'You want to come home?' and he said, 'They won't let me come home, I ain't ready yet.' They didn't get everything they wanted from him yet, was what it was. Then they did, and then he died."

"What did he die of?"

"They said it was his heart," Mrs. Plesser said in a tone that let Trace know what she thought of *that*.

"What do you think it was?" Trace asked.

"I don't know."

"Probably some secret stuff," Jasmine said. "Like they killed Elvis Presley with so he wouldn't talk. I read about it in the *Enquirer*."

"John Belushi, too," Trace said. "He was ready to rip the mask of hypocrisy off all the underhanded dealing in the videocassette industry."

"I din' read that," Jasmine said.

"Must have been an issue you missed," Trace said. "Do you have any reason to believe," he asked Mrs. Plesser, "that the sanatorium did something wrong? That maybe they even speeded your husband's death?"

"Speed, my ass. They killed him," she said.

"Mama," said Jasmine sharply.

The mother glared at the daughter, her beady little eyes glistening angrily. "I ain't supposed to say that, is what Jasmine means. Maybe you should be talking about all this to my lawyer."

"Did you discuss your suspicions with the police?"

"Aaaaaah, the police."

"What's the matter?"

"They're on the take too. A poor woman can't get no justice, excepting she's rich."

"You talked to the police but they took no action?"

"They didn't do nothing," Mrs. Plesser said.

"Do you know if they investigated your husband's death?"

"I don't know nothing except they didn't do nothing. Nobody wants to do nothing to help you. You get . . . poor people don't ever have a chance. Now we got nothing to live on except my social security and what Calvin brings home."

"Calvin?" asked Trace.

"Jasmine's husband. Leastways he's working now since Papa died."

The smell of sauerkraut was stronger in the room. Trace could hear the water boiling on the stove for coffee, but nobody bothered to do anything about it. He could imagine water boiling away in this kitchen, then empty pots standing over flaming gas burners until they melted, or turned brittle and shattered when plunged into water.

"Do you have a picture of Mr. Plesser?" Trace asked.

"What for?"

"I don't know. Sometimes in matters like this, it helps me to have a feel for the person. Like I'm not dealing in statistics but with a real human being."

Mrs. Plesser mulled this for a moment, then told her daughter, "Get them pictures of Papa."

When they came, Trace decided he would rather have been dealing with statistics. Mrs. Plesser took a small pile of photos from her daughter and handed them across the table to Trace one at a time for him to admire.

They were typical examples of the style of photography known as 1930s backyard art deco. There was Plesser, flanked on one side by his wife, on the other by his daughter, looking for all the world like a very slim volume pressed between two blowup bookends. All three of them stared resolutely into the sun, but it didn't take fright shadows down his face to reveal the late Frederick Plesser as a man of something less than striking beauty. His face looked like an undernourished ferret's and his thin hair was plastered down on his head. He was scrawny, with a protruding Adam's apple, and his clothes hung on his frame as if he had spent six months shrinking away inside them.

Each of the pictures was the same group: Plesser surrounded by wife and daughter.—What did you wear to the party, Mr. Plesser? —My wife and daughter and a look of grim despair.

If Plesser had ever smiled in his life, there was no indication of it in any of these photos, Trace thought as he looked at each of them.

And then the prize of the collection was handed him. These looneys had actually taken a picture of Plesser lying in his coffin. It was a washed-out-looking Polaroid print and Trace thought that what it really needed to be perfect was to be rendered on black velvet with granular paint by some artist in Tijuana.

"That's the last one of Papa," Mrs. Plesser said.

"I should expect so," Trace said.

He looked at it and didn't know what else to say. Should he tell them that the deceased looked good? That he looked like Randolph Scott? All men over fifty in their caskets looked like Randolph Scott.

But there was something else in the photo, some antic whim of a funeral director who either didn't know the dear departed or who had a sense of humor. Frederick Plesser was slightly smiling, a skill that seemed to have evaded him in life.

"He looks nice," Trace said because that's what everybody said when viewing a cadaver. He handed the picture back and Mrs. Plesser stared at it for a moment, as if to make sure they had gotten the right man.

"Undertaker did a good job," she said. She shuffled the pictures together and wordlessly handed them over to her daughter, who took them and left the room, presumably to return them to the crypt.

"Well, you've really been a big help to me," Trace said. He was afraid if he stayed longer, he'd be looking at locks of hair and relics from the body. "I'll be going now. I want to—"

He stopped as he heard a crash against the front screen door, then the baying of a hound, and then the galloping of hooves down the hall toward the kitchen.

A moment later, he was shrunk back against the wall. A

55

black dog, with saliva glistening on his fangs, as big as an understudy for *The Hound of the Baskervilles*, had his massive head next to Trace's chest and was growling.

"Devil, back off," Mrs. Plesser screamed.

"Quick, the tranquilizing darts," Trace yelled.

"Devil, back off," Mother Plesser yelled again.

The dog didn't budge and he didn't stop growling. He didn't even pause for breath.

"Devil, goddammit," Mrs. Plesser shouted. Trace thought maybe he was deaf. "Turn on his hearing aid," he hissed.

Mrs. Plesser and Jasmine started yanking on the beast's spiked collar, but it stubbornly held its ground. Its red-rimmed eyes never left Trace's face. The growls grew deeper in its throat. Its tail hung down.

Trace heard whistling in the hall. Somebody was whistling a tune. Here he was in danger of being eaten alive and somebody was giving a whistling concert in the hall. Stop. All music should cease until the life-and-death crisis had passed.

A man came into the kitchen. He was just a few inches over five feet tall but wiry and strong-looking. His black hair was thin, greasy, and uncombed, and he had a straggly black beard. He wore a plaid lumberjack's shirt and farmer's overalls and light-brown ankle-high brogans.

"Devil, stop fooling around or I bust your ass," he growled.

Devil backed off from Trace, whimpered once, and dropped to the floor in terror.

"Who's he?" the man said to Mrs. Plesser.

"Name's Morris. He's with the insurance company."

"Marks," Trace corrected.

"Shit, I ought to let Devil kill him," the man said.

"Stop joshing, Calvin," said Jasmine.

"Yeah, stop joshing," Trace said.

"This here's my husband, Calvin," Jasmine said.

Trace nodded and Calvin said, "Good thing you wasn't

trying to mess around with Mama or Jasmine. Devil'd rip you apart.''

''I can see that,'' Trace said. He omitted suggesting that so would the Legion for Good Taste. ''I was just leaving.'' He started to get up from the chair but froze when Devil growled at him.

''Devil, I kick your ass,'' Calvin said.

Devil covered his muzzle with his paws and closed his eyes.

''You going to get us our rightful money?'' Calvin asked.

If he said no, Trace wondered, would the dog be set free to tear him apart? If he said yes, could he live with the lifetime of shame caused by cowardice in the face of danger?

''Yes,'' he said.

''Good.''

Trace tried getting up again and this time Devil stayed quiet.

''Those people do anything,'' Calvin said. ''You be careful. If they find out you're onto them, no telling what they might do.''

''The people at the sanatorium?'' Trace asked, and Calvin nodded. ''Are they violent?''

''They killed Papa, didn't they?'' Calvin said.

''How do you think they did it?'' Trace asked.

''Just like Elvis Presley,'' Calvin said.

''And John Belushi,'' said Jasmine.

Trace could imagine these two lying side by side in their stall at night, reading the *Enquirer* to each other while Jasmine swallowed cases of Pepsi-Cola intravenously so she wouldn't have to get up.

Trace nodded and stepped gingerly past Devil toward the hallway. ''Well, I've got to be off.''

''Listen, Mr. Parks, you just stop in if you need any more help,'' Mrs. Plesser said.

"Sure will," Trace said. He started down the hall and realized that Calvin was following him. The smaller man stepped outside with him and they stood alongside Calvin's dented, body-cancered pickup truck.

"It ain't right, you know," Calvin said, "for Mama to get nothing from that insurance company."

"Seems unfair," Trace agreed.

"Sometimes women don't understand things too good, you know," Calvin said.

"What do you mean?"

"I just want you to know, you get us what's rightfully ours and you and I, maybe, could do some business."

"I understand."

"We look out for those who looks out for us."

"Right," Trace said. "Can you tell me something?"

"Sure."

"Was Mr. Plesser happy?"

"Like a clam. He had everything. This house, nice family. They shouldn't oughta killed him. There's nothing they wouldn't do up there."

"Why do you think *they*"—Trace emphasized the word— "picked him to kill."

"For the insurance, naturally. They knew they could get him to switch it over and then they could just kill him."

"Do you think they've tried it to other people?"

"I don't know. 'Cause we're poor, maybe they figured they could get away with it. Sometimes you wonder what the FBI's doing, when they don't have time to look into things like that."

"You asked them to look into it?"

"They're all on the take," Calvin said. "Every one of them. Since old J. Edgar died, ain't anything going right anymore in this country."

"You're right about that," Trace said, clapping the small man on the back. Then he glanced nervously toward the screen door to make sure that Devil wasn't watching and misunderstanding the gesture.

"What's your lawyer's name?" Trace asked.

"Mr. Yule. Best lawyer in town," Calvin said. "You gonna talk to him?"

"Probably."

"Tell him I'll be down to see him soon," Calvin said.

"All right. I'll be in touch," Trace said.

"We'll be waiting to hear from you," Calvin said.

Trace walked quickly to his car. Calvin smelled like sauerkraut too.

7

Harmon Hills police headquarters had an old-fashioned colonial facade over the front of the building, but it had bars on the windows and large green lights on either side of the front door. It was cute, but at least it was recognizable as a police headquarters. The trouble with up-income trendy towns like those in Fairfield County, Connecticut, was that everybody thought he was an architectural designer, and public buildings wound up looking like places that sold Frye boots.

Trace found Lt. Frank Wilcox in a basement office in the small building. He had read somewhere that a forty-five, a man had the face he deserved, but somehow Trace doubted if anybody deserved Frank Wilcox's face.

It was thin, pitted with the residue of adolescent acne, and his nose was long and so pointed that it might have served its owner as a letter opener. His eyes squinted so tightly, he might have been staring into the sun.

If Wilcox weighed 130 pounds, it would have surprised Trace, but it was a tough kind of skinniness that made him think of a jockey.

"Okay, Tracy, what can I do for you?" He looked at Trace's business card again. "Garrison Fidelity Insurance Company. What's that all about?"

"Well, Lieutenant, what I really came to talk about is the shocking murder committed at the Meadow Vista Sanatorium for insurance money, and the terrible coverup by the local police, you, the FBI, the CIA, and the State Lottery Commission.''

"I see you've been talking to the Plesser family," Wilcox said sourly.

"You mean you're going to deny it? You're not going to plead guilty?''

"Afraid not," Wilcox said. He smiled and showed a lot of yellow teeth with spaces between them.

"Shoot. I thought I had this all locked up," Trace said.

"Nothing to lock up. You *did* see the Plessers?''

"Yeah, just now.''

"You know, I'm getting tired of them. I think I'm going to talk to the town attorney and sue their ass for libel. Or slander. Or whatever it is. Defaming my character.''

"Do you have a courtroom big enough to hold them?'' Trace asked.

"We can hold the trial in a tent. You want some coffee?''

"Police-headquarters coffee?'' Trace said.

"Give it a try. We've got a new pot and this is one of the few police stations in the world where coffee tastes like coffee. You ever been a cop? You a private eye or something?''

"No. My father was a cop in New York, I guess I'm kind of a p.i. But I work mostly for the insurance company.''

Wilcox nodded and picked up the telephone. "Two cups of coffee," he said. "So you're here for the Plessers?''

Trace thought momentarily of mentioning the other reason for his visit, the worries of the Mitchell Carey family. But he seemed to have Wilcox in a good mood and he didn't want to change it yet.

"My office told me that the Plessers'll probably sue," Trace said. "Insurance companies take things like that seriously.''

"This one you can take unseriously. Let me lay it out for you. Meadow Vista is a good place. Well-run, highly regarded. No complaints in this town. Plesser died of heart failure. That was all. He was suffering from some kind of senile thing, but he was sane enough that he didn't want to go home. He told the staff at the hospital that if they made him go home, he'd run away, so they let him stay. They tried to treat him and maybe he was getting better and maybe he wasn't, but he died. You saw the family. Would you leave them money?"

"They'd just waste it on Pepsi and dog food. Was there an autopsy?"

"No. There wasn't any need for one. The Plessers didn't complain until after they tried to get the insurance money and your company told them the beneficiary had been changed. That's when they got all those murder ideas. Before that, everything was all right. After that, Plesser was already buried. For all I know, those ghouls may go down and dig him up and have their own autopsy."

"Did you talk to this Dr. Matteson who runs the clinic?"

"Yeah. Nothing," Wilcox said. "He's a nice guy. He remembered Plesser and thought he was a nice man and he was sorry he died. He doesn't know why Plesser decided to leave him money."

The door to the office opened and a tall, curvy brunette in a police uniform came in, carrying two cups of coffee. She placed them on Wilcox's desk, nodded to him, then turned and stared at Trace. There was a soft smile playing about her lips, and when she walked past him, her leg brushed against Trace's knee.

When the door closed behind her, Trace said, "How do you get away with that?"

"What?"

"Having women bring you coffee. I thought it was against the Constitution or something."

"It is," Wilcox said. "Except she's my wife. She brings me coffee home, why not here? She complains to the police union and I have her out doing traffic duty in the swamps."

Trace sipped hard at the coffee. "The Plessers say they've got a lawyer."

"You meet him?"

"No," Trace said. "Yule or something."

"Yule. Wait until you meet him. You'll understand he's the perfect lawyer for this case."

"I guess I ought to talk to him before I pack this whole thing in," Trace said.

"You go out the front door, make a right and down about three blocks. He's in the middle of the block, upstairs over the drugstore."

Trace sipped a little more of his coffee, then rose and thanked the lieutenant for his help.

"Anytime." When Trace was at the door, Wilcox said, "If you find out anything, let me know."

In the outer office, Wilcox's wife was sitting at a desk, looking through a pile of blue-sheeted police reports.

She looked up at him and Trace smiled and said, "You make good coffee."

She smiled back. "I do a lot of things well."

Trace's day was made halfway up the narrow flight of bare wooden stairs leading to Nicholas Yule's second-floor office. He heard a door at the top of the steps open, looked up, and saw a woman starting down the stairs. She was a tall redhead, with widely spaced large brown eyes framed by thick dark lashes. Her nose was thin, straight, and, Trace thought, perfect, and her lips, coated only with a light-colored gloss, were full and wide. She had high cheekbones and a complexion that looked so healthy it seemed to glow. She was wearing a white-linen suit, and as she came down the stairs, the jacket of the suit parted to display a gold chain belt, cinched tightly around her narrow waist. He stopped on the stairs, first to marvel at her, then to move aside to give her room to pass.

She saw him, but her face did not respond in any way.

Was she happy to see him? Angry? Preoccupied? He couldn't tell, and as she reached him on the stairway, he smiled and said, "Come here often?"

She looked hard into his eyes and snapped, "Not anymore, if you're going to be here," then brushed by him and continued down the stairs.

She went through the door and out onto the sidewalk without looking back, and Trace sighed. Was this what they meant by two ships passing in the night? But couldn't she at least have sounded her whistle when she passed? For a moment, he had the urge to forget Nicholas Yule and chase after the woman, harass her, importune her, beg her to take him home and make him a pet, but instead he turned and kept going up the stairs.

Before he opened the door, he heard a sound from inside. A trombone was playing "Nola" at top volume and he thought it was unusual music to be played in a lawyer's office. Muzak had certainly changed since the last time he had noticed it.

But when he went inside, he found it wasn't Muzak. A thin man with a balding head sat behind the lone desk in the office, his feet up on the desk, playing the trombone. The man was small, wore thick-lensed glasses, and looked as if he'd been dressed by a vote of the fans. He had on a red plaid shirt, a blue plaid tie, and green plaid pants. He wore white sweat socks and heelless Indian moccasins. Even from ten feet away, Trace could see that his shoulders were dotted with dandruff.

He looked at Trace, nodded, and kept pursuing "Nola" to the end, while Trace waited just inside the door.

Finally, the man stopped.

"I'm looking for Nicholas Yule," Trace said.

"What for?"

"Business," Trace said stubbornly. Start off by talking to trombone players and soon you'd be talking to everybody.

"Okay," the man said. He put the trombone down onto

the desk. "My rates are two hundred dollars a night. For that, you get four hours. We've got a piano, drums, bass, and I carry the lead on the trombone. We know a lot of ethnic stuff, so you tell us who's likely to be there, what kind of people, you know, and we can do whole Irish sets or "Hava Nagilah" or polkas or Neapolitan favorites or whatever. I only do a few German. You can't get a better band at any price, and I do the vocals too, and that saves you the cost of a fifth man. When's your party?"

"Are you Nicholas Yule?" Trace asked.

"Who'd you think I was?"

"I thought you were a lawyer."

"I am. I'm also the best musician in three counties. You want music or you want law?"

"Law," Trace said.

"Law sucks," said Nicholas Yule. "But if that's what you want . . . have a seat." The little man got up and carried his trombone across the small room and put it in a black cardboard trombone case. Trace sat down and looked around the office. There were two things on the walls: a diploma from law school and a bank calendar that was opened to the wrong month. A pile of file folders sat on the lone desk in the office, and half of them seemed to have fallen onto the linoleum floor. Most of the desk space was taken by a daily racing form.

Yule came back, rubbing his hands, and sat at the desk, facing Trace. He moved the racing form aside, "Now what can I do for you, Mr.—"

"Tracy." He handed the lawyer one of his business cards. "I'm here about the Plesser case."

Yule looked at the card and nodded. "Well, it's about time you people have come to your senses. When you send the check, send it to me. I have to deduct my fee first, you know."

"Actually, I'm not planning yet to send any check,"

65

Trace said. "I'm still looking into this matter. You're representing the Plesser family, correct?"

"That's right, and I've notified your people that we're planning to sue, and I've notified everybody else involved, and I'm going into court as soon as I get the papers drawn. It's a miscarriage of justice, that's what it is. It's worse than a miscarriage. It's an abortion. A willful vicious abortion."

"What is?" Trace asked.

"Depriving that poor Mrs. Plesser of what is rightfully due her. She was married to that man for thirty years; she's got dower rights to everything. You know what dower rights are?"

"No."

"Well, it's too complicated, but she's got them, and if your company doesn't pay up, it's going to have a lot of egg all over its corporate face."

He seemed about to go on and Trace said, "Mr. Yule, time out. I'm not the enemy. My company sent me here to find out what's going on and I've got to report back to them. When they get my report, then they'll decide what to do. So why don't you just tell me what's going on."

"What do you want to know?"

"Do you think pressure was applied to Mr. Plesser to get him to change his insurance?"

"I don't know."

"Oh. Okay. Do you think anything strange happened to him at Meadow Vista?"

"Like what?"

"The family seems to think he was murdered."

"I don't know."

"If you don't mind my saying so, you're not much of an advocate for your position," Trace said.

"I'm not interested in facts. This is an equity matter. What's fair. What's fair is that Mrs. Plesser gets that insurance money. That's what's fair. I told your company that and I told Dr. Matteson that, but if they're not going to pay up, then we're going to go into court and it's going to be this poor little old woman against the big insurance company and the big doctor, and you're all going to look like idiots."

"Suppose you lose?" Trace asked. "It happens in court."

"They can't take my trombone away from me. Or my voice. I have a beautiful natural tenor voice."

"I wasn't really thinking of you. I meant the Plesser family," Trace said.

"Do you know if they sing?"

"What?"

"There used to be two fat sisters who sang. I don't remember their names. Maybe I can get the mother and the daughter to put together an act. They could work with my band. Dolly and Polly I could call them. A novelty. Do you know if they sing? I'm looking for another singer."

"I think they do the Pepsi-Cola commercial," Trace said. "About this case. What would you like to see happen?"

"Your company to pay Mrs. Plesser the insurance. Send it to me first so I can get my fee. Or Dr. Matteson to turn the money over to Mrs. Plesser. He can—"

"I know. Send it to you so you can deduct your fee," Trace said.

"You think I'm in this for the fee, don't you?"

Trace shrugged.

"Well, I can make a lot more money leading my band," Yule said. "And another thing. I don't need cases. I have cases. These are all cases." He waved his hand toward the stack of file folders on his desk, nudged them by accident, and they all fell on the floor. Trace started forward to pick them up and Yule said, "Don't worry about it. None of them are pressing right now. I'll straighten them out later. You come from around here?"

"No. Las Vegas," Trace said.

"Oh, Las Vegas." Yule seemed interested. "I want to get my band to Las Vegas someday. How is it there?"

"Dry," Trace said.

"I mean to work."

"I don't know. I don't work," Trace said.

"You wouldn't know what they're paying lounge acts, would you?"

"No. Sorry."

Yule chewed his lips and shook his head. "Why'd they send a guy here from Las Vegas instead of from around here?"

"I've got friends in town. I volunteered so I could visit them. Maybe you know them. The Mitchell Careys."

"The old man's sick. You know that?"

"Yeah. I heard he's in Meadow Vista too," Trace said.

"Had a stroke. He's a friend of yours?"

"Yeah."

"Keep an eye on him. He might not get out of that hospital "

"What do you mean?"

"Mr. Plesser didn't," Yule said.

"You can't just tell me that and nothing else," Trace said.

"Watch me," Yule said. He smiled at Trace, who finally realized that Yule was not going to talk anymore and he got to his feet.

"Thanks for your time, Mr. Yule," he said. "If there's anything else you want to tell me, anything that you know might make my company think about settling, just let me know. I'm staying at the Sylvan Glade."

"Nice place."

"Yeah."

"Ask them if they want a band on weekends," Yule said.

Trace nodded and walked to the door. In the doorway,

he stopped and turned. Yule was taking his trombone out of the instrument case again.

"Mr. Yule?"

"Yes."

"That woman I saw leaving here. Who is she?"

"You don't want to know her."

"Yeah, I do."

Yule answered by playing "When the Saints Go Marching In," and Trace left.

8

"Mr. Tracy?"

"Yes."

"Do you know a Koko?" Dexter, the desk clerk, sniffed down the sizable length of his nose as he asked the question.

"Yes. Nestle's and Bosco. I like Bosco myself, but Nestle's is easier to travel with 'cause Bosco is like a mush. I broke a bottle of Bosco once in my suitcase and it ruined all my underwear."

"No, no, this is a person."

"Koko?" Trace said. "Chico?"

"It might have been. A woman."

"Yeah, Chico is a woman, all right. And if she caught you sniffing her name like that, she'd have a dirk between your ribs so fast your heart would stop before you knew you were cut. What about her?"

"She called and said she would call again at precisely five-thirty P.M. I think I should tell you, Mr. Tracy, that she was very insolent."

"What did she say? Be accurate. You may be called to testify at her deportation hearing."

"Well, she called me Buster for one thing."

"She calls everybody Buster. Go on."

"And she— Well, very rude— She said, I think she said that I was the dumbest person she ever talked to."

"What did you say?"

"I told her I would not dignify that statement with a comment."

"Good for you. That'll teach her."

"Mr. Tracy?"

"Yes."

"You're not really here for the Vatican, are you?"

"Of course I am. Who told you otherwise?"

"Oh. Oh. Oh." Dexter's face lit up with happiness. "I hope you're finding everything here to your liking."

"I certainly am," Trace said.

"If there's anything you need . . ."

"Thank you, Dexter."

It was five minutes after five, and when Trace got to his room, he showered, first placing his tape recorder and the two tapes he had made that day on the dresser.

The telephone rang at precisely five-thirty. It was one of the things he liked about Chico; to her, five-thirty meant exactly five-thirty.

"Where are you?" he asked her.

"Memphis, of course."

"Tennessee?" he asked.

"Don't start. Of course, Tennessee."

"Listen," he said. "This is important. How did you find me?"

"A little Oriental guile. Why?"

"Because if you found me this easily, Svetlana, my ex-wife, can find me too. I can't have that."

"She doesn't even know you're in New Jersey," Chico said. "And her name's Cora."

"You don't know what she knows," Trace said. "That woman knows every move I make. A chance word in the lobby of our condo . . . a talkative bellhop. I tell you, that woman can find out. It might have gotten out and maybe something was in the social columns. Jim Bacon might have written a piece. 'Mr. Devlin Tracy and his Sicilian fortune cookie are traveling east to New Jersey.' I tell you, that woman subscribes to a clipping service. She turns the reports directly over to the Mafia. I've got a contract on my head. How'd you find out where I was?''

"I remembered the town, so I called police headquarters and asked for the name of the hotels. I figured there'd be a couple and I'd call person-to-person for you, but the cops said there was only one and there you were. How do you stand that desk clerk?''

"Dexter? Actually, he's kind of charming. If you don't mind being treated like rancid meat. He liked you a lot.''

"Mutual, I'm sure,'' Chico said. "How are you doing anyway?''

"I'm just about all done with this thing. There's nothing that I can see to that old guy's death at the sanatorium, and all I've got to do is stop in and pay my respects to the Carey family and I can go anytime.''

"You going back to Vegas?'' Chico asked.

"Absolutely. I don't want to be around here, I told you. When are you coming back?''

"Probably not for a few days,'' she said.

"Oh. How's your sister?''

"Sist— Oh, sure, she's fine. We're having a wonderful time. I didn't know how many relatives I had down here.''

"Want me to come down and do the tea ceremony with them?''

"The last time I put you near my family and you wanted to do a tea ceremony, you larded up the tea with vodka and everybody threw up.''

"Come on, I'll behave this time,'' he said.

"No,'' she said quickly. "Just me and the sister. We don't get much of a chance to be together.''

"So I have to fly back to Vegas alone?''

"Don't pout. Why not? You've done it before.''

"Never by choice. All those old women with blue hair, they're lurking on those planes, just waiting for one like me. And they eat all the chicken and all I get is codfish. Ah, the hell with it. You're not interested in my troubles. Where are you staying anyway? Where can I reach you?''

"That's why I called back," she said. "I'm at a public phone. Sis and I didn't like our motel room, so we moved out. We haven't found another one yet, so I don't have a number.''

"All right," Trace said flatly.

"So I'll call you, if you're still there. Otherwise, I'll see you back in Vegas.''

"Whatever you want.''

"Cheer up. I've got a question for you. How high is Mount Fujiyama?''

"Who cares?" Trace said.

"It's 12,365 feet high. You know how I know?''

"'Cause you used to live there when you were master-minding World War Two. How do I know?''

"Because there's twelve months in a year and 365 days in a year: 12,365. That's the height.''

"That's ridiculous," Trace said. "Does it grow a foot every four years for leap year?''

"Disregard leap year.''

"How can you disregard one year out of four?" he asked.

"If I knew you were going to be crabby, I wouldn't have called.''

"Why should I be crabby? Enjoy yourself in Memphis, Tennessee. It's all right. I'll sit here in this old folks' home, drinking myself into oblivion.''

"Yeah," she said. "That's the answer to everything, isn't it?''

"What do you mean by that?''

"You're an alcoholic, Trace.''

"I know it.''

"There's no future in alcoholics," she said.

"The hell with the future. Live for the present, I always

say. Tomorrow you may be on a plane to Las Vegas, by yourself, flying with a lot of women with blue hair who are eating up all the Muslim food.''

"Why don't you try not drinking for a while?" she said.

"Why don't you try coming back up here?"

"So long. I'll call you when my plans are firmed up," Chico said.

"Yeah, sure," Trace said as the telephone clicked off in his ear.

9

Trace's Log:

Tape Number Two, Devlin Tracy in the matter of Frederick Plesser et al. It is seven P.M., Tuesday, in the twilight of my life and what the hell do you do in Harmon Hills when you face another empty evening?

Well, not much longer. Thank whoever's in charge that there's nothing to this Plesser business. That's one very good thing and it is going to get me out of here tomorrow. It's also a very good thing, because if there was something to the Plesser matter, and I was instrumental in getting old G-F Insurance to send money to the Plessers, I might have Widow Plesser and Daughter Plesser and Son-in-law Plesser come to visit to thank me, and that might just make me die. Can you die of an overdose of sauerkraut smell?

With luck, I will never see them again. People that ugly shouldn't be given money anyway. It encourages them to go on, and I'd like to think of the Plessers marching down to a lake or ocean or something and wandering out, like Norman Main. Yeah, I know it'll hurt the sales of Pepsi and the *Enquirer*, but the junk drink and junk information cartel be damned. Some things in the world we have to support because they add to our overall sense of beauty and order. Commerce has to take a back seat.

So there are two more tapes in the master file.

The first one is my interview with the Jukes . . . oops, the Plesser family and their dog, Devil. They've got a lawyer now 'cause they think we're cheating them. But Old Man Plesser wasn't feeling good. His doctor said he was just getting old. Christ, I can't blame him. Five minutes with that family and I felt old. Old and dead. His company paid for him at the sanatorium. Cause of death was a bad heart, but the Plessers don't believe it. Ahah, they said that about Elvis Presley too and we know, don't we, just how much truth there was in that.

You know, it's a terrible thing when the only picture anybody has of you smiling is in your coffin. I may be an alcoholic—anyway, Chico says I am, and she's always right about things—but when they carry me off, some people are going to remember me smiling. At least little smiles. If they want big smiles, they'll have to go look at my ex-wife. My death should be worth a year's guffaws from her. They'll have to shield her teeth with Polaroid filters so they don't blind passersby.

Well, anyway, the Plessers did me a favor. They warned me to watch my ass because Meadow Vista's hired killers will be coming after me as soon as they know I'm in town.

Groucho, you'll be glad to know I turned down a bribe. You see, all I've got to do is convince you to send the Plessers a hundred thou and Calvin will take care of me. That probably means he'll send me a six-pack and a gift certificate for two at Burger King. Don't worry, Groucho, I didn't take the deal.

What do I have between me and my Calvin?

Nothing, if I can help it.

And on tape two we have Lt. Frank Wilcox, who doesn't put any stock in anything the Plessers say. I don't know if his wife does or not, but I think if I wanted to call her up some midnight and ask her to spend time going over her views with me, she wouldn't mind. And she does make good coffee.

Anyway, Wilcox has a high regard for the sanatorium and for Dr. Matteson. Nothing there.

And we finish up our selections of the evening with the Tommy Dorsey of Tort, Lawyer Nicholas Yule. He says the Plessers have dower rights, whatever the hell they are. But he doesn't know about any pressure on Plesser or anybody doing him in, he just knows his clients ought to get money, send it to him first, so he can take his cut. Groucho, I think we can settle this whole matter cheap. You give Yule a contract to play at the next two office parties, and I think he'll hand up the Plessers on a silver platter. If you don't want him at two parties, you give him one and I'll get him booked for a night into the Araby Casino lounge. Think it over, Groucho. This may be our big chance.

Yule says that I better worry about Mitchell Carey because maybe he won't get out of the hospital alive. 'Cause Plesser didn't. He was trying to be cute with me, but dandruff and trombones ain't cute. Yule's an idiot. But he has pretty company.

A woman walked out of his office who was worth coming to New Jersey to see. Somehow, I don't think she fell deeply in love with me at first sight. If I were going to hang around town, I'd really find out who she is. But I'm going to be gone tomorrow.

Flying back to Las Vegas alone, while Chico's playing around in Memphis, Tennessee. She says I'm a drunk. No, she didn't. She said I was an alcoholic. They're not the same. Well, she's right. I am. And she's a whore, and I'm not buying that she's in Memphis, Tennessee, with her sister, and she doesn't have a hotel room, so she doesn't have a phone. What would Churchill have said here? 'Madam, I'm drunk. But when I sober up, you'll still be a whore.' It's too depressing.

So are my expenses. I'm tired of itemizing everything every time I have to go on one of these stupid assignments.

From now on, we're starting a new system. My expenses for the day are one hundred dollars. Anything under that, I get to keep. Anything over that, I'll itemize. Don't complain, Groucho, I save the company millions.

And now if you'll forgive me, I'm going downstairs to see my friend Hughie. In the restaurant. A man has to eat, doesn't he?

10

There was a guard on duty in a small booth alongside the wide iron gates of the Meadow Vista Sanatorium, but the gates were open, and when Trace slowed down his rental car, the guard barely glanced up before waving him on.

The road curled around to the right of a three-story brick building, and when Trace followed the road into a parking lot, he saw four identical brick buildings, each three stories high, the fading pink brick ivy-covered, jutting out from the parking lot like the spike marks on a compass.

He parked his car and followed a weatherbeaten sign that pointed to THE ADMINISTRATION BUILDING, and inside, a bright-looking young clerk pointed him down the hallway toward Dr. Matteson's office.

The walls in the hallway were of pink marble and the floors of a polished white stone with black swirls in it and Trace suspected that the sanatorium had been built originally by some governmental unit, because private owners and builders didn't generally put out that kind of money for floors. Only governments never had to worry about the bottom line because the bottom line was always the same: raise taxes.

There were two women inside the office behind the door that was labeled simply DIRECTOR. The young woman near the door looked up brightly as Trace entered. The second woman, older, was pounding away at a typewriter. She had a pencil clasped between her teeth and she typed so rapidly she sounded like a Teletype machine Trace had once heard in a newspaper office.

Trace handed the young woman one of his cards. "I'd like to see Dr. Matteson."

"Do you have an appointment, Mr. Tracy?"

"No."

"Can I tell Dr. Matteson what it's in reference to?" she said. She was still smiling.

"It's an insurance matter regarding one of his patients. Look, do me a favor. Don't keep smiling at me. I'm not ready for smiling today."

"Okay. Just wait a minute, please." She went into an inner office and just a few seconds later came out and said, "Dr. Matteson will see you right now."

"I'm in luck," Trace said.

"I warned him that you're grouchy," she said, and held the door open.

Trace slid by her into a large airy office that overlooked a grassy field that swept down to a stand of trees that bordered the edge of one of the small streams that maundered through that part of New Jersey. The view was peaceful but the rest of the office was busy. The carpet was bright orange and the walls a particularly disgusting lemon yellow, plastered with posters and prints that were vaguely modern and seemed to Trace to embrace every social cause from protecting seals to free abortion on demand to anyone, regardless of age, religion, or even gender.

Piles of medical journals and newspapers were stacked on small tables around the walls of the room. A tape recorder on one of the tables was blasting Gilbert and Sullivan's *Mikado*. Three diplomas, in frames, hung askew on the wall behind Matteson's desk.

Dr. George Matteson was sitting at the desk in the far corner. He had a small well-trimmed beard that seemed to clash with the wild curled frizz of his hair. He wore no jacket and his shirt sleeves were rolled up to display heavy muscular forearms. His collar was open. His suit jacket hung on a plain wooden coatrack behind him, with a tie carelessly looped over the top of the rack. Trace estimated that Matteson was in his mid-thirties.

The doctor didn't look up as Tracy entered. He was busy jabbing a stiletto-shaped letter opener down into his desk, *thump, thump, thump.* Trace couldn't see what he was stabbing at because two rowdy stacks of books were in his line of vision.

When the door closed behind him, Trace said, "Roach problem?"

Matteson seemed to respond to the unfamiliar voice in his office because he stopped his last thrust in midstroke and looked up.

"No, goddammit," he said. He took the letter opener and held it by the tip and Trace glanced sideways to see if there was something to hide behind in case Matteson should be an accomplished knife thrower.

"You ever get the feeling that the world is out to get you?" Matteson asked.

"All the time."

"Well, this, goddammit, this letter opener's out to get me. I don't know who makes things like this. It's got a point on it like a freaking laser beam and every time I try to open an envelope with it, the goddam point gets under my fingernail and I feel like I'm being tortured in Attica. This sucks."

"Is that how you've worked out your revenge?" Trace asked. "Using the letter opener to punish your desk?"

Matteson looked annoyed and puzzled. "Oh. No. I wasn't jamming it into the desk. I was jamming it into this wooden ruler. I'm trying to dull the point before it freaking kills me." He popped his left index finger into his mouth and sucked on it. "Everytime I try to open a letter, it leaves me bleeding. Freaking thing must be made of titanium steel. It won't get dull.''

"Throw it out," Trace said. "Open your letters with your teeth, like I do.''

"I can't. The girls gave it to me. They'll be heartbroken. Maybe you can steal it when you go." He picked up a business card from the desk. "So, let's see, you're Devlin Tracy, Garrison Fidelity Insurance Company. What can I do for you? But if you tell me you're investigating a murder, I don't want to talk to you. What do you want?" He dropped the letter opener and drummed his fingers impatiently on the desktop.

Trace looked around for a chair, but there was none, so he went across the room and sat on the sofa.

"I don't have a chair. It encourages people to hang around and then you never get any work done. You know how hard it is to run a hospital?''

"I'm here about Frederick Plesser," said Trace.

"I knew it. I just knew it. This is going to go on forever, isn't it? I'm going to be hounded year after year for the rest of my life. No rest. No place to put my head. Until I finally confess.''

"Confession's good for the soul," Trace said. " 'Fess up.''

"I've got nothing to confess.''

"You mean I've wasted this whole trip?" Trace said.

"Have you talked to my lawyer yet?''

"No, who's he?''

"She. Jeannie Callahan. She's got an office in town.''

"No," Trace said. "I'll talk to her next if you want. I just wanted to get a sense of what you were like.''

"Just exactly what do you do?''

"Sometimes I check out claims for good old Gone Fishing.''

"Gone fishing?''

"Garrison Fidelity," Trace explained. "We heard about

the suit the Plessers are filing, and since it all looks like it's going to wind up in court, they wanted me to check it out and find out what's going on. Nothing sinister. No accusations. Do you mind if I turn down this damned screaming?''

"No, go ahead. You don't like Gilbert and Sullivan?''

"They're to music what hockey is to sports,'' Trace said. He turned the tape player down to a faint hum.

"What are you talking about?''

"You ever watch a hockey game? I used to watch them. I watched them for a while and then I realized I never saw a goal being scored. Then I used to watch them on the TV news, and I never saw a goal. Even on the instant replays, the slo-mo, I still couldn't see the goal, it was all just too fast. Gilbert and Sullivan are like that. I've never heard one of their lyrics. It's just an exercise with words, to see how many words you can fit into four beats. It's a trick, like a hockey goal. Ya-ba-ba-ba-ba-ba-ba-ba-ba-ba. That's not music; it's articulated noise. I hate Gilbert and Sullivan. You were going to tell me what's going on.''

"What's going on is this— You mind if I smoke?'' Dr. Matteson said.

"It's your office. I don't care if you tap-dance on the desk,'' Trace said.

"I know it's my office, but a lot of people don't like smoking nowadays. I don't smoke but once in a while, it's good.''

"If people don't like it, let them stand outside your window and yell in to you,'' Trace said.

"You've got a good attitude on life,'' Matteson said. He lit a cigarette and took a deep inhalation and his face glowed. Trace wondered if he himself ever looked that content and happy. He lit a cigarette too and coughed.

"I was saying, what happened is this. Frederick Plesser came into the hospital. He was suffering from general atherosclerosis that—''

"Hardening of the arteries," Trace said.

"Right. Call it that. It was reducing the blood supply to his brain and that gives off symptoms like senility. At least, that's the theory we work under. We were treating him with heavy oxygen therapy. That's what we do here. We try to saturate the brain with oxygen to try to minimize, maybe even reverse, any damage that might have been done. Also we put our patients on a good stiff exercise program so their heart and blood system improve and they can start pushing oxygen to the brain better by themselves."

Trace nodded.

"Anyway, Plesser was making really good progress. Did I tell you he was a nice man?"

"No."

"He was a sweet guy. He helped out a lot around the hospital, helping other patients, talking to them. A nice man. I thought he could probably go home and continue his therapy there. We had him pretty well straightened out. But he didn't want to go home."

"Did he say why?" Trace asked.

"Kind of."

"Why was that?"

"He said that he didn't have any fun at home and he liked being here. It was still covered by his hospitalization insurance and his company, so I let him stay. And, er, Tracy, right?"

"Yeah."

"It wasn't like I was gouging Blue Cross or anything for extra money for the hospital. The simple fact is that any other hospital in the world might have kept him in forever. I had good-enough medical reasons for letting him stay."

"I don't work for Blue Cross," Trace said.

"Okay, just explaining. I told you, he was a nice guy, so we let him stay. He was a real help to everybody around here, and then one day, I didn't know it, he changed his insurance policy and made me the beneficiary. One of the nurses and a doctor witnessed the change for him.''

"And they didn't tell you?" Trace asked. He reached into a jacket pocket and fished out a paper.

"They didn't know what it was. He had written this letter, see. I guess to your company and then he asked them to witness his signature and he signed it and he had them sign it, but he had the top of the letter folded over so they couldn't read what it was. I was going to jump all over them when I found out about it, but they didn't know anything."

"That was, let's see, a Dr. Darling and a Nurse Simons," Trace said, reading the names from the paper.

"That's right."

"Then what?"

"Nurse Simons mailed the letter and everybody forgot about it and then, eight days later—that was about a month or so ago—Mr. Plesser died."

"Just up and died?"

"Yes. He had a massive heart attack in his sleep. He wasn't in intensive care or anything, so he wasn't hooked up to any kind of monitor. He was dead when the nurse found him in the morning. She called me, but it was too late to do anything."

"Why a heart attack?" Trace asked. "I thought you had him on an exercise program and all."

"I did. A good, tough one too, dammit, but anybody can have a heart attack anytime. It happens to people, some little valve or something just gets tired and it closes down, and good night, sweet prince. He just died. And I didn't know anything about the insurance until I got a call from somebody at your company explaining to me how claims are filed and blah blah blah. I nearly fell out of my chair, so one of your guys came around and talked to me. I didn't know, I thought maybe he had some other insurance or something, and then those bastards decided to sue me over it.''

"Have you met the Plessers?" Trace asked.

"Not since Mr. Plesser's death. I met their lawyer."

"Trombone McGinty? From the firm of Sleazebag and Crud?" Trace said.

"You said it, not me. He came here and said I should just turn the insurance money over to the Plessers."

"What'd you say?"

"I told him I'd think about it. Then the next day I got a threatening letter in the mail and that shyster called and kind of threatened me with exposure, about running a murder mill, and who was going to be the next victim, and I lost my temper and told him to go to hell and sue me."

"What'd the threatening letter say?"

"I don't remember. I threw it out. I nearly took my finger off with this damned opener trying to open it. Something like God will punish murderers. Don't take advantage of the sick and hurt their loved ones. Crap like that."

"You think it came from the Plessers?" Trace asked.

Matteson shrugged. "Who else? I mean, I haven't murdered anybody else recently."

"You need the money?" Trace asked suddenly.

"No. I don't know anybody poor enough to need a hundred thousand dollars. Of course, I need the money." Matteson hesitated. "No, actually, I guess I don't. Somehow I stayed single and I live here in the hospital and I don't have a lot of expenses and no family, so, no, I don't need the money, but damn sure I'm going to take it now."

"If you get it. You have all the medical records?"

"I gave them to my lawyer."

"Anything there that can hurt us?"

"Nothing at all. The treatment was absolutely consistent with the best medical practices."

"Chances, are, then, that we go to court," Trace said.

"Guess so," Matteson agreed glumly.

"Would you mind if I talked to"—Trace checked the sheet of paper in his hand—"this Dr. Darling and Nurse Simons."

"No. Talk. Keep me out of court. Anything you want."

"You know, I'm surprised at this place. When you hear the word 'sanatorium', you instantly start thinking of some kind of funny farm, but this place is really a hospital, isn't it?"

"Yeah. A poor thing but 'tis my own," Matteson said.

Trace said, "Mind if I ask you a question?"

"I haven't minded so far. You've asked about a hundred."

"Why do you have all this crap on your walls?"

"I don't think it's crap," Matteson said. "I happen to believe in those things."

"You believe in seals?"

"I never got sued by a seal," Matteson said. "Yeah."

"Can you tell me where to find Darling and Simons?"

"They're both in the East Building on the first floor."

"I'm sorry," Trace said. "I only know east when I stay up all night and see the sun coming up. That's east, right?"

"Yeah, but I don't want you staying in my office until daybreak. So go out the front door and—"

"Wait a minute," Trace said. He walked to the window and looked out, but the sun was almost overhead.

"Okay. I can't count on the sun for help. Tell me where to go."

"We've got four buildings here. This is the North Building. That's 'cause it's on the north side of the parking lot. So when you go out and walk to the parking lot, the building on your left will be the East Building."

"And on my right would be the West Building?"

"Right. And across the parking lot will be the South Building. You're not really this dumb, are you?"

"I think I've got it," Trace said. "Could I have your phone number to call you in case I get lost?"

"You wear a watch?" Matteson asked.

"Yes."

"On your left wrist?"

"Yes."

"All right. When you get to the parking lot, turn in the direction of your wristwatch. Got it?"

"Got it," Trace said. "Oh, before I leave, there was something else."

"What's that?"

"While I'm in town, my boss asked me to look up an old friend of his. A Mitchell Carey. I found out that he's here, one of your patients. You know him?"

"Sure. I know Mr. Carey."

"How's his health? I'd like to tell my boss."

"I'm sorry," Matteson said. "I can't really talk about him to you. His medical condition's a matter for his family."

"I'm going to see them."

"If Mrs. Carey wants me to talk to you, she can call me. Otherwise . . . well, I'm sorry."

"I understand," Trace said. "It was nice meeting you." He shook Matteson's hand and walked to the office door.

He opened the door, waited until the receptionist had turned to look, then called back to Matteson, loudly, "And thanks for the help about Mr. Carey. I appreciate it."

He closed the door before Matteson could say anything, and turned to the receptionist. "Mitchell Carey's room number?"

She spun the Rolodex on her desk.

"He's in the East Building. Two-thirteen. That's the second floor."

"And the East Building is on the right when I reach the parking lot?" Trace asked.

"On the left," the receptionist said. "There's a sign next to the door says EMERGENCY ROOM. Just remember E for Emergency, E for East."

"It's very simple, the way you explain it," Trace said.

"No. Today is Wednesday. Wednesday. Tomorrow is Thursday when we have a movie. So today is Wednesday. Yesterday was Tuesday and the day before that was Monday. On the day before, Sunday, we had a lot of visitors at the hospital. Write it down. Put Sunday at the top, then Monday, then Tuesday, then Wednesday. And tomorrow is Thursday. Write it down."

The woman speaking was blond and pretty. She wore a hospital smock and Trace could see the fringe of a red skirt peeping out from under it. She had nice legs, but her voice was brisk, hard, and chilly. Trace stood in the back of the room and watched as she turned her back on the two dozen elderly patients and wrote on a blackboard.

Sunday.

Monday.

Tuesday.

Wednesday.

Thursday.

"I want you to copy this down in your notebooks," she said without turning.

She had nice hips, Trace thought. He liked the way women's bodies moved when they wrote on blackboards. American students' SAT scores started dropping when men entered the teaching profession in great numbers and there was no reason anymore for anyone to look at the blackboards. This was one of many facts in his head that Trace held to be incontrovertible.

When he had first entered the room and handed her his card, the woman had nodded to him to wait. Now she turned around, after finishing writing out all the days of the week, and told the patients, "I want you all to look at your wristwatches now and figure out how long it will be before dinner. We eat dinner at six o'clock. Figure it out and no cheating. I'll be back in ten minutes. Look at that on your watches too. Ten minutes.''

She walked briskly toward the back of the room and let Trace follow her out into the hallway, where she asked him, "What can I do for you, Mr. Tracy?"

"First, tell me, why were you yelling at those poor people?"

"I wasn't yelling," she said. She had a soft smooth voice and in normal conversation it was buttered with a slight Southern accent. Her eyes were very blue.

"Sorry," Trace said. "My mistake. It's just that I thought when people raised their voices and shouted, it was called yelling."

"It's called emphasizing and just who are you? Are you here to criticize my teaching techniques?"

"No. I just came from Dr. Matteson. He said to talk to you about this Plesser insurance thing. I'm representing the company."

"Oh, that again," she said, and sighed. She glanced around and said, "Come on across the hall. I think that office is empty."

Trace followed her into a barely furnished office with just one desk and one chair and a bookcase that was largely empty.

Dr. Darling sat in the chair and Trace perched on the desk and pressed the record button on his tape recorder.

"Now what is it you wanted to know?"

"You were a witness when Mr. Frederick Plesser changed the beneficiary on his insurance policy. When he changed it over to Dr. Matteson."

"Yes."

"Did he say anything while he was doing it?"

"What kind of question is that?" she asked.

"Pretty straightforward," Trace said. "Did he say anything about the insurance or about Dr. Matteson?"

"No. We didn't even know what we were witnessing. He just folded the paper over and then we witnessed his signature. He signed it first and then we signed it."

"He didn't say anything about it?"

"Well, he did say something. He said this is going to make two people very happy. Something like that."

"What did he mean by that?"

"I don't know," she said.

"Do you have any idea, Dr. Darling? What did you think he meant at the time?"

"I didn't think about it," she said. "What do *you* think he meant?"

"I think he meant he was going to make Dr. Matteson happy if he died, and probably himself too."

"Then that's it," she said.

"What did you think of Mr. Plesser?" Trace asked.

"He was okay," she said without much conviction.

"I heard he was the salt of the earth, helping with patients, cleaning out bedpans, that kind of thing."

"Yes. He did that."

"And?"

"He was always grabbing at me," she said.

"I applaud his taste," Trace said.

She ignored the remark. "Sometimes people with borderline senility get strange ideas. He had this notion that because his wife was a couple of weeks younger than he was, he was the scourge of younger women." She shrugged and said, "It's not abnormal, I guess, but it was a little disconcerting. I could never let him get behind me."

"How did he get along with Dr. Matteson?" Trace asked.

"Fine. Why shouldn't he? I mean, Dr. Matteson was his— Oh, wait, I get it. You think there's some kind of nonsense going on and George twisted him around to get him to leave the money.''

"People have been known to do it for a hundred thousand," Trace said blandly.

"George doesn't care about money," Dr. Darling said. "If he cared about money, would he have started this place?"

"I never heard of a hospital director starving," Trace said. "If he doesn't care about money, what does he care about?"

"He cares about old people, Mr. Tracy. That's what we do here. Do you know he went into hock to buy this old place from the county? This used to be an asylum and he took every penny he could raise and pumped it into here. To treat the elderly. The only reason we do anything else, like that emergency room, is because that was part of the price the county wanted when they sold the place. This is the only emergency room for miles around."

"Why does Matteson do it?" Trace asked.

"Because he cares. This kind of work is his life."

"Is it your life too?"

"Yes, it is. And one more thing while we're at it. You were wondering why I was yelling at those patients out there. Well, I wasn't yelling. I was lecturing and you have to do it the way it works. I could mumble and smile and pat them on their heinies, and by next week they wouldn't know what day it is and the week after they'd forget how to tell time. You keep them alive by making them keep working and I don't appreciate any cheap shots from you, particularly when you don't know what the hell you're talking about. I'm talking about keeping these people functioning. You want polite, go talk to a rutabaga. I'm not into vegetables and I'm not into letting people turn into them."

Trace got to his feet. "I'm sorry, Dr. Darling," he said. "I've got to go back. Anything else?"

"Just tell me where I can find Nurse Simons."

The angry look on her face mellowed. "Come here," she said, and led him outside. She pointed down the corridor. "Far corner back there is her office."

"Thanks for the help," Trace said.

Nursing Supervisor Thelma Simons was in her early fifties. She wore nursing whites so highly starched that they looked stiff enough to support a person born without bones. Her graying hair was pulled back into a severe bun and Trace knew that he could get to her anytime just by telling her that her hair was coming undone. Her face jutted forward, a prominent chin, a needle nose, and a forehead that seemed to loom over her eyebrows. She gave the impression of having stayed too long too close to a strong suction. It was as if her face were a full inch in front of where it should be.

"Well, Mr. Tracy," she said after he explained who he was, "you know I can't just talk to anybody who comes in here, don't you?"

"I know that. That's why I went to see Dr. Matteson first. He said it was all right."

"Well, we'll just check on that, won't we?" Trace wondered if she began all sentences with "well." She sounded like a British schoolteacher taking the cat-o'-nine-tails from the closet. "Well, we'll see about your behavior, won't we?" He also hated, on general principles, people who ended sentences with "won't we?"

She seemed to hesitate in reaching for the phone and Trace said, "Would you prefer I waited outside?"

"Well, yes. If you would," Nurse Simons said.

In the hallway, Trace started chatting with a young nurse who was filling out reports at a desk. The telephone rang on her desk, and when she answered it, Trace saw her face blanch. She said, "Yes, ma'am," and hung up. "Nurse Simons will see you now."

"Sorry if I got you into trouble," Trace said.

She mumbled under her breath, "Being under fifty got me into trouble."

"Not with me."

Inside the office, Nurse Simons said, "Well, we've talked to Doctor and Doctor says it's all right to answer your questions, so let's get right to it, shall we?"

"One important question," Trace said.

"Yes?"

"Why do nurses call doctors Doctor?"

"What do you suggest we call them? Milkman?"

"I suggest that you call them 'the doctor' or 'Doctor So-and-so.' 'We've talked to Doctor' doesn't make any grammatical sense."

"I see no need to change anything that has served our profession well for so many years, Mr. Tracy."

"My father used to feel that way about his undershirts until my mother got him to Undershirt City," Trace said. "Then he finally got straightened out. Family liked him a whole lot better then too."

"Have you come here to tell me disgusting stories about your relatives?" she asked.

"No, and you're lucky. If I got to telling really disgusting stories like the time my aunt Billie fell off the wagon and barfed in the soup tureen, well, we'd really find that disgusting, wouldn't we?"

"Doctor told me to answer your questions. He did not tell me to let you waste my entire working day. Good day, Mr. Tracy."

"Just one question," Trace said.

"Please hurry."

"Why did Patient name Doctor as his beneficiary? Did he tell you?"

"No. He never said a word to me."

"Did Patient say he was unhappy with Family?"

"We did not have many personal discussions, actually."

94

"I can believe it. Did Patient say he was happy with Hospital?" Trace asked.

"You're really very insolent, Mr. Tracy. Yes, Mr. Plesser said he was happy here and I do believe that you can leave now."

"Thank you. You've been very kind," Trace said.

"Well, you've been most obnoxious."

"Investigator apologizes," Trace said as he left.

11

As he walked down the long hallway, Trace sensed the steely eyes of Nurse Simons still burning into his back. He turned casually into the corridor leading toward the front door, then ducked quickly into a stairwell and walked upstairs.

Mitchell Carey was in Room 213.

It was a large private room with two assortments of fresh flowers on a small table across the room from the foot of the bed. Carey lay in the bed, sleeping or unconscious, and Trace could see he was a large man, burly and robust. Big hands and thick wrists protruded from the sleeves of his rough-textured white hospital gown. But the man's face seemed puckered and tired, the look that seems to come onto the faces of politicians and popes who are shot and never regain their look of full vigor. Carey had a lion's mane of white hair, and Trace thought he looked like the kind of man you'd expect to see in a meadow, with a shotgun folded over his arm, looking skyward for ducks. There was a green oxygen tank standing next to the bed, and on the wall over Carey's head was a small panel that looked like the channel selector box for cable television, which held a half-dozen monitor lights. All the lights were green.

The man hissed noisily as he breathed.

Trace looked at the cards on the flowers. One said, "You are always loved. Amanda." The other read, "Same message as the last time. Get better. These flowers are expensive. Will.''

Trace looked around the room. There was nothing to see, really. He walked to the cabinet next to Carey's bed and opened the top drawer. Sure, he thought, it's going to have a hundred legal documents changing the beneficiary of his insurance and the heirs to his estate. It contained a small box of Kleenex.

He closed the drawer softly, and as he turned toward the old man, Mitchell Carey's eyes opened wide and he stared at the ceiling, as if in horror, as if death had just entered the room and roughly shook him awake. Trace knew the feeling. It was the sense one gets waking up in the middle of the night and knowing, despite all evidence to the contrary, that there is someone in the bedroom.

The man stared, unblinking, at the ceiling for a moment. The eyes were pinched with fright or terror. Trace reached out and touched the man's hand with his.

"Easy, old-timer," he said softly. "It's all right."

Slowly, as if the act took every bit of his strength, Carey's unblinking eyes turned toward Trace. He stared at the big man, seemingly unable to focus his eyes. Trace saw his lips move slightly.

"Just take it easy," Trace said. "Everything's okay." Should he call a nurse? Should the man be awake?

Carey's lips began to move, the movement of a toothless man gumming a soft piece of bread. A soft low sound emanated from his mouth. Mitchell Carey was trying to speak, and as Trace leaned over, putting his face near the man's mouth, he instinctively pressed the record button on his tape recorder.

The sound Carey made was not much more than an exhalation and the words were slurred and indistinct. But Trace could pick out most of them.

"Hundred . . . two hundred . . . dying . . . dying . . .

97

hundred hundred . . . no more . . . take it away . . . more dying . . . dying . . . dying.''

There was a long pause and Trace lifted his head. The lips were still moving, but no sound came out. Then Carey's lifeless eyes riveted to him. There was a hiss and more sound came out of his mouth. Trace bent over to listen and suddenly he heard another voice: ''What's going on here?''

It was a woman's voice and Trace turned to see an elderly nurse standing in the doorway.

''Who are you?'' she said, even as she walked over to Carey's bedside and looked down at the old man. His eyes had closed now, but he appeared to be breathing regularly.

''Walter Marks. I'm a friend of the family. Just stopped in to see how he was doing. He was trying to talk.''

''Visiting hours are this afternoon and you get passes at the front desk,'' the woman said crisply. She was adjusting the covers over Carey's body. She took his pulse and nodded to herself in satisfaction.

''Is he all right?'' Trace asked.

''He's fine. Just come back when you're supposed to be here.''

''I will,'' Trace said as he left the room.

Out in the hallway, he could find no men's room, where he could change the tape in his recorder. He went into a door marked EXIT and walked up the steps to the next floor. A sign outside the door read: THREE EAST. NO ADMITTANCE. Trace pushed open the door and was facing a uniformed guard.

''Yes, sir?'' the guard said.

Trace smiled sheepishly. ''My aunt Lulu's eating cigarette butts again. I was just checking the place out.''

''Sorry, sir, this area is restricted. You'll have to arrange a visit at the front office.''

''Sure,'' Trace said. ''How come it's restricted?''

"Special patients," the guard said brusquely. "Ask at the front desk."

"Thanks a lot."

Outside the door to Three East, there was a pay telephone on the landing, and Trace decided to call Sylvan Glade to see if he had any messages. He searched through his pockets until he found a dime, but when he tried to dial the number, an operator came on and told him the call was twenty cents.

"I thought a short call was a dime."

"It's twenty cents in New Jersey. Deposit another ten cents please."

"I'm just calling down the block."

"The call is twenty cents. Please deposit another ten cents."

"I don't have another dime. Can I mail it to you? Send you a stamp?"

"I'm afraid not, sir."

"You're no fun," Trace said as he hung up. His dime was not returned.

In the parking lot, Trace noticed a Mercedes Benz parked next to his rented Ford.

Visible through the right front windshield, lying on the dashboard, was a yellow piece of cardboard marked PARKING.

The windows of the Mercedes were open and Trace reached in and filched the parking pass.

He turned and saw a uniformed maintenance man sweeping the sidewalk behind him. The man's uniform hung on him as if it had originally been purchased to hold two like him. Trace wondered if he had noticed anything, and he tossed the parking pass into his car and walked over toward the man, who smiled a gap-toothed grin at him.

"Got a light?" Trace asked.

"Sure." The man rested his push broom against his

wheeled trash can and dug an old Zippo lighter from the shirt pocket of his uniform.

Casually Trace said, "I was just over in the East Building and I got lost. What's on Three East anyway?"

"Hey, heh, you don't want to go there, son," the man said. He flicked the lighter and held it up so Trace could light his cigarette.

"Why not?" Trace said. "What's there?"

"That's the nuthouse," the man said with a cackle. "For the crazies. You go in there, maybe you never come out, heh, heh."

"Are they dangerous? They've got a guard up there."

"Everybody's dangerous around here," the old man said.

"What do you mean? Who's dangerous?"

"They're all dangerous." The man looked around to make sure no one was watching him. He leaned his face close to Trace's. His whiskey breath could stop a horse coming out of the starting gate.

"They put saltpeter in the water so you can't get it up," the old man said.

"Oh, the dirty dogs," Trace said.

"Been doing it for years now." He looked around again and fired another blast of breath toward Trace. "Don't tell them I said anything."

"I won't."

"And I won't tell them you stole Doc Matteson's parking pass," the old man said.

"Thanks," said Trace.

"And stay out of Three East."

"I'll try," Trace said.

12

Shaken emotionally by his bedside meeting with Mitchell Carey and the old man's strange words, Trace stopped at a small roadside bar a half-mile from Meadow Vista Sanatorium and ordered a vodka on the rocks.

The tavern was empty and the bartender was busy watching a televised game show and seemed uninterested in intruding in Trace's drinking. He tossed down his drink rapidly, called for a refill, and went into the men's room, where he untaped the recorder from under his shirt and unhooked the wire leading to the golden frog microphone.

He took the recorder back into the bar. The bartender had refilled his glass and, having decided that Trace was going to be more than a one-drink customer, apparently figured he would help enrich his customer's life with joy and camaraderie. And talk.

"What's that, a tape recorder?"

"Yeah. You're missing your show."

"I hope you're not with *Candid Camera*," the bartender said. "I didn't wear my best shirt." He smiled at Trace.

"Go watch your show."

"Ahhh, I hate this show. It's stupid. They get these two families on, see, and then they try to get them to—"

Trace coughed in the direction of the man's face, then said with agitation, "Oh, Jesus, I'm sorry. You'd better go wash your face off right away."

"Whatsa matter?" The bartender put a tentative hand to his cheek.

"Honolulu herpes," Trace said. "I've got it and you can get it just by breathing the same air as me. Christ, I'm sorry. Quick, wash. I'll leave you my card. If you get it and your wife wants to know why, I'll tell her it was innocent."

"You've got a hell of a nerve coming in here."

"If you want to waste time talking, that's your business. But I'm telling you. Wash. Right away."

The bartender glared at Trace for a moment, then walked to the other end of the bar, ducked under the counter, and walked quickly to the men's room.

"Gargle too," Trace called.

Alone in the bar, now quiet except for the insipid yelping of a television emcee who thought, quite mistakenly, that he was charming, Trace rewound the tape recorder and turned up the volume.

It started playing in the middle of his interview with Nurse Simons and he fast forwarded it to the end of that section. Then he heard Carey's voice.

"Hundred . . . two hundred . . . dying . . . dying . . . hundred hundred . . . no more . . . take it away . . . more dying . . . dying . . . dying."

Then there was a pause and then the old man's voice started again. Softly, in the background of the tape, Trace could hear the voice of the nurse who entered the room. "What's going on here?"

But the microphone was close to Carey's face and his words came out clear, even though faint.

"They're killing me," the old man said. "Help me. Help me."

Trace played the strip of tape back again, just to be sure.

"They're killing me. Help me. Help me."

Trace finished his drink, then popped the tape out of the

recorder, slid it into his jacket pocket, and inserted a fresh tape. A few minutes later, the bartender came out of the bathroom and Trace walked toward it.

"I don't want you touching nothing in there," the bartender snapped.

"Nothing that belongs to you."

Inside the men's room, he restrapped the tape recorder to his waist and hooked up the microphone again.

He washed his hands carefully. Who knew what strange diseases the bartender might have?

When he went back outside, he drained the last drop of his drink and put a ten-dollar bill on the bar.

The bartender was sitting at the far end, warily, near the cash register.

"I don't want your money," he said.

"This money's okay. I've had it treated."

"I don't want it. I might get something. Idea of some guy comes in here with something and doesn't—"

"I'll leave the money. Use it to pay somebody you don't like."

Outside the bar, he looked through the glass window and saw the bartender use a napkin to pick up his glass and drop it into a garbage pail. Then he used the same napkin to pick up the ten-dollar bill, and he put it into his cash register, at the bottom of his pile of tens.

13

From the roadway, there was nothing to distinguish the Mitchell Carey home from all its affluent neighbors, but when Trace came up the driveway and parked in the open area in front of the large garage, he could see that the house stretched back from the visible front section in a long-legged el. The addition was easily twice as big as the section of house visible from the roadway, and inside the el there was room for a swimming pool and tennis court and elaborately manicured gardens. Trace saw a dog kennel in one far corner of the property with two beautiful black and copper Gordon setters lounging inside.

There was no street behind the Carey house and the property rolled away to a large clump of trees. Far in the back, he saw what looked like a large pond.

The doorbell was answered by a woman wearing a housedress of red-striped cotton and a kerchief around her head.

"My name is Tracy. I'd like to see Mrs. Carey."

"Oh, yes?" the woman said, and then waited.

Trace hesitated, then said, "I'm a friend of a friend's. Bob Swenson. From Garrison Fidelity Insurance?"

"Oh, Mr. Tracy," the woman said. "How is Bob? It's been so long since I've seen him."

"You're Mrs. Carey?"

"Yes, of course." The woman took the kerchief from her head and shook loose her naturally graying blond hair.

Her face was smooth, and although she had to be in her sixties, her skin was soft and unlined.

"I'm sorry," Trace said. "Bob's well. He's at a convention in Europe."

"He always did like to travel, that one. Don't just stand out there. Where are my manners? Come on in."

She led Trace to a sitting room in the far corner of the house, large enough to seat a small orchestra and its audience. Through the large front windows, Trace could see the road that passed in front of the house.

"Would you like tea?" Mrs. Carey asked.

"Do you have coffee?"

"Yes. It'll just be a minute."

She left the sitting room and Trace stood up from the sofa and looked around. It was a warm, personal room with good oil paintings hanging side by side with inexpensive prints. The shelves held expensive carved jade and little cloth stuffed mice. It was a room that said real people lived there, not manikins from a magazine insert on how to decorate your home like the stars.

On one of the shelves was a large ball of crystal, four inches thick, and Trace held it up to the light to look at it. He loved the look and feel of crystal and he was disappointed when he saw air bubbles and little imperfect dark spots inside the glass. When he replaced it, he saw on the shelf two small black wax candles and a saucer with half-burned incense cones in it.

When Mrs. Carey came back with a tray, Trace said, "Servants' day off?"

"Servants? Oh, we wouldn't have servants. What would I do in this big house if I didn't clean it myself? And Mitchell wouldn't think of hiring somebody to fix something that he could fix himself."

The woman was altogether too nice, Trace thought. She reminded him a little of one of the aunts in *Arsenic and*

Old Lace who went tippy-toeing happily around while the bodies of the poison victims piled up inside the cellar.

The thought brought him up short because he again remembered Carey's words: "They're killing me. Help me." Did that have anything to do with this pretty little woman who was bustling about with teapots and coffeecups?

"So tell me, how is Bob?" she asked again with a smile.

"He's fine. He's on a convention," Trace said again. "In Europe."

"He always did like traveling," she said.

Nuts, Trace thought. The woman was either nuts or the dullest conversationalist in the history of the world.

"Bob asked me to stop by and see how you and your husband were getting on," he said.

"Oh, we're fine," she said.

"Of course, Bob was sorry to hear your husband was ill."

For a moment, she paused. "Oh, yes. It's an awful thing. He's been so sick."

She sat in silence for a few moments, and finally Trace asked, "Did Bob and Mr. Carey grow up together?" The long pauses in the conversation made him uneasy. It was a trick he often used with other people, letting the air hang dead and silent; it made people uncomfortable and they started jabbering just to fill the dead air. But with Amanda Carey, he felt that unless he said something, they might just sit in silence until they decayed.

"Oh, no," she said. "Bob and I were friends. We went to school together from childhood. Bob didn't meet Mitchell until I married him. Bob and I were from another town, near here, but he didn't know Mitchell. My, my, how Bob always liked to travel."

"How long's your husband been ill?"

"April sixth. Three months ago. He had a stroke. Right after we learned it happened."

106

"Learned what happened?" Trace said.

The woman sipped her tea silently and then began to rock gently back and forth in her chair. She was humming softly to herself, still smiling at Trace, but smiling as one might when looking at a favorite painting, not expecting a smile back.

She began to sing softly to herself and Trace could make out some of the words. " '. . . prettiest tree you ever did see, and a tree in the woods and a limb on the tree, and a branch on the limb and a twig on the branch and the green grass grew all around, all around, the green grass grew all around.' "

He was about to interrupt when Mrs. Carey said, "That was her favorite song when she was little."

"Whose favorite song?"

"Belinda. Our daughter," Mrs. Carey said. "She's dead now," she added with a finality that hinted that it had answered all questions and solved all puzzles.

"I'm sorry," Trace said, silently cursing Walter Marks for not giving him any information on the Carey family.

"Yes. April sixth. It was an automobile accident. In Europe."

"And that's when Mr. Carey became ill?"

"He had a stroke right after it happened." She was talking to Trace but staring past him at the large windows in the front of the room through which the high-noon sunlight poured. Softly she said, " 'And the green grass grew all around, all around, and the green grass grew all around.' Do you like that song?"

"It was one of my favorites when I was growing up," Trace said.

"So young," she said, and then she seemed to snap out of it and asked Trace, "So how is Bob Swenson?"

"He's fine. He's at a convention in Europe."

"Oh, my, how that boy likes to travel. When we were growing up, he always said that he wanted to see the whole world. It wasn't really any surprise when he joined the navy right after high school."

"How is your husband now?"

"He's not well. I don't think he really wants to get better anymore. You don't know how he loved Buffy."

"Buffy?"

"Belinda. Everybody called her Buffy." The old woman's face brightened. "That's her picture over there." She pointed to one of the cabinets in the room, but Trace could see no picture.

"Where'd that picture go?" Mrs. Carey said. "It was there." She shrugged, as if putting the picture out of her mind forever. "Buffy's picture was there. She's dead now," she said, almost as an afterthought, and suddenly Trace felt very sick about the way he made his living. When he had first gone to Las Vegas, he had gambled for a living, and while a lot of people thought that was degenerate, at least it was just him against a vast impersonal casino. Now he had to traipse his way with muddy feet through the tragic lives of other people and it made him sick sometimes. He wanted a drink.

"Do you mind if I pour myself a drink?" he said, nodding toward the liquor cabinet.

"No, you go right ahead. Mitchell always liked a drink when he came home from the office. That was before he became ill."

There were no ice cubes, so Trace just splashed vodka into a large tumbler. "Bob Swenson said you were concerned about the treatment your husband might be getting at Meadow Vista," he said.

Mrs. Carey looked at him, her large brown eyes wide open in surprise. She had lovely eyes, Trace thought. When younger, she must have been something to dream about.

" 'Who is Hecuba that all the Swains adore her?' " he said softly.

And Mrs. Carey said, "No, no, it was Sylvia, not Hecuba. 'Who is Sylvia? What is she that all our swains commend her?' *Two Gentlemen of Verona*."

"Yes, you're right. I was thinking of something else," Trace said. "We were talking about the treatment your husband is getting at Meadow Vista."

"Oh, it's fine. I'm sure they're doing all they can for him— Well, it's all right. His business is being sold and Mitchell won't be going back there. I guess he won't have to worry about that anymore." Her voice trailed off at the end of the sentence and she sipped her tea and began to hum again.

Trace found looking at her painful, and turned away. He sipped his vodka and with his free hand picked up the crystal ball.

The door to the room flew open and Trace looked up as a young woman snapped, "Put that down. Who are you? What do you want here?"

"Before you go barking at me, champ, count the spoons. They're all still there," Trace snapped back.

The woman was in her early twenties. She wore jeans rolled halfway up her calf and a tight-fitting man-style shirt. Her hair was blond and frizzed out wildly around her face in a hairstyle that Trace found revolting. But the girl was beautiful. Even without makeup, she looked fresh and appealing.

"Oh, Muffy, don't be cross," Mrs. Carey said. "This is Mr. Tracy. He's a friend of Bob Swenson's. You remember Bob. From the insurance company?"

"Oh," the woman said, and paused, then she walked into the room and extended her hand toward Trace. "I'm Melinda Belknap," she said. Her handshake was surprisingly strong.

Mrs. Carey was on her feet and said, "Muffy, I'll make you some tea."

"Yes, Nana, please," the young woman said.

109

Mrs. Carey left the room and Trace said, "I'm Devlin Tracy, I'm with Garrison Fidelity Insurance."

"I'm sorry for barking at you just now. I just didn't know who you were and I don't want people bothering her. She's not strong."

Trace had placed the crystal ball back on the shelf and Muffy moved it slightly, as if to its correct position, then sat in the chair Mrs. Carey had just left.

"Now you know who I am," Trace said. "Who are you?"

The woman smiled at him. She had large white even teeth and it was a good smile. "I was a friend of Belinda's," she said. "The Careys' daughter." She licked her lips as she spoke. Her lips were full and shiny and Trace wondered if lips like that came naturally or if she slept with her mouth pressed into a saucer of salad oil.

"We were in Europe on Easter vacation when she died," the woman said. "We were friends, always together, all through college. Belinda and Melinda. They called her Buffy and me Muffy. Buffy and Muffy."

"I had two friends when I was growing up," Trace said. "They used to call us Huey, Louie, and Dewey. How come you don't sound like a Muffy?"

"What's a Muffy supposed to sound like?" the young woman asked.

"Like you've got lockjaw. From biting down hard so the silver spoon doesn't slip out of your mouth."

"Like this?" She curled her lips back so they showed her tightly clenched teeth, and she spoke with a voice that came from deep in her throat, like a series of glottal stops. "So, I said, Lyle, I said, Lyle, I told you I was a *sailor*, and this shabby scow has a motor, for Gawd's sakes, a motor." It was a devastatingly accurate impression of moneyed, female preppie speech, and despite his instant dislike of the young woman, Trace laughed aloud.

"That's too good to be an act," he said.

"All act. I only got to be Muffy after I met Buffy. Belinda and Melinda, I guess it seemed logical to make me Muffy. But the only silver spoon I ever saw was when Buffy'd take us out to a good restaurant for dinner. I grew up on pitted stainless steel."

"How'd she die?" Trace asked.

"A car hit her. I was sleeping late. I usually do, but Buffy got up early and she was out shopping. She liked to go out early and buy apples and fruit and stuff. So she had her arms filled with bags and she was crossing the street, that was in Rome, and one of those lunatic kamikaze drivers ran her down. She died right away."

"What happened to the driver?"

"Who knows?" she said. "He was arrested, but what happened, I don't know. I came back here with Buffy's body and Mr. Carey had gotten sick and I could see Mrs. Carey needed me, so I thought I'd stay to help her."

"Do you know anything about Meadow Vista? Where Mr. Carey is?"

"What did Amanda say?"

Trace shrugged. "She didn't seem to mind it."

"Well, I don't like it at all," Muffy said.

"Why not?"

"Mr. Carey was getting better in the other hospital after his stroke, then they took him to Meadow Vista for some special kind of therapy."

"Oxygen enrichment," Trace said.

"Yeah. But he's not getting any better and then I find out about that guy who changed his insurance to the doctor who runs the place. I thought, suppose it's all a dodge and that's what they do with these poor unfortunates. What would happen to Nana if Mr. Carey dies and she finds out that this doctor inherits his estate. Not just his insurance, but everything."

"You think they do that? As a regular practice?"

111

"I don't know," she said. "Maybe they do. And maybe they make sure that people who sign things over to them don't get well. I don't know if they do that and I'm not saying that they do, but maybe they do."

"That's called murder for money," Trace said.

Muffy shrugged.

"What does Mrs. Carey think about this whole thing? She's the one who mentioned it to my boss."

"You've talked to her. She can't concentrate real well on things anymore. I'm not going to let anything—"

She stopped as Mrs. Carey reentered the room holding a tray with two cups.

"For you, dear," she said as she put a cup of coffee in front of the young woman. "And I made you more coffee, Mr. Insurance, I forgot your name. That must be cold." She cast a disapproving eye at the black coffee that Trace had not touched, and put it on the tray.

"You two must be busy, so I'll leave you alone. Muffy, I'm going to trim the rose bushes back. Is that all right?"

"Of course it is, Nana. Just be sure to wear gloves and be careful of the thorns."

"All right," Mrs. Carey said as she left with the tray.

"You see what's she's like," Muffy said after the door again closed. "She doesn't really think a lot about her husband's condition. I don't know what to do. He's in like a coma and she's in a fog."

"You told her to mention Meadow Vista to Swenson, I take it," said Trace.

"That's right. I met him at the funeral. Of course, Mr. Carey was in the hospital then. But later, afterward, she told me that Mr. Carey had a lot of insurance with your company. Then your boss called her last week, and I told her to mention to him about that man who died and the insurance. I guess that's why you're here, isn't it?"

"I guess so. Anybody else you mention your suspicions to?"

"No. Well, yes, I talked to the family lawyer, but she didn't seem concerned about it. I didn't think much of her."

"Who is she?" Trace asked.

"Callahan, her name is. Jean Callahan, I think. She just didn't seem to think it meant anything. Sort of told me to get lost. I guess I lose my feminist merit badge over this, but I don't trust lady lawyers."

"Male or female," Trace said with a shrug. "What do you think I can do?"

"Have you been to Meadow Vista?" Muffy said.

"Yes. Today. I talked to Matteson."

"Then you've probably already done it. Just kind of let them know somebody's watching what they're up to. It should work out. And we hired a private nurse to be with Mr. Carey at night so nobody tries anything off the wall with him, you know, so let's hope."

"You think I scared them off?" Trace asked.

"Probably. Did you ever have an easier job from your office?" she said with a smile. It was a good warm smile filled with large perfect pearlescent teeth.

"Actually, it's not my office. I work for the insurance company just on special cases. Did you talk to the police?"

"I didn't have anything to tell them." She hesitated. "I just don't want anything bad to happen to Mrs. Carey."

"And you got all this in your head from that family suing Dr. Matteson over the insurance?"

"I saw it in the paper and it started me thinking," she said. "Think about it. Mr. Carey was doing well and now he's getting worse. How do you explain that when that oxygen therapy's supposed to make him better? I just didn't want to take a chance."

"Have you ever seen the Plessers? Or talked to them?" Trace asked.

"No."

113

They sat in silence for a few seconds and Trace tried to sip his coffee, but his stomach didn't really favor it.

Muffy said, "So you'll be leaving."

"In a little while, I imagine," Trace said. He stood up and finished his vodka. Muffy stood up also.

"I appreciate this," she said. "I think you and Mr. Swenson may have done a real good turn for Amanda."

She followed him to the front door.

"I'll tell Mrs. Carey you said good-bye," she said.

"Oh, by the way," Trace said, "I saw Mr. Carey at Meadow Vista."

"Oh really," the girl said politely.

"Yes. He spoke to me."

"He did? What did he say?"

"He said he was dying," Trace said.

14

Jean Callahan's law offices, on the second floor above a trendy small shopping arcade, looked like they might be the wave of the future in automated offices: all furniture, no personnel.

The walls were warm and woody and there were six empty desks neatly placed about, and Trace wondered where the secretaries and receptionists were. He heard a faint noise in the back of the office and found one young woman, sitting inside a glass cubicle, tapping away at the biggest typewriter he had ever seen.

He waited outside the glass wall for her to look up, but she was so intent on her keyboard that she didn't until Trace rapped on the glass.

She saw him and a momentary frown shaded her face. Then she pressed a button on her desk and her voice came out metallically through an amplifier over his head. "Yes? Can I help you?"

Trace didn't see any microphone into which he was supposed to respond. He didn't like this anyway. He liked to talk mouth-to-ear, like live people, not microphone-to-microphone.

He moved his lips quietly, letting no words come out as he mouthed the syllables, I want to see Miss Callahan.

"I can't hear you," the young woman's voice blasted back over the speaker.

Trace shrugged and again silently mouthed, I want to see Miss Callahan.

"The microphone's over there," the girl shouted. She pointed to one corner of the large glass window of her office and Trace saw a small microphone implanted in it. He walked toward it, lifted his head, and cupped his hand alongside his mouth as if shouting. Then he again mouthed, I want to see Miss Callahan.

"Goddammit," the girl yelled, and got up from behind the enormous typewriter.

Trace heard another voice.

"Is it your usual custom to try to make secretaries crazy?"

Trace turned and saw a statuesque redhead standing in the doorway to another office. She was beautiful, even more beautiful than he had thought when he had seen her yesterday coming down the steps from Nicholas Yule's office. Her voice was crisp, but there was a smile in her large dark eyes. Behind her, Trace could see a file cabinet and soft leather chairs.

He smiled sheepishly. "I guess I'm just not willing to join the electronic age," he said. He turned and saw that the young woman in the glass cage had returned to her machine and was again tapping away silently at the typewriter keyboard.

"Now that you've disturbed us, what is it you want?"

"You're Miss Callahan?"

"Yes."

Trace handed her a business card, which she stared at suspiciously for a moment.

"Are you a lawyer for Garrison Fidelity?" she asked.

"No. Some things I wouldn't do even— Never mind."

"Exactly what is it you do?" She was a tall woman, and in her high heels her eyes were almost on a level with Trace's.

"I'm kind of a claims investigator," he said.

"Kind of? What else are you?"

"Well, not all of them for Garrison Fidelity. I'm a drunk and a reformed degenerate. I'm firmly committed to the libertarian principles of government. I believe in low tariffs and that you should not crucify man upon a cross of gold."

"Any position on gun control?" she asked.

"I firmly oppose gun control, except as it relates to everyone else's guns."

'Are you armed and dangerous?" the lady lawyer asked. She had a small smile on her very full wide lips.

. "I'm disarmed and ingenuous."

"You don't talk like a gumshoe."

"You don't look like a lawyer."

"Fair enough. I still don't know what you want with me, but come on inside anyway."

Trace followed her into the office, and when she sat behind the large oiled-walnut desk, he settled into a soft glove-leather armchair in front of her. The office walls and carpet and furniture were all muted, subtle colors, and a small refrigerator on one side of the room and a file cabinet against the other wall seemed to Trace like jarring contradictions to what could otherwise be a millionaire's study.

"You're here, I take it, about the Plesser matter."

"That's right," Trace said.

"Honestly, Mr. Tracy, I thought your company'd send a lawyer, since it's probably going to be involved in this suit."

"My friends call me Trace."

"I'll save that privilege for when I'm sure we're friends."

"Shot down before I ever had a chance to fly," he said. "The company usually sends me out to check things out before they commit lawyers and such to the battle."

"Listen," she said, "you're not the advance guard for

117

some army of minor functionaries who are going to be trooping in here every day for the next year, are you?''

"No. I'm the secret power behind the insurance throne in the United States. When I speak, heads of big conglomerates tremble.''

"Good. What do you want to know?'' she asked.

"What were you talking to Nicholas Yule about yesterday?''

"So that's where I saw you,'' she said. "On the stairs.''

Trace nodded. "When I tried to pick you up.''

"Right. What did you think of Yule?'' she asked, and Trace noted that she had not answered his question.

"I kind of like the idea of a lawyer who plays the trombone.''

"Why's that?''

"It's a cradle-to-grave service. Look at the versatility of it. When you buy a house, he can pipe you aboard after the closing. When you get divorced, he can take you out dancing and make sure you like the music. When you die, he can play taps before he reads the will. I hope you play the guitar or something. If he gets you into court and it's you against him *and* his trombone, I don't know what'll happen to you.''

"Don't let the trombone fool you,'' she said. "Nick's a very effective lawyer.''

"I noticed you didn't say 'good,' you said 'effective.' That means something.''

"It means that he gets his way most of the time because everybody's afraid of him. He'll do a striptease in court. He sings his summations to the jury. He'll cross-examine a witness in rhyme. I walked past a courtroom once and he was playing an accordion. The judges are afraid of him. At first, they just thought he was quaint, but now they've created a Frankenstein. The press loves him, and if one judge goes against him now and tries to put a lid on him, it could bring a batch of stories about what he's been getting away with in everybody's courtroom and that'd bring the wrath of God and the state supreme court down on all the judges' necks. So they kind of leave him alone and let him do what he wants. They don't know what else to do, so he gets away with murder, and sometimes so do his clients.''

"Maybe we should surrender now," Trace said.

"Not this time."

"Why not?"

"Nick can get away with a lot, but he can't manufacture something out of air. There's nothing there. He can walk into court with John Philip Goddamn Sousa leading the Boston Pops and he's going to lose this case."

"You don't think he's got a case?"

"Nothing," she said. "Dr. Matteson's treatment was medically correct for Plesser. No one exerted any influence on him to turn his insurance over to George. There's absolutely no wrongdoing in this case and Nick doesn't have a chance of winning it. That's what I told him yesterday."

"Do lawyers around here generally go visit other lawyers to tell them they're going to lose?" Trace asked.

She nodded. "One for your side. No. I went and offered him a two-thousand-dollar nuisance settlement for him to drop the suit."

"But he wouldn't deal?"

"No." She hesitated for a moment and said, "Look, I'm telling you this because we're on the same side. I heard that Nick has got a problem with money shorts, that he owes a lot more than he can pay. That's why I thought I might be able to buy him cheap. But I couldn't. He said he didn't need money."

"I still say surrender," Trace said. "Especially if we're facing a lawyer who won't take money."

"Don't get sarcastic," she said.

"Sorry. What else did he say?"

"He said he couldn't wait to parade the Plessers in

court. A poor family against a rich powerful doctor. He's writing the headlines already in his mind,'' she said.

"Did you ever see the Plessers?" Trace asked.

"No."

"They're not going to impress anybody in court."

"You talked to them?" she asked.

"All of them. Mother Plesser, Jasmine, Boofus T. Boofus, the son-in-law, and Rex the Wonder Dog. Rex is the smartest. They showed me pictures of Plesser. The only one with a smile was him lying in his coffin.''

"Jesus, you've got some job,'' she said. "Did it look like they were willing to deal?"

"Ordinarily, I think you could buy them and seven generations of their family for eleven dollars,'' Trace said. "But I got the feeling that Yule has them snowed, that they're convinced they're going to get the hundred thou. Less his fee, of course."

"We'll just have to wait and see, then,'' she said. "I don't mind telling you that when this thing gets closer to court, I'm going to move to have George removed from the case because he's got nothing to do with it. The Plessers' argument is with your insurance company and with the dead man, not with Dr. Matteson."

Trace nodded appreciatively. "Very shrewd."

"You figured that out, huh?"

"Yep. You save your options. Later, you can always have Matteson sue the insurance company if the first case doesn't go in your favor."

"You're smarter than you look,'' she said. She got up from behind the desk and walked to the refrigerator. Inside, Trace saw only an apple.

"Did you eat lunch yet?" she asked him. She kept staring into the refrigerator as if hoping that somehow its contents would magically change, and then she slammed the door shut.

"I haven't even eaten yesterday's lunch yet,'' he said.

"Well, there aren't any real restaurants in this town, but I know a cocktail lounge down the street that makes a reasonable sandwich. You interested?"

"Yes."

"Follow me, Trace," she said.

The woman had led Trace into the ratty little lounge where everybody had greeted her by her first name and the waitress had brought her a brandy and water without its being ordered.

Now as they sipped their drinks, she was explaining why she had only one girl working in her office.

"I took it over, the practice, from my father when he died last year. Before that, I was his associate. Well, he had all these people working there who'd been there since the time of the Flood and he'd never let them go. He used to have to go out every hour and shake them to make sure they were still alive. When I took over, I knew that one girl with a computer could do the work of all the rest of them, so I let everybody go."

"Is it working out?"

"Until today, when you tried to make Betsy crazy with that microphone nonsense," she said.

"I won't do it anymore. Did you just fire all those poor people who worked for your father? Christ, you're heartless."

"Fire? Pension, me bucko. My father had the biggest private pension plan in the world, I think, outside of General Motors. They'll collect forever, but at least I don't have to watch them sleep. Don't worry, Trace, nobody got hurt in the deal and I get more work out in a day than I used to in a week."

The waitress came back for a food order and watching the lawyer agonize over the menu made Trace think of Chico. Like almost all trim and beautiful women, Jean Callahan paid a lot of attention to her calories. She finally settled on a hamburger with no roll and no catsup and hold the french fries. Chico was the exception; she ate like a Russian weight lifter, ordering almost everything on the menu, eating it all, then starting to steal food from the plate of whoever she was eating with. Yet her lithe dancer's body never seemed to add an ounce. Whatever works, Trace thought. He'd hate to have to live on the difference between the two women.

"Listen," Trace said when the waitress had left, "I've got to call you Jean. I had a teacher once named Miss Callahan."

"Was she a good teacher?"

"I hated her. She kept praying mantises in a plant on her desk."

"Why?"

"I don't know. I think she taught biology or something. I don't remember 'cause I spent all my time trying to look up her dress. She caught me one day and she kept me after school. She told me that the last kid she caught trying to look up her dress, she tied to the desk and left him there overnight. When class started in the morning, there was nothing left but a skeleton. The praying mantises ate him. It almost made me queer, so if I have to call you Miss Callahan anymore, it'll ruin my lunch."

"Try Jeannie. Everybody else does. I'm glad you recovered." She signaled the bartender for two more drinks.

"Coming up, Jeannie," he called back.

"Better be careful," Trace said. "You're going to get whacked and I'm going to take advantage of you."

"Make that four more drinks," she said sotto voce, and smiled.

She was nice to look at, Trace thought, and she was wonderful to listen to. She had a whispering throaty voice that seemed as if it should naturally be talking in your ear. From a distance of no more than two inches. Preferably while lying down.

He decided he'd better stick to work.

"So tell me about Mitchell Carey," he said abruptly.

"Mitchell Carey?"

Trace nodded and she said, "What's he got to do with this?" He could almost sense her bristling.

He realized he'd been clumsy and quickly he said, "They're friends of my boss. He heard that Mr. Carey was sick and asked me to look in on the wife. So I go over there and I run into some blonde with Bride of Frankenstein hair and she tells me some story about there being a pack of killers running amok at Meadow Vista and she mentioned your name."

"You can't stop people from mentioning your name," the woman said. "The insolent little twerp."

The waitress brought the two new drinks and the hamburger, sitting alone on a small plate.

"This Muffy kid doesn't sound like one of your favorites," Trace said.

"She's not," Jeannie said just before she filled her mouth with a hunk of hamburger.

He waited until she had finished chewing before asking, "Why not?"

"She came to see me with that story, that she was afraid that something might happen to Mr. Carey because she saw that Plesser story in the paper. I told her to butt out, that nothing was going to happen."

"What'd Mrs. Carey say?" Trace asked.

"Nothing. She just sat and listened."

"I don't think she's all that well herself," Trace said. "Did you tell the kid you were representing Matteson?"

"No. That would really have made her bonkers."

"Shouldn't you have told her?"

"It's none of her business. Listen, Trace, Mrs. Carey's like an aunt to me. Her husband and my father were close friends all their lives. When I was really little, their house was practically a second home. Then they had Buffy. She came very late—"

The waitress came back with two more drinks, which she set on the table. "Frankie bought you these."

"Thanks," Jeannie said, and waved to the bartender, who nodded back. "Do you know what that little bitch did?" she said.

"What little bitch?"

"That Muffy or whatever her name is. The first time I saw her, she wasn't in town a week, and I was out at the Careys' house and she almost chased Amanda from the room. Then she starts pumping me about having Mr. Carey declared incompetent and how do you draw wills. Jesus Christ, like she had already taken over. Is that nerve or what?"

"I'd say it's nerve," Trace said. "Mrs. Carey was telling me the business is closing down or being sold or something?"

"Being sold. Mr. Carey made plans for the sale before his stroke. I'm handling all the arrangements. You know, it's funny, he called and told me about selling and I went up to his house to talk to him about it and he kept calling me Littlejean like he did when I was little, and I know he kept thinking about whether or not I'd be able to handle a big sale like that but he was going to go through with it because of loyalty to my father. I hope he lives to see that I handled it well."

"He's not getting any better," Trace said.

"It's tough after a stroke," she said.

"Not because of Dr. Matteson?" Trace asked.

"Forget it," she said. She nibbled at the hamburger and said, "I think I'm getting drunk. I've talked too much."

"Exactly my plan," Trace said. "What are you doing for dinner?"

"Waiting for an invitation."

"Will you have dinner with me?" he asked.

"On one condition."

"I hate women who impose conditions. What condition?"

"We eat at my house. I love to cook."

"Okay. I'll bring the wine."

"Bring red," she said.

15

Dexter, the clerk, called out to him as Trace walked through the lobby of the Sylvan Glade Country Club toward the steps to his room.

"I have a message for you, Mr. Tracy," he said. As he fumbled through papers under the desk, he asked, "And how are you finding our town?"

"Very nice. A lovely town."

"Do you think your principal will approve? That is, if you're allowed to say."

Principal? Trace realized Dexter was talking about the Vatican. "I think I'm going to give them a report that will have you blushing," he said.

Dexter smiled. "Oh, I hope so." He handed Trace a pink message note. "That Chico person," he said. "You must have spoken to her. She was very polite this time."

"I told her you were my right-hand man," Trace said. "Thanks, Dexter."

He read the note as he walked away. It said simply, "Will call tomorrow," and Trace thought it was significant that she had left no return telephone number.

He took a shower, then lay naked on his bed and called Walter Marks' office at Garrison Fidelity.

"Mr. Marks' line," the vice-president's secretary said.

"This is Devlin·Tracy. Let me talk to Groucho," he said, as he always did.

"Just a moment. I'll see if he's in," the secretary said, as she always did.

Trace didn't have the energy to argue with her, but he wondered why secretaries always made that particularly nonsensical statement to callers. Anyone with half a brain knew that the secretary would know whether or not her boss was in. Therefore, she was saying, in essence, I'll see if he wants to talk to you. Didn't it embarrass secretaries to come back on and say, He stepped out, can you leave a message? It would embarrass anybody with any sense.

Therefore, secretaries did not have any sense. A neat little syllogism, perhaps not so elegant as the ones his Jesuit professors in college had taught him: God created everything in the world, including evil; anything created by God has a worthwhile purpose; therefore, evil has a worthwhile purpose. This, Trace had found out early, was part of an intellectual package deal. You had to accept that and then the second part of the package, namely: only God can understand why He has done certain things; we are not God; therefore, we cannot expect to understand everything God has done.

Trace had suggested to his professor a new syllogism: only Jesuits can pretend, with a straight face, to believe Jesuit theology; I cannot swallow this crap with a straight face; therefore, I am not, and never will be, a Jesuit.

The priest-professor had responded in turn: only those who understand will graduate this school; You do not understand; therefore you will not become a graduate of St. Luke's College. Q.E.D.

And Trace had changed his major the next week to accounting. At least, the errors in accounting were correctible. Nobody ever launched an inquisition because it took two tries to make a balance sheet come out even.

Marks came onto the telephone. "What is it, Trace? Don't you ever call anymore?"

"We only talk when I call you; we are talking; therefore

127

I have called you. That's called a syllogism, Groucho. All A is B; C is A; therefore, C is B. You see what you missed out on when you passed up Catholic college. You could have found a way to make the insurance business seem noble and worthwhile. If you had done that, you'd be the president emeritus of every insurance company in America. Even Jesuits would buy insurance. Just in case they were wrong.''

"What are you talking about? Is this going to be one of those nasty conversations?''

"No. You give me 110 percent of everything I demand and I'm pretty sure we can conclude this conversation on a high note of friendship, accord, and mutual respect. Where's Bob Swenson?''

"Mr. Swenson's in Europe. You know that.''

"And since I know that and you know I know that, you also know that that's not what I mean. Where in Europe is he?''

"Why?''

"Because I want to talk to him about this Mitchell Carey thing. I want to find out who told him what and why. Every time he gives you a message for me, it's garbled and it's worse than having no message at all.''

"I told you everything he told me,'' Marks said.

"You told me everything you think he told you. There's a difference.''

"What's going on that's so important anyway?'' Marks asked.

"I think killers are massing at Carey's door,'' Trace said perversely, "ready to do him in, should we drop our guard. What've we got, a half-million-dollar insurance on him? I'm trying to save us money.''

Marks sighed. "Okay. Let me look up the number.''

He was back a moment later and gave Trace the telephone number of a hotel in London.

"Mr. Swenson is there in Room Ten-forty-two. Where

are you anyway, in case Mr. Swenson calls, he can reach you."

"I'm staying at the Sylvan Glade Country Club in Harmon Hills. But, Groucho, if you tell my ex-wife, my ass is grass. She doesn't know I'm in New Jersey. She finds out and I leave."

"I know about the love between you and your ex. I wouldn't tell her anything."

"Good. And as long as you're so agreeable, I've got something else for you."

"What's that?"

"I'm tired of itemizing my out-of-pocket expenses every time I do something for you people. From now on, I'm putting in for a steady hundred dollars a day. Anything big I spend'll be over that."

"Best news I've had in years," Marks said.

"Huh?"

"Just put in the hundred dollars."

"Why?"

"Because, dammit, I just got a statement from accounting and your average out-of-pocket is $147 a day. Put in the hundred. We'll both be happy."

"Aaah, I hate insurance men," Trace said.

He dialed London, charging the call to his credit card, and was surprised to find that it was late night there. He was always surprised because he could never figure out if it was later in the east or in the west. But there was no answer in Swenson's room and Trace declined to leave a message. There was no telling when Swenson might come in and Trace didn't want to be awakened in the middle of the night.

As Trace dressed, he whistled cheerily and then realized he was in such a good mood because he was indulging in one of mankind's oldest, most noble pleasures: revenge. He had no delusions about where Chico was and what she was doing. She was in Memphis, Tennessee—not Egypt—and she was tipping on him with some other man. If she hadn't been, she would have left a number where he could call her back.

It had been a good run and what did he expect? Eternity? Four years wasn't bad.

There had been some kind love between them, the unusual love of a part-time hooker and a full-time ne'er-do-well, but friendship had come first. And now she was trampling on that friendship by lying to him. How do you lie to friends and still call them friends? It was more of a question than he could answer right now. He just knew that somehow things were different, and once things started going differently, they kept going differently. Maybe it was time to look for a new roommate.

He thought of Jeannie Callahan. Or maybe to fall in love.

The telephone rang. Maybe Chico, he thought as he walked to the bedside. It wouldn't be Marks. Maybe Swenson.

It was none of them.

"Hello, Devlin," said a whiny voice. "This is your mother, Mrs. Patrick Tracy of Manhattan."

"Yes, Mother. I recognize the name," Trace said with a sigh.

"Did you know that tomorrow is Cousin Bruce's birthday?"

"No, Mother. Somehow it must have slipped my mind."

Trace tried to remember Cousin Bruce. All he could summon up was the image of some middle-aged moron who was fifty pounds overweight, waddled like a duck, had a bald spot, and laughed like a hyena, sometimes at nothing more humorous than a burned-out light bulb. Then Trace realized that could describe all his cousins, all the offspring of his mother's siblings beyond number, all named either Bruce or Barry.

She was talking. ". . . no wonder it slipped your mind out there in Las Vegas with that woman, I guess you've got more important things to do than think about your family, your real family."

"That woman's name is Chico and you can call her that and I'd rather study remedial Swahili than think about . . . Who is it? Bruce?" Trace said.

His mother sniffed as if Trace had confirmed all her suspicions. "I hate it when you're nasty with me, but never mind that. The reason I called is that we're having a birthday party for Cousin Bruce."

"Stop calling him Cousin Bruce," Trace said. "Just plain Bruce will do nicely." Who in hell had cousins named Bruce? What had his father been thinking of when he married this woman?

"I said we're having a birthday party for Bruce. I want you to come."

"For Christ's sakes, Ma, Bruce must be fifty years old."

"Forty-eight. And is that a reason not to have a party?"

"It would be for someone with some taste or decency. I can't make it."

"You don't even know when it is."

"I still can't make it."

"It's next Wednesday, a week from now."

"I'll be back in Las Vegas then," Trace said.

"Oh, sure. You've got lots of time for that woman and gallivanting around the countryside, but no time for your family," Mrs. Tracy said.

"Mother, I'm here working. That's the male equivalent of your shopping. Let me talk to Sarge."

"I'll get him. And I'm expecting you at that party."

Trace heard her put the phone down, and a few moments later his father's laconic voice asked, "Hello, son. What's up?"

"Sarge, what's gnawing at her craw now? I know she didn't call to invite me to that baboon's birthday party."

"Her birthday was last week. You forgot to call."

"I sent flowers. You know I can't remember dates. The florist has a steady order. Every year, same time, he sends a dozen roses."

"She would have liked a phone call."

"Next year, I'll call and skip the flowers," Trace said.

"That'll really piss her off," his father said with a chuckle.

"Good. Serves her right. Listen, Sarge, you talk her out of being mad, but no way I'm going to Bruce's party."

"I wish I had an excuse not to."

"Square it for me," Trace said. "Tell her my oral exam for the priesthood is that day."

"You'd better tell her that one yourself," his father said. "I'm not crazy."

"I know. You're the only one of us who isn't. Don't drink too much."

"You too, son."

16

Trace's Log:

Tape recording Number Three, Devlin Tracy in the matter of Plesser, Carey, and other assorted pains in the ass and aggravations in my life.

Two more tapes in the Master File, and mightily though I tried, there are going to be more. But I want to get all this stuff out of the way early because I am having dinner tonight with a beautiful woman and I don't want my overdeveloped sense of duty and responsibility to keep intruding and telling me I have tapes to make.

I've got problems here. The big problem is that everything seems like a nothing, and then I've got that poor old man telling me that somebody's trying to kill him. Delirium? The babbling of somebody junked up with drugs? I don't know. I don't think so.

So there I am at Meadow Vista and we've got Dr. Matteson, who sits in his office surrounded by pictures of whales and seals and Jane Fonda and listens to Gilbert and Sullivan, for Christ's sakes. He thinks that letter openers are out to get him. Maybe mild paranoia. I wouldn't say he's worried by the Plesser lawsuit, but he's annoyed by it. And Plesser, he said, didn't want to leave the sanatorium. Having been in that sauerkraut factory of a house, I can buy that.

So Plesser asked to stay even when Matteson could have let him go. Maybe oxygen therapy works for senility and some brain damage. I don't know. It could be Matteson's a quack, but his idea seems logical. If you can cut off oxygen to the brain, it dies; so maybe if you saturate it with oxygen, it lives better. I know it helps with hangovers. When I used to tourist it in Las Vegas, sometimes I'd go to those hotels with the big spas and take fifteen minutes of oxygen to clear the head. Maybe.

Even if he does look like a hippie that never got off the shelf, I like Matteson. And I believe him when he says he didn't know anything about Plesser changing his insurance policy over. Could a man who drives letter openers into his desk because they prick his fingers, I ask you, could that man lie?

Plesser just had a heart attack and died. Anybody can have a heart attack anytime, that's what Matteson said. Well, thank you, Doctor. What about us who can't brush our tongues? If you can't do anything about hearts, if it's always going to be anything can just happen, then why not concentrate on tongues? Find a medical breakthrough so I can scrub three packs of tar off my tongue every morning. And another thing. I can't put Q-tips in my ear without gagging. Has anybody thought about doing something about this? I'll tell you, world, medicine isn't what it's cracked up to be.

Matteson gets a point for telling Plesser's lawyer, that Yule, to go to hell. And I guess there isn't any doubt that the Plesser tribe wrote Matteson that threatening letter. God punishes those who steal our insurance money or whatever it said. They wrote it. At least that's my humble opinion and this is my tape recorder, so you're stuck with it.

Anyway, I'd feel better about Matteson if he had different posters on the walls. He's got pictures for Save the Seals. Come on, cut me a break. They started that lunacy in California, where else? So they save the damn seals and the water is six feet deep with seals. Then what happens?

Wherever you've got seals, you're going to have sharks. Suddenly, the waters are flooded with sharks. They're eating seals and they're eating people too. So we save a couple of goddamn seals and people are getting killed. I hate environmentalists.

That's another sign I'm going to make for my backwards billboards on cars. *Save the people first.*

Starting with me.

Anyway, that's what I think about Dr. Matteson, and what I think about his assistant, Dr. Barbara Darling, is I don't know. I don't care if what she's doing is all the latest rage in working with old people, I think she takes just too much pleasure in yelling at them. But hand it to her, she shot me down neatly when I blew off my big mouth, and I deserved it. Anyway, she confirmed what Matteson said; she just witnessed Plesser's signature and she didn't even see what she was signing. Somehow if Plesser was as senile as everybody was making him out to be, he was thinking pretty well about how to be secret and change his insurance. And what'd he say? Make two people happy? She tells me that Matteson runs that sanatorium out of love for the elderly. Well, maybe. Maybe him. I don't know about her.

I don't want to talk about Nurse Simons. If I ever meet her in a bar, she'll have to buy her own vinegar and water. "Well, we'll see about that, won't we?" God, I hate people who talk like that. I don't like Nurse. But she gave me the same story as Darling. What an entry. Darling and Nurse. They sound like Hollywood's last two bad summer comedies.

So, so far, nothing, right? But then there's Mitchell Carey. I still get chilled thinking about this big old buck of a man, lying there like a helpless child, and then seeing the torture in those eyes. What did he mean? "Hundred, two hundred, dying, dying, hundred hundred, no more, take it away, more dying, dying, dying."

135

And then he said, "They're killing me. Help me. Help me."

I want to, Mr. Carey. I just don't know how. I don't know what and I don't know who and I don't know how to do it, and that's why I'm afraid I'm going to be around here awhile, until I find out just what's going on.

Groucho, if I'm dead and you're listening to this, you'll be happy to know I almost landed in Three East. That's the nut factory at Meadow Vista. If I do wind up there, tell Chico that I'm all right and staying out of trouble, 'cause they put saltpeter in the water. Never mind, don't tell Chico anything. She doesn't deserve explanations. Besides, I'll be safe. I never drink water.

And then there's the Carey family. I learned a lot there. How that Bob Swenson always liked to travel. Aaah, that's a crappy thing to say. The poor old lady isn't all there anymore. Mitchell Carey had a stroke when he found out that Buffy got killed. I think Amanda Carey suffered worse and nobody knows it. I was thinking about that misquote of mine. "Who is Hecuba that all the swains adore her?" and she reminded me it was Sylvia, not Hecuba. So what was I thinking about? I remembered. It was a line about Hecuba from Homer. "An old gray woman that has no home." That's what Amanda Carey reminds me of.

What the hell's a crystal ball and incense doing in their house? I'll have to ask Melinda, call her Muffy, an ersatz, no-money Muffy, and isn't that just too cute for words. That one I can do without, and not just because she's a blonde. But she's the one getting Mrs. Carey worked up about Meadow Vista. She thinks I've done my job by coming here and being seen at the sanatorium. Now they won't try anything. That's just a little too smart by half.

Newspapers can cause a lot of trouble. Muffy saw that story about the Plesser family and it got her thinking. I don't think anybody under twenty-five should be allowed to think.

Dammit, I'd like to know why Mr. Carey has been going downhill since he got to Meadow Vista. "They're killing me. Help me." Why'd he have to say that to me? I could be out of this place.

I've got another piece of tape with Jeannie Callahan, but I'm having dinner with her tonight so I'll save it and do it later, in case anything else comes up. Chico, you listening? I hope mightily that something else does come up.

And I hope this is all done fast. My mother knows now where I am. Damn Groucho's eyes for squealing.

Expenses. A hundred dollars for routine. Fifty more for expensive stuff that came up but I lost the receipts. Total, a hundred and fifty.

17

Jeannie Callahan lived on the top floor of a low apartment building on the outskirts of Harmon Hills. There was parking alongside the building, and when Trace rang her doorbell, she answered right away and told him to come up.

Her apartment was at the end of the corridor, her door was open, and Trace found her in the kitchen, holding a brandy snifter and looking into the refrigerator.

"Nice to see you again," she said. "Where's the wine?"

"I forgot the wine."

"Good. I forgot to cook. Make yourself a drink and go sit at the table. I hope you like roast beef. I bought some at the delicatessen."

"I love roast beef."

"Rye bread all right?"

"With seeds?"

"Of course with seeds. Without seeds, is it rye bread?"

"Good." Trace went inside with his vodka and set the drink on the glass-topped dining table on which two candles of unequal size were burning, then he went to the stereo and found two albums of Charlie Parker with Strings and put them on the turntable.

When he sat at the table, she called, "What do you like on your roast beef? Mayonnaise?"

"God, no. That's awful. Catsup."

"Nobody uses catsup on roast beef."

"Everybody does who knows anything about roast beef," Trace said.

She came into the room a few minutes later with a platter of roast-beef half-sandwiches that she set on the table. The rays of the setting sun cut through the window and made her hair glow as if aflame.

She was just beautiful, Trace thought, almost too beautiful.

A few moments later, she was back with another tray containing cole slaw, catsup, mayonnaise, and her drink. She sat down and watched him put catsup on his sandwich.

"That's really disgusting," she said.

"Actually it's very logical. Roast beef is red, right? So you put red stuff on it. If you had something white, like chicken or turkey or tuna, you put white stuff on it: mayonnaise. Brown stuff like bologna or hot dogs or kielbasa slices, that takes brown stuff: mustard. Once you learn it, it makes life very simple."

She thought about that for a moment and was about to say something when he added, "Of course, like any other good rule, it has a few exceptions. Liverwurst, for instance. That's brown and should take brown stuff, but it takes mayonnaise."

"How do you deal with the exceptions?" she asked him over the top of her brandy glass.

"By not eating liverwurst. It's really a good system. It's only got one design flaw."

"What's that?"

"Cheese. It doesn't work for cheese. You would think that cheeses take mayonnaise, but they don't. They all take mustard."

"If you use light-yellow salad mustard instead of the spicy brown, you can make it work," she said.

"God, I love lawyers' minds," Trace said. "I wouldn't have thought of that in a thousand years. Of course. Light-yellow mustard on light-yellow stuff. Wonderful.

I'll drink to that." He leaned across the table and they clinked glasses.

They hardly put a dent in the sandwiches, but they drank a lot, and later they sat on the sofa and looked out the window where the last faint pink fingers of the vanished sun clawed up at the sky. It reminded Trace of a drowning, of someone's hand reaching convulsively for something, anything, to hold on to, before it settled slowly beneath the surface of the water.

Jeannie refilled her drink and Trace said, "You're drinking too much."

"Does it bother you?"

"No."

"It's the curse of the race, you know," she said. "God created alcohol to stop the Irish from conquering the world."

"My Irish father used to tell me that," Trace said.

"Is he an alcoholic?"

"He's in retirement, kind of. Once in a while, a sip of beer or a glass of wine. Or occasionally, a one-night toot. Most of the time, nothing."

"My father was an alcoholic too," she said. "He was a neat one, though. He'd have his martinis for lunch and he'd sit around the house drinking his cocktails before dinner and his wine with dinner and his brandy after dinner, and then he'd have just a couple of pops during the evening and maybe a schnapps before bedtime and he pulled it off for years. Your father like that?"

"No," Trace said. "He was more of a rip-roaring, bingeing, empty-out-a-saloon drunk. He was a cop. He told me once he answered a call, it was some rape thing, but he was traveling with half a bag on and he pegged a shot at the rapist, but he missed and the guy got away. He couldn't deal with that so he stopped drinking on the job, and then when he retired, he just kind of drifted into stopping drinking off the job. I think he was trying to set a good example for me, but it was too late. Doesn't drinking bother your law practice?''

"Oh, no. I don't really have a problem. I drink when I want to. Like this afternoon and tonight, I just really felt like it.''

"And tomorrow?'' Trace said.

"If I feel like it,'' she said. She put her feet up on the cocktail table, then put them down, squirmed out of her shoes, and put her feet back up. "Your father named you after relatives?''

"Yeah.''

"It's a nice name. Devlin Tracy. If it was the other way around, you'd sound like a quarterback. Tracy Devlin. But Devlin Tracy's got a nice ring to it. Like a prime minister. 'Prime Minister Devlin Tracy announced today . . .' Names are important.''

"They sure are,'' Trace said. "Mozart.''

"What about Mozart?'' she asked.

"Well, his middle name was Amadeus. That's Wolfgang Amadeus Mozart. It's Latin, you know.''

"I know,'' she said. "I'm not an idiot. It means God's love. So what?''

"Suppose his middle name was German. In German, God's love would be Gottlieb. Wolfgang Gottlieb Mozart. You think that rings? You think anybody's going to do a Broadway show named *Gottlieb*? I tell you, there's a lot to this name business.''

She mumbled agreement and said, "You married?''

"I used to be.''

"Any steady interest?''

"I live in Las Vegas with a hooker,'' Trace said.

"That must be fun.''

"It used to be. I don't know anymore.''

"I was almost married once,'' she said. "I was just out of law school and I was clerking with this firm in New York and I was going out wth one of the very junior

141

partners. Then one night I went to have dinner with his parents. Very Upper East Side. So after dinner, the father asked around for brandy. I said yes and had a brandy with my coffee and a cigarette, and his mother looked down her goddamn East Side nose at me and said, 'I always hoped Frank would find a woman who didn't smoke or drink.' ''

"What'd you do?" Trace asked.

"I looked down my patrician New Jersey nose at her and said that actually I had always hoped to marry an orphan. Well, Frank, the asshole, he jumps to her defense and I poured my brandy on his permanent-waved hair and left. Then I went to clerk for my father."

"Good for you."

"You staying around town long?" she said.

Trace reached down and through his shirt turned on his tape recorder. "Looks like I'm going to be around for a couple more days."

"More work?" she asked.

"I was talking to my boss tonight, the one I told you is the friend of the Careys, and he wanted me to stay around a little longer, just to make sure that Mr. Carey's all right."

"He's all right," she said.

"He's not getting better at Meadow Vista. In fact, he's getting worse."

"Not because of anything that's happening at the sanatorium," she said. "He's old, he had a stroke. Sometimes they recover and sometimes they don't."

"You're sure it's like that? No maniacs at the funny farm pulling the plug on patients?"

"None."

"No lady lawyers who've been looting company funds for years and are afraid they're going to be found out?"

"Not me," she said. "I'm too dopey to steal."

"No business partners who want to bump him off because he knows too much?"

It seemed to Trace that she hesitated one beat too long before answering "No."

"Who's Mr. Carey's partner?"

"Wilber Winfield. Nice old guy. They've been together since Hector was a pup."

"And they don't get along," Trace said.

She sipped at her drink, then got up and walked to the kitchen to refill it. Trace noticed that she was walking unsteadily. She kept talking from the kitchen.

"They've been fighting every day for forty years," she said loudly. "They argue about everything. They love each other."

"You can love and still kill," Trace said.

"Hey," she said, sticking her head around the corner of the kitchen wall. "What is all this kill stuff? Mr. Carey's sick. He had a stroke. What kill? You're not buying that Plesser bullshit, are you?"

"No. Sorry. I guess I've just got a morbid turn of mind."

"A drink'll cure that," she said, and came back into the living room and snatched his glass up to refill it.

When she was back in the kitchen, Trace called out, "What's the real reason you don't like that girl living with the Careys?"

"I told you the real reason. I think she's a bitch."

"Why?" he asked.

" 'Cause I think she's a parasite, living there for months, reminding Amanda of her dead daughter. And I don't think it's any of her business worrying about having Mr. Carey declared incompetent or how you draw up wills or whatever. Who the hell is she?" She looked around the corner to see if he was agreeing with her. He nodded and she went back into the kitchen.

She came back with both glasses filled to the top and most of the contents reached the coffee table safely.

After she put down the glasses, she stood looking down

at him, then she knelt on the couch and kissed him hard, pressing him back against the sofa cushions.

"I think I want you to make love to me, Trace."

"Should I wait until you make up your mind?" he asked.

"No. Seize this mad moment of weakness," she said. She kissed him again, then pulled away and surveyed him as if he were a coat on sale. "Let's take that tie off," she said. "You're always wearing that tie. And that stupid frog on your tie. Your shirt, let's get you comfortable." She reached for his shirt and Trace let her fumble with his shirt buttons for a moment before pulling her hands away. Any more and she would notice his tape recorder.

"I think we ought to stick at what we're best at," he said. "I undress me."

"And I undress me? How dull."

"No. I undress you next," he said.

They were perfectly matched, Trace thought. Each of them brought their glasses into the bedroom and put them on the end tables. They both made sure they had cigarettes and ashtrays, and then occasionally, they would take a break during lovemaking to sip from their drinks or smoke a cigarette.

She had her hands around Trace's naked waist.

"What's that sticky stuff?" she said.

"Don't be disgusting," Trace said. "That's a by-product of successful sex."

"I mean that goo on your back."

"Oh. That's from a mustard plaster." He reached back and moved her hand from the sticky area where he had adhesive-taped his recording machine.

She giggled. "Shouldn't it have been a mayonnaise plaster?"

Later, they lay side by side in the bed, smoking. Trace looked at his jacket hanging from the top of the door and could almost sense the tape recorder running silently inside his pocket.

"Trace, how old are you?" Jeannie asked.

"Going to be forty, thank God."

"Why thank God?" she asked. "What's so good about forty?"

"No more getting erections on buses," Trace said. "It almost makes being forty worthwhile. How old are you?"

"Thirty-two," she said. She stubbed out her cigarette in the ashtray on his naked belly, slung an arm across his throat, and fell asleep in seconds.

It was after midnight when Trace extricated himself from her grip, took a shower, and then dressed quietly in the darkened apartment.

When he was ready to leave, he knelt on the edge of the bed and kissed the beautiful redhead lightly on the forehead.

"Good night, lady lawyer," he said softly.

She opened her large eyes. In the dark room, glints of moonlight reflected from them. "You're leaving?" she said.

"It's either that or come back to bed with my suit on, and I hate getting wrinkled."

"Be quiet going out," she said. "You'll ruin my reputation if anybody sees you."

"I was planning on whistling the March from *Aïda* down your halls."

"Hold it till next time. We'll do it together."

She reached her arms up for him and brought him down and this time he kissed her a long kiss before walking quickly to the door of the bedroom. She stopped him by calling his name.

"Trace?"

"Yes."

"You believe in love at first sight?" she asked.

"Maybe a little bit," he said. "Maybe now."

"Me too," she said. "I feel something good about you."

"I know," he said, and let himself out. In the hallway, he made sure the door to her apartment locked tightly behind him, and then he walked down the two flights of stairs to the ground floor.

He lit a cigarette outside the building and looked up at the sky. It reminded him of the night sky in Las Vegas, not when looking from the Strip or Downtown: there was so much other light around that one could hardly see the sky. But from the outskirts of the town, where the city drifted away into just sand and open desert, where the roads were unmarked and unlit, the sky hung over the earth like a twinkling ceiling. It was the kind of night that made Trace wish he owned a telescope, even though he had owned one once as a child and had never been able to see much of anything through it, except a woman in a building two blocks away who liked to undress in front of her window.

His father had caught him on the roof one night, peeping-tomming at the woman. He was still in his police uniform, but he was off-duty with a beer can in his hand.

"What are you doing?" Sarge had said.

"Just looking around," twelve-year-old Devlin had said nervously, but before he could move the telescope, his father had said, "Let me see," and Police Sgt. Patrick Tracy had looked through the eyepiece and Trace had felt himself shrinking away as his father kept looking and going "Unhuhhh, uhuhhh" softly under his breath. Then he had stood up from the telescope.

"When I bought you this, this wasn't exactly the kind of heavenly body I had in mind," he said.

"No, sir," Trace had said.

His father nodded. "Your turn," he said, and young Devlin had hesitated and his father had said, "Quick, before she's done."

As Trace again watched the woman through the scope, his father had spoken softly to him. "Now some people might think that what we were doing is wrong, but that's

146

nonsense," he said. "That woman undresses in front of a window because she wants people to look at her. Can you imagine how terrible she'd feel if nobody outside saw her?"

Without looking up, the boy said, "So we're really doing good?"

"That's right, son. She do that every night?"

"Most nights. Weekends, she must go out or something 'cause the lights are out by the time I've got to go to bed."

His father had nodded. "Well, I'll try to take care of things on weekends, because I stay up later than you." He had hesitated for a moment. "I think I saw that woman on a wanted poster at the precinct."

"Really? A criminal?"

"I think so. But in police work, you've just got to be sure. A lot of people have been hanged because of mistaken identity."

"Should we call the police?"

"I am the police," his father had said. "I think we better just keep checking her out until I can be sure of my identification."

"All right."

"Don't tell your mother anything. I don't like to involve her in my professional duties. It could be dangerous."

"Okay, Pop."

"It could be dangerous for you too, but I trust you to be careful and not breathe a word of this to anyone. That way, you won't be a target."

"I understand, Pop. Sort of an undercover investigation."

"That's exactly what I had in mind," his father said, and then added sternly, "But don't neglect the sky either. Everything is up there." He pointed skyward. "The past and the present and the future. Everything."

"Sure, Pop. I just have trouble telling one constellation from another one. They all look alike to me."

"Practice, Devlin. Practice."

For the next week, Devlin had gotten used to his father coming up on the roof to share his views of the sky and their interesting blond neighbor.

One night, when his father was working a different tour of duty, covering for someone who was ill, the boy had seen the police squad car park down the block from their house and seen his father walk toward their building. A few minutes later, he had joined his son on the roof.

"She home tonight?" the father had asked. His breath reeked of whiskey.

"Yeah, there she is. You think she's the criminal?"

"What criminal?" his father had said, moving to the telescope.

"You know, the one you're looking for."

"Oh. Hard to tell at this distance." The man had looked for a few moments, then said he had to get back on duty. "You should be getting to bed now," he said.

"Okay, Dad. I'll close up now and go downstairs."

"Don't tell Mother I was home. She'll think I was sick or something."

"I won't," Devlin had said.

His father left, and when he saw the squad car head down the block, Devlin had stayed on the roof, watching the blonde. She was sitting in her lingerie on her sofa, facing the window through which the boy looked, reading a magazine.

Occasionally, she stretched, and it was the stretches that he waited for. But she seemed to be restless tonight, and if she didn't undress for bed in a few more minutes, he was going to carry his telescope downstairs and go to sleep.

As he was watching, the blonde suddenly cocked her head, then got up, tossed a satin robe around her, and went to her front door. The door of the apartment was set back from the window and the boy could not see who was there.

He could see the blond woman, though; she seemed to be talking to someone for a long minute or two, and then she reached out and turned off the main overhead light. There was still a small lamp burning near the sofa.

Trace saw a big figure, a male, move toward the window, but he could see only the man's silhouette. The man stood alongside the window, still not visible from outside, reached his hand up, and pulled the shade down. In the flash of light from a streetlight, young Devlin saw something glitter on the man's sleeves.

He kept watching, even though he could see nothing now except vague amorphous outlines of shapes on the window shade. He saw two persons and then, as he watched, they seemed to merge into one.

A few moments later, another light came on in the apartment. It was in her bedroom, because it was the light that always went on after the blonde had undressed in front of her window. The light was on for a few minutes and then it too went off.

The boy waited a few more minutes, then folded his telescope tripod and carried it downstairs to their second-floor apartment. His mother was dozing on the couch and he went right to bed. But as he lay in bed, something gnawed at his mind and he got up, dressed quickly, and taking the key from behind the door, let himself out.

He ran the two blocks to the street where the blond woman's apartment was. He stood in a doorway on the corner, looking at the building. Parked in front of it was a police cruiser and behind the wheel was Patrolman Eddie DeRose, his father's regular driver.

His father was not in the squad car, but young Devlin knew where he was. He knew what had glittered on the sleeve that had pulled the blinds in the blonde's apartment. The flash had been the brass buttons on a policeman's sleeve.

Devlin ran back home and let himself into the apartment. His mother was still sleeping on the sofa.

The next night, he was back on the roof, but the woman's

shades were drawn. As they were every night from then on. And from then on, his father did not visit the observatory on the roof, and young Devlin was forced to try to look at stars.

A month passed before his father came up to the roof where Devlin was looking at the sky, charting the stars against a map from an encyclopedia.

Without preamble, the boy asked, "That blond woman?"

"What about her?"

"Was she the criminal you thought?"

The older man shook his head. "No. You know, I went over there one night under false pretenses. Told her we heard about a burglar in the building. But close up I could see right off she wasn't the woman. Sorry, son. I thought the two of us were going to be in on an arrest. You still watch her?"

"No. She pulls the shade down at night now."

"Too bad," his father said. "Well, you know, women come and women go. But the stars, they're always there." He pointed overhead and said excitedly, "Look, there's Cassiopeia."

"Where?"

"There."

"Pop, that's the Big Dipper."

"I knew it was one of them," his father said triumphantly, and went back inside.

The memories came into Trace's mind as he stood outside the front door of Jeannie Callahan's apartment building, looking up at the summer sky. He could still recognize the Big Dipper, but that was all. The rest of the constellations looked to him like nothing but stars spilled at random across the evening sky.

He remembered he had bought What's-his-name a telescope on his eighth birthday. Or maybe his tenth. How old was his son? He didn't remember. And he had put the kid on the roof of their apartment building and he had showed him how to focus the telescope and had told him to keep an eye on their neighbors, but the kid had never spotted anybody to compare with Trace's blonde. Or, if he had, he had kept it to himself. The swine. How could anybody like a kid like that?

Trace remembered his father's rooftop words, "Women come and women go," and he flipped out his cigarette and strolled down the length of the building toward the parking lot and the green Ford he had rented. As he approached his car, he thought he heard something, and stopped, but the only sounds he could recognize were New Jersey night sounds—insects, a faint breeze through the trees that bordered the narrow road, and far away the sound of a train whistle.

He shrugged and walked toward the car, fishing in his pocket for the keys, which were jammed in under his tape recorder.

He was inserting the key in the door lock, reminding himself that he was in rural New Jersey now, not in Las Vegas, and he could leave his car parked without locking it, when he heard the sound again. It was the sound of footsteps and he wheeled, just in time to get a fist crashed into his jaw. The punch knocked Trace backward, and he helped it by rolling, spinning along the front fender of the car, to get a split second to clear his head and to put some space between himself and his assailant.

As he rolled straight up off the fender, he saw there were two of them. They wore ski masks and he raised his fists as they charged him; he caught one of them with a straight right-hand punch directly in the face. The man stopped as if he'd run into a wall, but the other one was on Trace, driving punches home into his belly, *rat-a-tat-a-tat*, and as Trace spun toward him and drove his own fist into the man's stomach, the second man jumped on Trace from the back, slipping his arms around Trace, trying to stop him from punching. Trace slammed himself backward toward the car and the man let out an *oof* of air as he was sandwiched between the fender below and Trace's 210 pounds atop him; but the second man slammed a right hand into Trace's jaw, and even as the man beneath him released him, Trace rolled off the fender and onto the pavement of the lot. He got up quickly. Being on the ground was no way to win a street fight, but the two men turned and ran as he lumbered back to his feet.

He saw them turn the corner of the building and he yelled after them, "You're in trouble now. My kids live in Jersey. They'll never forgive you for letting me live."

He felt himself with his hands. Nothing seemed broken or seriously injured, but his stomach felt as if people had been using it for test borings. He checked the tape recorder in his jacket, but it seemed undamaged.

He heard a car door slam heavily and a motor start up, and a moment later a car without lights sped from the back of the building, out into the street, and turned left, away from him. He could only barely make out the car's outline, and even if he had, it wouldn't have made any difference because he was convinced all car manufacturers shared the same set of plans so all their cars looked exactly alike. All he could see was this car was dark green and had some kind of sporty sloped back roof.

Trace's key was still in the door lock, and as he turned it, he glanced toward the back of the car.

"Shoot," he exclaimed. The left rear tire was flat. For a moment, he thought of saying to hell with it and going back upstairs to barge in on Jeannie Callahan, assuming he could wake her up, and impose on her hospitality, but he didn't want to. He had said good night to her, just right, just enough, and he didn't want to change it.

He opened the trunk of the car and hoisted out the spare tire, putting it down next to the bumper while he rooted about inside the neat carpeted trunk for the jack. He thought that it was probably a major American cottage industry, people sitting around trying to find ways to hide jacks and lug wrenches so they could never be found by anyone but an automobile salesman. As he leaned into the trunk, his knee brushed the spare tire and it rolled away from the bumper and he lunged to grab it. It wobbled to the ground, and as he picked it up, he noticed something else. His right rear tire was flat also.

"Sumbitch," he growled, and tossed a kick at the car's rear fender, just as an auto's headlights illuminated him from behind. He turned but couldn't see anything because the car had stopped only feet from him and its headlights were blinding him.

Was it the two men come back? If it had been and they wanted to hurt him, wouldn't they have just slammed him into his own car, crushing his legs?

His eyes adjusted and he was able to see that the car was a police cruiser. The door opened and a woman's voice hailed him. "What's going on here?"

The woman was tall and Trace moved out of the path of the lights and saw she was wearing a police uniform.

"My tires are flat," he said.

"Is that how you fix them? By kicking your fender?" she said. "Oh, it's you. What's your name, Tracy or something?"

Trace recognized the woman now as Officer Wilcox, the wife of the lieutenant he had seen when he first came to town. The woman with the roving eyes.

"That's right. Tracy. You're Officer Wilcox?"

"Yeah. You say 'tires' are flat?"

"Both rear ones. I think it was vandals."

"From that blood on your lip, it looks like you caught them."

Trace reached up his hand to the side of his mouth and his fingers came away sticky. He decided impulsively that he did not want to involve the police in any of this yet, so he said, "I rapped myself on the trunk lid." He wiped his mouth with his handkerchief.

"What are you doing here anyway?" she asked.

"I was visiting."

"Who?"

"A friend."

She hesitated, then said, "I guess we can let it go at that."

"Is there an all-night garage around here?"

"No. There's no all-night anything in this town. Well, hardly any all-night anything. Best I can do, I'll give you a lift somewhere. You can call somebody in the morning."

"I appreciate it," Trace said.

He turned around to replace the spare tire in the trunk, and as he did, in the glare of the squad car's headlights he saw a small piece of paper on the ground near his flattened right rear tire. He picked up the paper and jammed it into his pocket, and he noticed that the valve cap had been taken off the tire. The tire had not been punctured; someone had just opened the valve to let the air out.

He locked the spare tire in the trunk, then put his car keys on the floor under the front seat and locked all the car doors, first making sure the driver's front vent window was unlocked and an arm could reach through it to the door lock.

"I left the keys under the seat for whoever comes," he said.

Police Officer Wilcox drove carefully, her eyes on the road, and Trace had a chance to admire her profile, classic and sharp. She looked to be in her early thirties, perhaps fifteen years younger than her husband.

"You think vandals got your tires?" she said.

"I think so. The valve caps were off. I think somebody just let the air out. I'm staying at the golf-course hotel."

She nodded. "There were a dozen cars in the lot. Why'd they pick on you?"

"Maybe my ex-wife sent them to harass me. She's capable of it."

"You're divorced, huh?"

"Yeah."

"What's it like being divorced?"

"How do you mean?"

"You know. Is it hard to get back to a normal life?"

"Marriage wasn't ever normal for me," Trace said. "I like to come and go when I feel like it. I'm surprised to see you out in the car at night. I thought you were a house mouse."

"A house mouse?" she said. "What's that?"

"A woman cop who's on desk duty all the time. At least, that's what my father used to call them."

"Oh. Somebody turned up sick and I decided I could use the overtime. I do it a lot."

"Your husband like your being out?" Trace asked.

"He does his thing. I do mine. Damn, this hot weather makes you thirsty."

"Yeah."

"Reach under the seat," she said. "There's two cans of beer there. Get them out."

"Your command is my command," he said.

"Don't say things you don't mean. That could get you into trouble."

Trace popped the tops of the beers and handed her one. She tilted it to her lips and drank a long swallow, then placed the can on the flat dashboard of the car.

"You got many friends in town?" she asked.

"The Mitchell Careys. Their family," Trace said.

"They don't live out this way."

"That was another friend," Trace said.

"I'll need the name for my report."

"You going to report this?"

"Vandalism to a private car? Think I ought to," she said. She was driving now with just her left hand on the

155

wheel. Her right hand rested on the seat between them and then casually touched his leg.

Trace did not move and she said, "Nobody's waiting for you at your hotel, is there?"

"No."

"Good." She made a sharp left turn and sped off down a narrow dark road.

Trace reached into his pocket and turned on his tape recorder. "What do you have in mind for me?" he asked.

"Can't you guess?" she said as she turned off into an unpaved lane off the highway and killed the car's engine.

"I haven't done this since I was a kid," he said.

"I have. Don't worry. I'll refresh your memory."

"I guess it won't do any good to tell you I'm almost forty years old?"

"Not a chance."

"Okay, Officer. I'm at your mercy," he said.

She began to unbuckle his belt. "I think you can call me Lauren now," she said.

They were almost back to the golf course when she said, "Well, I'll say this for you. Making it with you is interesting."

"What do you mean?"

"All you want to do is talk about Meadow Vista. Then when I touch you, you complain your stomach is sore. Lots of fun."

"What about me?" he said. "You think it's fun with that police radio squawking every ten seconds and me expecting to get caught in a crossfire any minute? I tried my best."

"Actually you did very well."

Trace said, "I don't think you ought to report what happened to my car."

"Why not?"

"If you do, you'll have to report this rape."

"There's no rape without a complaint," she said.

"I'm not complaining," he said.

"Neither am I."

It was almost three o'clock when she let him off in front of the country club's main building. "If you're around for a while, I hope I see you again," she said.

She smiled at him, and as she drove away, Trace mumbled, "Not if I see you first."

Dexter was not at his usual spot behind the desk and Trace wondered why he should be surprised. The man had to sleep some time. He leaned over the counter but saw no messages in his box.

Upstairs in his room, he hung his jacket on the back of a door. Then he remembered the piece of paper he had found near his car and fished it from his pocket.

It was crumpled and Trace suspected that someone might have used it to unscrew the valve caps on his tires, in a totally unnecessary effort to avoid leaving fingerprints.

He unfolded the sheet of pink paper. It was the top of a billhead and printed on it clearly was: MEADOW VISTA SANATORIUM, Harmon Hills, N.J.," but the paper had been torn and there was no name or invoice number on the sheet. Nor was there any marking on the back of the paper.

He undressed, took another shower, and wondered what all this scrubbing was doing to his body's natural oils. If he started to wrinkle, he was going to think about sex-by-mail.

He was surprised to get a dial tone on his room telephone and he made a credit-card call to Bob Swenson at his London hotel.

The voice was crisp, sharply clear even over three thousand miles of distance as it snapped "Hello" into the phone.

"Bob, this is Trace."

Trace knew immediately that Swenson was drinking

because he lapsed into his hearty ho-ho-ho voice that sounded like a cross between W. C. Fields and a drunken Mr. Magoo.

"Hello, my boy. What brings your voice here at this vile hour?"

"You been to bed yet?" Trace asked.

"I don't remember. I love these conventions," Swenson said.

"I know. You love to travel. You always did."

"Someone's been spilling personal secrets," Swenson said.

"Listen, Bob, I'm in Harmon Hills checking on the Carey family."

The bluff heartiness of the voice vanished and Swenson was crisp as he said, "I talked to Walter Marks about it. Amanda is an old friend of mine."

"Did she tell you she was worried about her husband's safety at that sanatorium? Think. I need to know."

"She told me something about somebody changing their insurance beneficiary."

"Yeah, but was she worried? Did she really sound worried?"

There was a pause before Swenson said, "Maybe not really worried. But she did mention it and I thought it was worth looking into."

"Do you think that maybe she was just mouthing somebody else's words?"

"Possibly. She's a nice woman. Maybe. She wasn't hysterical or anything, if that's what you mean. What's going on there?"

"I don't know. I don't think there was anything fake about that guy who changed his insurance beneficiary."

"Good. That ends it, doesn't it?" Swenson said.

"Not quite. I was at the hospital and Mr. Carey said that somebody was trying to kill him."

"Who?"

158

"I don't know. He might just have been delirious, and I don't think he knew what he was saying. He's in a coma most of the time. So I would have discounted it, except some goons turned my ribs into a marimba band tonight, so I don't know."

"What are you going to do?" Swenson asked.

"Hang around until I find out some more."

"How is Amanda? Have you seen her?"

"Yeah. I think she's taking that daughter's death pretty hard. She's not really functioning," Trace said.

"Trace, I like the Careys. Don't let anything happen to them."

"I'll try not to. Listen, from now on, if you've got things for me to do, will you talk to me directly? Marks didn't even tell me the Careys had lost a daughter."

"His feelings will be hurt if I don't talk to him," Swenson said.

"Then talk to both of us. But me directly."

"Okay," Swenson said.

"When you were at the funeral, did you meet that girl who's staying with Mrs. Carey?" Trace asked.

"Yes. What's her name?"

"Muffy."

"Yes, I met her."

"What'd you think of her?"

"I think she had too much hair, as I remember," Swenson said.

"Okay," Trace said. "I ought to let you go. These calls are expensive."

"Nonsense. I just saw a commercial. Calling overseas to chat with friends is one of the real bargains left in the world."

"No," Trace said. "The only bargain left in the world is coffee filters."

"Coffee filters?"

"Yeah. You ever try to finish up a box of coffee filters? They last longer than most marriages."

"Trace, what time is it there?"

"I don't know, three-thirty or so."

"Have a drink and go to sleep."

"I'm cutting down on my drinking," Trace said.

"You're fired."

"Well, maybe I could force just one down."

"Good night," Swenson said.

Trace sat on the bed and rewound a few inches of tape on the recorder, then pressed the play button.

He heard his voice. "I'm six-three and I don't fit in these cars. I stopped fitting in these cars when I was sixteen."

He heard Lauren Wilcox's voice. "You're fitting just fine. Oh, yes. There. There."

And his own voice. "I aim to please."

And her voice. "Your aim is very pleasing."

He turned the machine off, sighed, and got up to get a fresh tape from his jacket pocket.

18

Trace's Log:

Tape Recording Number Four, Devlin Tracy in the Land of Nod, at, oh, God, four o'clock on Thursday morning.

So maybe I fall in love, right, and two hours later I'm unfaithful. So, okay, it was a nymphomaniac cop and how do you reject a woman with a gun but why do these things always happen to me? If human beings someday hear these words, remember, I was more to be pitied than censured.

Hold it all. I said falling in love. I don't know if I believe in that, in love at first sight. Lust at first sight, I know about. Even like at first sight. But love? No. Therefore, machine, I can tell you now with absolute surety that I am not now in love, nor have I ever been in love, with Jeannie Callahan. Well, I don't think so anyway.

In the Master File are two more tapes of my meetings with Jeannie Callahan and I don't think I'm ever going to let Chico listen to these tapes. And I am not going to think about the Lawyer Callahan *versus* Michiko Mangini, part-time hooker and roommate who is out someplace cheating on me. It is really more than I care to deal with right now.

Jeannie is a much nicer lady than you would suspect about somebody whose office help is a computer and a typist with a temper. She's ready to defend Matteson in the Plesser case, and if nothing else comes of this, I'd better remember to tell Groucho to have our lawyers contact her, since sooner or later they're all going to be working together anyway.

She says that she will peel **Nicholas** Yule's skin if she ever gets the Plesser lawyer in court, but she was willing to try to make a two-thousand-dollar settlement with him. He turned her down. How could anyone turn that woman down for anything? And what kind of a lawyer doesn't need money?

My stomach hurts and my ribs are no prizes either. I don't like getting hit. Fortunately, it hurts only when I breathe.

Lawyer Callahan doesn't like Muffy 'cause Muffy came to pester her about Mr. Carey and making wills and such. She was probably right in not telling Muffy that she was also representing Matteson in the case.

So she's the Careys' lawyer too, and they're more than clients, they're lifelong friends. So you know she's not involved in any scheme to hurt old man Carey. Right?

Right.

Why do I trust this woman when it's an article of faith with me that I don't trust lawyers? Is my personal opinion getting in the way of my professional judgment? Probably, and why not? My personal opinion's as good as anything else I've got in this case. If it is a case.

Jeannie is making a deal now to sell Carey's business. I better check that out 'cause I'm not even sure what Carey's business is.

And then I had dinner with her. Chico, if I'm dead and you're listening to this, the woman cooked a magnificent roast beef for me. What did you ever cook for me besides my goose? And my faith in womankind?

Jeannie is sure nothing is happening to Mr. Carey at Meadow Vista. What'd she say, though? He's been fighting with his partner for forty years? Wilber Winfield is the partner and he goes on my list to talk to tomorrow, if my stomach lets me live until tomorrow.

Muffy talked about having Mr. Carey declared incompetent. Let's see. If she gets that done, then Mrs. Carey is in charge of everything and Muffy is in charge of Mrs. Carey. It all makes sense to me.

Maybe.

I just don't like that frizz-haired blonde. Maybe it's 'cause she slides so easily from calling Mrs. Carey "Nana" to her face and "Amanda" when she's out of the room. We'll see.

And then there's a lot of stuff on the tape of a highly confidential, personal nature and maybe I'll erase it.

Unfortunately, there is no record on the tape of me getting the shit kicked out of me in the parking lot. Why let the air out of my tires? Why beat on my belly? Why drop a Meadow Vista billhead near the car? That's too stupid for words.

At least I clocked one of the bastards. If I see somebody with a light-bulb nose walking the streets, I may have found my man.

Keep on the lookout for a dark-green car with a sporty back. I don't know cars. When I was young I knew every car. Now I don't know any of them. Maybe this was a Camaro. Or maybe a Firebird. Sure, and maybe it was a 1922 Hispano-Suiza and Juan Fangio was driving it. What do I know?

And then I got a ride home from Police Officer Wilcox and I pumped her mightily. About Meadow Vista, that is, and she didn't know anything bad.

It's funny. When Chico used to tell me the truth, the whole truth, I used to launder these tapes and lie a lot. And now that she's started lying to me, it seems like I can tell the truth on the tapes and not have to lie anymore. Maybe this is a good thing.

And Bob Swenson says that he didn't like Muffy and she could have put Mrs. Carey up to talking to him about Meadow Vista and worrying about her husband. Why such a big deal? Muffy admitted it to me when we met the first time.

If there something wrong with Jeannie? Why hasn't she ever been married? Unless she's too smart to get married, in which case she's obviously too smart to have anything to do with me. This is a quandary.

Why did Mitchell Carey tell me somebody was trying to kill him?

I should have told Jeannie about that. Probably I didn't because I find it hard to trust people who put mayonnaise on roast beef, even if they are heavy drinkers like Jeannie. I'll think about it all some more tomorrow.

And so to bed.

My stomach still hurts.

19

Squawk, squawk.

It was a flock of geese. No. No, definitely not geese. Moose. A herd of moose.

No, not moose. It was telephones. A bank of telephones. Ringing, *squawk, squawk*, near his head.

Trace picked up the telephone and struggled to open his eyes. His stomach still hurt.

"Hello."

"Hello, Devvie," a woman's voice said.

"Cora, how many times do I have to tell you to stop pestering me this way?"

"I haven't talked to you in six months."

"That's what I mean. I can't turn around without you being on the phone. What do you want?"

"Since you're in New Jersey, come and see your children."

"I saw them last night."

"No, you didn't."

"Yes, I did. When they jumped me in that parking lot. I'm ashamed to see how you've raised them, Cora."

"Stop it, you damn fool. You haven't seen your children in three years now. They're your children too, you know."

"They're pretty old now, aren't they? Pretty big," Trace said shrewdly.

"Yes. You'd hardly recognize them."

"I didn't recognize them in the parking lot. But I guess What's-his-name was the big one who kept punching me in the stomach. I hope the girl likes her broken nose."

"What the hell are you talking about?"

"You're just lucky I didn't turn you in to the police. Let the three of you spend the rest of your life behind bars."

"Devvie, it's not asking too much for you to stop by to see your children. Maybe you'd like them to visit you in Las Vegas?"

"Definitely not. Las Vegas is no place for children. Even if they are muggers."

"Do you remember when you saw them last?"

"Yes. At my mother's, Thanksgiving Day, three years ago. The date is emblazoned in my memory. I could tell they hated me. You poisoned them, Cora. You poisoned them against me."

"Nobody's poisoned them. Come and see them."

"No. I was just leaving town. I've got a plane to catch in twenty minutes."

"I feel like driving out there to see you and bring them with me."

"All you'll see are the wingtip lights on my departing airplane. How did you get this number?"

"From your mother."

"I knew that woman hated me," Trace said.

"You'd better tell me right now. You're never going to see your kids again?"

"I know what you've got in mind. It's like *The Manchurian Candidate*, isn't it? You're going to say to them, What's-his-name, Girl, this is your father, and like a bell, it's going to bong off in their heads, 'father,' and they're going to bear me to the ground by the sheer size of them and stab me like Caesar. Confess, damn it. That's what you've got planned, isn't it?"

"Devvie, you are the sickest, most evil-minded, rotten bastard son of a bitch I have ever met."

"Trying to be nice to me now won't change a thing," Trace said. "I'm leaving town."

"I'm really sorry for you. You're sick, and you're making a big mistake."

"I've only made four mistakes in my entire life," he said.

"I guess I'm supposed to ask what they are," she said.

"Yeah. You. What's-his-name. The girl. And the clap. I was lucky there. I got rid of the clap."

His ex-wife hung up, but Trace knew it wouldn't end there. She would be on his trail now, forever, like Inspector Javert.

He needed a drink. He needed a car. He looked at his watch. It was nine-thirty A.M. He needed a night's sleep. He thought of Cora. He needed to be up and done with this whole matter and out of this town before she made good on her threat.

Dexter was on the desk when Trace called downstairs, and the clerk said he knew a very good garage that would pick up Trace's car, pump air into the tires, and deliver it to the country club.

"You're being very helpful," Trace said.

"Nothing but the very best service for our treasured guests," Dexter said.

He was on his way out the door when the telephone rang.

"Hello, Tracy, this is Nicholas Yule."

"Yeah?"

"Is your name really Tracy?"

"Yes."

"My clients said it was Marks. You told them your name was Marks."

"I lied. I lie a lot."

"Oh. I was wondering what your company's planning to do."

"About what?"

167

"About the Plesser matter. I was hoping I could save Fidelity Garrison some embarrassment."

"It's Garrison Fidelity, and don't worry about their being embarrassed. They've got me working for them; they're used to it."

"If you can tell me without violating your professional oath . . ." Yule began.

"I didn't take an oath," Trace said.

"Okay. Are you going to recommend to your company that they settle with my clients?"

"No."

"Why not?"

"Because I've talked to the lawyers for the other side and they don't think you've got a case."

"You've been talking to that Callahan woman?"

"As often as possible," Trace said.

"Have you talked to the people at the sanatorium? Dr. Matteson? Those people?"

"Yes," Trace said.

"And what do you think of them?"

"I like them all a lot," Trace said. "Nurse Simons reminded me of my mother."

"They're really not to be trusted, you know," Yule said. "Those people would do anything." He hesitated. "I'd take anything they tell me with a grain of salt, if I were you."

"Thank you for the advice."

"Listen, you going to be in town for a while?" Yule asked.

"A little bit more."

"Think about it," the lawyer said. "We could probably make a deal that'd make your company very happy and would satisfy my clients."

"Okay, I'll keep it in mind," Trace said.

"One more thing," Yule said.

"What's that?"

"Did you get a chance to ask them at the country club if they need a band?"

"I'll do it today," Trace said.

"Let me know," Yule said.

When Trace entered his office at the sprawling plant of Carwin Enterprises on the edge of the small town, the first view he got of Wilber Winfield was of his rear end. The man was on the floor, crawling around, apparently trying to reach something under his desk.

"Can I help?" Trace asked.

"Feef," Winfield said without turning.

"What?"

"Vropp ma feef."

Trace got down on the floor to help look.

He finally found it. *It* was a beautiful set of false teeth, sitting up on the rug as majestically as an ox skull resting on the dried bed of an old salt lake.

"There they are." Trace tapped Winfield on the shoulder and pointed. The man turned to him. He wore thick eyeglasses whose lenses looked like they had been cut in slabs from champagne-bottle punts. The glasses exaggerated the size of his eyes and it gave Trace the impression that he was watching a man drowning slowly, helplessly, inside a goldfish bowl.

Winfield picked up his teeth, then sat on the floor, his legs extended like a fat little child, and inserted the dentures into his mouth.

"There," he said triumphantly. He clicked his teeth together, apparently to verify that they still made sound when clicked together. "Now what can I do for you?"

He was still sitting on the floor, a fleshy, well-fed man in his sixties, with thinning hair combed sideways across the top of his head, thick glasses, and false teeth. He was wearing a suit, but Trace noticed that he was also wearing ankle-high shoes.

"You mind if I sit down when we talk?" Trace said. "In a chair?"

"No. Go ahead. Over there, son." He pointed to a chair a few feet in front of his desk, and then, as if remembering who he was and where he was, he got to his feet and walked to the swivel chair behind his desk.

"My eyes aren't so good anymore and I dropped the damn choppers. I do it a lot and they always wind up rolling behind the leg of the desk or something where I can't see them. Who'd ever think teeth would roll like that?"

"Peanut butter," Trace said.

"Huh?"

"Like when you make peanut-butter-and-jelly and you drop it, it always lands peanut-butter-side-down. Didn't you ever notice?"

"That's because of the density of the peanut butter compared with the bread. It makes it heavier and the heavy side gets to the bottom. What you got to do, son, is, work over a counter, not over the floor. That way when you drop the bread, it doesn't have enough space to turn over in before it hits bottom. Save a lot of peanut butter that way."

"I like to work over the floor," Trace said. "Maybe I could make peanut-butter-and-jelly while I was kneeling down. That'd cut the distance."

"You still liable to drop it when you stand up. Kneeling's not the answer. Work over the counter. Me, actually, I don't have that problem 'cause I can't eat the crap 'cause it cements my dentures together."

He folded his hands over his chest for a moment, looked off into space through his big fish-eye lenses, then nodded as if he had considered it and could find no logical flaw in his argument. "Anything else? What is it—Tracy?"

"Yeah. Tracy. Actually I didn't come in to talk about peanut butter."

Winfield was looking right past him. "Look at that," he said. "Peanut butter."

Trace turned and saw a cuddly, rounded blonde in a tight pink sweater standing at a file cabinet outside Winfield's office.

"Peanut butter?" Trace said.

"That's my new secretary," Winfield said. "I'd like to lather her up with peanut butter and go to work on her."

"Your dentures'd get stuck."

"What a place to get stuck," Winfield said. "Not much chance, though. I heard her making fun of me the other day, calling me a dirty old man. You were saying why you were here."

"I'm with Garrison Fidelity Insurance Company. I'm checking on your partner, Mitchell Carey."

"He didn't die, did he?"

"No. Not yet."

"Be like him to die and nobody tell me. Nobody tells me anything. This place runs itself and nobody tells me anything. That's why I'm talking to you, 'cause I don't have anything more important to do."

"I'm honored by the faith you've shown in me," Trace said. "You and Mr. Carey been friends a long time?"

"Friends sometimes, but we've been partners forever. He's the worst crab-ass man I ever saw. If he ain't dead, what are you doing here for whatever-it-is insurance company?"

"Trying to see that he doesn't die. You know anybody'd who'd want to see him dead, Mr. Winfield?"

"You mean besides me?"

"Well, start by including you. You want him dead?"

"Yes. No. Hell, I don't want him dead, I just want him the hell out of my life. You get him out of my life, you can keep him alive forever if you want. Stuff him and implant a motor, I don't care."

"You two sound like you've got real business problems between you."

"You know, we ran this business thirty-five years without a contract, just on a handshake. Then five or so years ago, Mitch comes to me and says we're not getting any younger. I say, I thought *you* were getting old, and he says we've got to put everything down on paper, this is no way to run a big business."

Trace nodded, he hoped, sympathetically.

"So we put everything on paper. Old Elmer Callahan, he drew everything up. Son, if you ever deal with lawyers . . . Well, don't deal with lawyers."

"What happened?" Trace asked.

"Elmer works it out so that Mitch gets fifty-one percent of the company and I get forty-nine. He says this is so that we can make decisions without being deadlocked. I got some extra money for the extra one percent, I forget what it was, but something. And there was some other stuff in there about who gets what when one of us dies and like that, and I didn't think anything about it and then all of a sudden, last year, Mitch says he wants to sell the company and retire. His daughter's getting out of college and it's time to retire, he says. I tell him I don't want to retire; he wants to retire, go ahead. I'll keep sending him checks and he says, no, that won't do, because there's capital gains and some bullshit to think about and I don't know what the hell he's talking about; so anyway, he goes ahead and tells little Jeannie, old Elmer's dead now, he tells her to start selling out the company and he's got us a buyer. So now, dammit, she's doing it. What do you think of a guy who does like that?"

"I don't know," Trace said. "It doesn't sound fair."

"It's not fair. We built this business together. Mitch is real good with planning and stuff and design, and he leaves managing men and like that to me. We worked fifty-fifty and we split fifty-fifty and now he wants to sell it and I don't have anything to say about it. I don't think that's fair and maybe I should be wishing him dead."

"If he dies, what happens?"

"Why you think somebody wants him dead?" the old man asked.

"He told me. I was up to see him and he told me."

"What'd he say? I didn't think he could talk."

"He was just counting numbers and then he said they're trying to kill me."

"Who's they?" Winfield asked.

"I don't know."

"And you think maybe it's me?" Winfield asked.

"Is it?"

"Hell, no. I'd rather grumble than murder. You want a motive, I'll give you a motive. If Mitch dies first, I get one-third of his stock in the company. His estate gets what's left. If I die first, the same thing. He gets one-third of what I got, and my family, goddamn their eyes, gets the rest."

"Would that change anything?"

"That'd change everything. If I got another seventeen percent of stock, I'd own, what, sixty-six, and first thing I tell young Jeannie, no sale."

"What's your company worth?"

"I don't know, fifty, sixty million, something like that. We make a lot of money here. Say sixty million. Mitch dies, I get one-third of his, that's an extra ten million to me. Would you murder for ten million?"

"I'm working for an insurance company. I'd do anything for money."

"I wouldn't. Mitch lives, I go retire. Christ, I'll probably have to go down to Florida with my two no-good sons and their no-good wives and I'll sit on the sand down there and look at titties and be old in two weeks and dead in six. And then those vultures come swooping up here to see everything they can get from my corpse. You want murder, those two sons of mine will give you murder. Their wives. Wait till you catch their act. If you got any of them insured, best keep an eye on them."

"Have you seen Mr. Carey?"

"I go up to the sanatorium once in a while. I used to go every day, but he doesn't do anything but lie there and it gets depressing. Now I send flowers."

"What do you think of the sanatorium?"

"It's a horseshit place to visit, but it beats the hell out of living there."

"I heard that Mr. Carey was getting better at the hospital."

"That's right," Winfield said, "and then he went to the sanatorium and he got worse right away, like always in a coma."

"Why do you think that is?" Trace asked.

"I think after his daughter died and all, I, I don't know, I just don't think he gives a shit anymore."

"You know Dr. Matteson? He runs the place."

"Seen him around," Winfield said. "Seems all right to me. You got a rotten job, mister."

"I've got a rotten life too," Trace said. "Does Mr. Carey have any enemies?"

"You know, maybe you ought to talk to me." Winfield stopped talking for a moment and gazed past Trace through the glass window. Trace turned and saw the blond secretary stretching like a cat waking from a nap. "Peanut butter," Winfield said. "You know, I was saying, you say that maybe somebody's trying to kill Mitch 'cause he told you up at the cuckoo-clock factory he's in. But that doesn't explain why you're in town. You didn't come here just so you could stumble over Mitch in the hospital and have him talk to you. Why don't you talk to me?"

Trace thought a moment, then said, "It goes like this. There was some old guy up at Meadow Vista named

Frederick Plesser. He died, and all of a sudden they find out that Dr. Matteson is the beneficiary of his insurance policy. A big policy. All right, so now Mitchell Carey goes up there. His wife is a friend of my boss's. They went to school together. And that girl who's living with the Careys, I think she got Mrs. Carey worked up, and she mentions to my boss that she's afraid that somebody up at the hospital is going to get Carey to change his insurance or his will or everything and then pull the plug on him. So my boss asked me to check it out.''

"What did you find out?" Winfield asked.

"Nothing. The Plesser family isn't much.''

"I know that family since I was a boy. They never amounted to anything.''

"Right," Trace said, "and I think he changed his insurance out of his own free will and left the money to Matteson just to spite his family. So nothing checks out. Then I talk to Mrs. Carey and Melinda—''

"That's the girl living with them?" Winfield asked.

"Yeah. Muffy they call her. A school chum of the dead girl or something. It's obvious that she's pushing Mrs. Carey around and trying to run the world, but I can't find out anything. Carey's still up there and still alive and he's got round-the-clock nurses now, I think.''

"Maybe you ought to go home," Winfield said.

"Except Mr. Carey told me somebody was trying to kill him, and somebody beat me up.''

"Must've been one big sucker to beat you up.''

"Actually, it was two of them and they dropped a piece of paper with Meadow Vista's name on it. And I find out that Jeannie Callahan is the Careys' lawyer, and your business lawyer, and she's also Matteson's lawyer in that insurance suit, and I don't know what's going on. So I'm asking you. Anybody want Mr. Carey dead?''

"Try a for-instance," the old man said.

"You, for instance, to keep control of your company?''

"It's a possibility," the old man said. His eyes did not even blink behind the thick lenses.

"Or maybe because you've been stealing from the company for years and now you're going to be found out if it gets sold?"

"Not bad," Winfield agreed cheerfully. "Except Mitch is a genius with numbers. I stole a dime, he'd find out in ten minutes. Anybody else?"

"Matteson, because he wants the money."

"He won't get anything unless he gets a will or insurance or something made out to him," Winfield said. "Anyway, don't you people check that out, all you insurance companies? Wouldn't it look funny if he suddenly started showing up on a lot of insurance?"

"I guess so," Trace said.

"Try somebody else. You're really cooking now."

"Mrs. Carey or Melinda. Maybe they want to inherit a lot of money and don't want to wait. Especially Muffy. Melinda."

"Wouldn't put it past her. She's a nasty little bitch. Was up here one day, nosing around, and I threw her the hell out. But she's not an heir, and Amanda's not the sort."

"Jeannie Callahan," Trace said.

"Why her?"

"Maybe her old man looted the company when he was the lawyer and she's covering it up by stopping the sale. Maybe she's hooked up with Matteson."

"I think if that was so, Mitch'd probably be dead already, don't you?"

"You're not helping a lot. I wanted you to answer everything for me and you didn't do me a bit of good," Trace said.

"Sorry. If I think of anything, I'll give you a call."

"You do that."

"Maybe I'll give you a call anyway if I feel like talking to somebody about peanut butter."

"I forgot to ask you. What is it you do here? What is Carwin Enterprises?" Trace said.

"Computers. We used to make big fat heavy adding machines. Now we make little skinny light computers. Not nearly as much fun."

"Nothing is, anymore," Trace said.

Outside the office, he stopped at the desk of the blond secretary, who looked up, then smiled at him.

"Can I help you?"

"You can help yourself," Trace said. "I just want to give you a tip."

"Go ahead."

"Mr. Winfield was just telling me he's looking for somebody to fill a new job, like head office manager. I think he's got his eyes on you for the job."

She started to glance around toward Winfield's office, but Trace said, "Don't look now. It'll look fishy."

"Why are you telling me this?" she asked.

" 'Cause you look like a nice girl. You can probably handle the job. So maybe you ought to be even better around here than you are now. You know, help Mr. Winfield make up his mind." He winked.

"You're serious, aren't you?" she said.

"I've never been more serious," Trace said.

20

Trace liked mirrors behind bars. He could watch, without appearing to, what was going on around and behind him. And if his ex-wife and her litter should come in, he might spot them before they recognized him, dive over the bar, and hide in the ice chest until they had gone.

He was thinking about this, looking in the mirror of the golf course's bar, when he saw a familiar face. He turned in his swivel seat and looked toward the far corner of the room.

Jeannie Callahan was leaning across a table, talking very warmly with Dr. George Matteson. Her left hand was on the table and Matteson's hand was resting on hers.

Trace pursed his lips. So much for love. So much for lawyers. And he felt rotten.

He had a very strong urge to get up, go over, and punch Dr. Matteson in his bearded face.

In the mirror, he saw Jeannie lean farther across the table and kiss Matteson on the forehead. Trace had turned and was looking down into his glass when her voice said, "Hello, Trace."

He turned and saw her smiling at him, her dark-brown eyes looking liquid and mirthful. She reached out to touch his sleeve.

"Well, if it isn't the ubiquitous barrister."

"You make me sound like a margarine."

Biting off the words, wishing them back even before he said them, he snapped, "The low-priced spread."

Her hand dropped from his sleeve. "What's the matter with you?"

"Shouldn't you be getting back? Your playmate back there must be getting impatient." He turned away.

"Playmate? Oh, George. My client, remember. You came to my office snooping around about him?"

"I remember you telling me he was a client. Just a client. Is the huggie-feelie therapy part of the new lawyer-client relationship?"

"Will you stop? God, I feel a fool standing here talking like this to a man who won't even look at me," she whispered angrily. "Look at me, dammit."

"Sorry, lady, I don't think I'd like what I saw."

He stood up, scrawled his name on the bar check, and without turning to the woman, walked from the bar.

He hoped that out in the parking lot, he would find some besotted teenager tap-dancing on the hood of his rented car. Because he wanted to hit somebody.

Anybody.

Both Carey cars were in the garage, but there was no answer to the doorbell. Trace leaned on it a long time before giving up, then walked to the end of the garage, whence he could look down on the rest of the Careys' sprawling property.

He saw Mrs. Carey sitting on the ground at the edge of the small pond, seemingly staring out at the water. A moment later, Muffy broke the surface of the water, wearing a face mask and on her back a scuba tank. A moment later, she submerged again beneath the waters of the pond.

Trace thought a moment. Neither had seen him. Not even the two Gordon setters in their kennel had barked. He stepped back quickly and, inside the garage, found a door that led into the Careys' house.

It was unlocked and he walked inside.

"Hello?" he called out. "Anybody home?"

When no one answered, Trace turned on his tape recorder and, as he started through the house, began to describe the contents.

"Here I am, breaking the law again, for no good goddamn reason at all and where's my brains. Hello. Anybody here? Good. Nobody here."

He glanced quickly into the rooms on the first floor, a formal dining room, a large living room, the study where he had met with Mrs. Carey and Muffy, then he bolted up the stairs. At the landing window, he looked out.

"Muffy's still underwater. Maybe she'll drown. That'd be too good luck, not for me, not the way my life's going."

There were only two very large bedrooms on the second floor, each with its private bath.

"The Careys' bedroom, all flowers and chintz, and I feel like a fucking ghoul doing this."

He walked down the hall and entered the second bedroom.

"This must be Muffy's bedroom, and I guess before she died, it was the kid's. Two large beds. Beatles posters on the walls. This corner of the room looks lived in. A partially made bed. A desk with a lot of papers lying around on it. Somehow I don't think Muffy stays in this bed in this corner out of any respect for her friend's memory. Probably it's just easier to keep the room clean this way. So Muffy's desk, what've we got?"

He glanced out a window, overlooking the rear property and the roof of the long one-story wing of the house that extended back alongside the swimming pool and tennis court. Muffy was just walking toward the bank of the pond.

"Better hurry. So what have we here? A receipt from the Harmon Hills Photo Center. What does it say, copy negative? So what? And a photo album. Look quick,

Trace, they're coming back. This must be Buffy. Funny—in college she had the big head of hair and Muffy wore hers straight. The two of them on the merry-go-round. On the steps, I guess, of the college. This must be Muffy as a cheerleader. Do they have cheerleaders in college? No, probably high school. She's young. And a page that's blank. It says Petey and there used to be a picture here, but there's no picture anymore. They're coming back to the house. A lot of blank spots in this book, all of them Petey. Who the hell's Petey? Put that away.

"Interesting book on the shelf. *All About Making Wills*. She's got wills on the mind, this girl. Oh, oh, the dogs are coming back to the house with them. Let's get out of here, Trace. She must fill her scuba tanks from this big green tank in the corner. Isn't it dangerous having this crap around the house?

"Hurry up."

Trace took the steps three at a time, ran through the kitchen, down the hallway, and out into the garage.

As he went into the garage, one of the black and rust Gordon setters came padding, big-footed, around the corner of the garage. It stopped short when it saw Trace, then its long feathered tail started to wag and it galloped toward him and licked his hand.

"Good watchdog, Fang," Trace said as he walked out toward his car.

Trace leaned against the fender of his car, idly petting the dog's head and smoking a cigarette until he figured the two women had had enough time to get back into the house. Then he flipped out the cigarette and rang the doorbell again.

Muffy answered it. She was still in her bathing suit, and close up now, Trace saw that she filled it nicely.

"Hi, Muffy. You didn't have to dress for me," he said.

"Oh. Still in town, huh?"

"Apparently. Mrs. Carey in?"

Before she could answer, Mrs. Carey called out, "Who's that, dear?" and Trace called back, "Devlin Tracy. From the insurance company."

The woman appeared in the hallway. "How are you today, Mr. Tracy?"

"Fine, Mrs. Carey. I was talking to Bob this morning and he told me to give you his regards. He said that when he comes back from Europe, he'll stop in and see you."

"Isn't that nice? He's in Europe, is he?"

"Yes, ma'am," and because he didn't really want to hear how Bob Swenson always loved to travel, he said, "I was going up to the sanatorium today to see Mr. Carey."

"Oh, so are we," Mrs. Carey said.

"When?"

Muffy seemed annoyed at being talked across and she said, "In an hour."

"Well, good. I'll see you there," Trace said.

"That'd be very nice," Mrs. Carey said.

"Sure," said Muffy without enthusiasm.

Trace was hungry, so he stopped at a tavern on the way to Meadow Vista and ate four chili dogs. Chico always complained that he never ate, but if he could get chili dogs everywhere, he'd do nothing but eat.

He killed an hour eating and watching a rare daytime baseball game on television, then drove to the sanatorium, where he breezed past the guard waving his stolen parking pass and met Mrs. Carey and Muffy in the parking lot.

Mrs. Carey was holding a paper bag and Trace carried it for her as they strolled toward the entrance of the East Building. Muffy had gone ahead and she didn't bother holding the door, but just walked inside.

Nurse Simons was at Carey's bedside when Trace and Mrs. Carey arrived. Muffy was already in a chair, next to the coffee table, looking bored. Mitchell Carey's eyes were open, but he was just staring blankly at the ceiling.

The nurse was fluffing up the pillows under Carey's head and she said pleasantly, "How are you, Mrs. Carey?" but her expression chilled over when she saw and recognized Trace. "You?"

"Friend of the family," Trace said. "Nice to see you again. How's Patient doing?"

"You'll have to ask Doctor," she said, and left the room.

He stood at the foot of the bed next to Mrs. Carey, looking at the unseeing, unfeeling form of her husband. The old man's eyes seemed to stare off, unfocused, into space and his body was so still it might have been made of plastic.

Mrs. Carey said, "Do you think he looks a little better? Maybe his complexion is brighter?" There was a terrible request in her voice for confirmation and Trace said, "I think so, from the last time I was here."

But his mind told him, No, he doesn't look any better. He looks the same. He looks dead. He looks like all the dead I've ever seen. Life has a lot of forms but death always has the same face and he's got it. Only the accident of a heartbeat and respiration allows him to be called alive.

He put his arm around Mrs. Carey's shoulders and squeezed her affectionately, then stepped back and sat in the other chair at the small coffee table. He watched Mrs. Carey, but she seemed to have forgotten everyone else's presence in the room. She stood, still holding her bag in her arms, staring at her husband. Muffy looked disgusted.

"I guess you don't like this much," Trace said softly.

"What's to like? He's a vegetable. He's always going to be a vegetable."

"Shhhh," Trace said.

"She won't hear. She's in a trance," Muffy said. "I see it every day. Listen."

She was silent and Trace could hear the soft voice of Amanda Carey.

". . . brought your new pajamas, the ones with the silly-looking cuffs on the sleeve. I remember how angry you were when you bought them and I thought they were funny-looking. You knew I was fooling, didn't you, Mitch? Anything you wear is all right with me. Actually, they were kind of dashing. Just as you always are. You're very handsome, you know. You just swept me right off my feet. So long ago . . ." Her voice trailed off and got softer, and Trace felt as if he were under a bed listening to two people make love. He looked at Muffy, but she showed no sign of embarrassment and Trace chalked it up to a generation that seemed to have reached its high point of elegance with bathrooms that no longer had locks on the doors.

He got up. "I'll be outside," he said, and he took his cigarette out into the hall and sat on a long bench, next to the ashtray.

He wished he had a case to solve, something to put his mind to. This whole job was a nothing. It was as if Bob Swenson had sent him here to wait for Mitchell Carey to die and there was nothing Trace could do about it. There was no murder plot, no reason for him to hang around.

All right, then. Why don't you go?

Because, dammit, I can't. Because Mitchell Carey told me they're killing him. Because Amanda Carey is an old gray lady who has no home. Leave me alone.

He stared off emptily into space as he smoked, his mind far away, until he noticed a pair of men's shoes on the floor in front of him.

It was Dr. George Matteson.

"Tracy, isn't it?"

"Yeah."

"You all right?"

"Just daydreaming. I'm here to visit."

"Good. I wanted to talk to you a minute. Mind if I sit down?"

"It's your hospital," Trace said.

Matteson sat down alongside him and Trace noticed again how thick and muscular the man's wrists and forearms were.

"I wanted to talk about Jeannie. Jeannie Callahan."

"She send you?" Trace asked.

"Not exactly. Her last words about you, as I recollect, were, I think, 'Screw that rotten bastard, I hope he dies.' "

"Oh. That was at lunch today?"

"Yeah. She was upset when she came back to the table," Matteson said.

"I hope she wasn't so upset that it interfered with your game of kneesies."

"You know, Jeannie was my lawyer when I bought this place and opened it up two years ago. She's my friend as well as my lawyer. I guess she was my first friend in town. That's all. Friend. Not lover. Not ex-lover. Not girlfriend. Friend."

Trace pressed the record button on his tape recorder.

"You looked very friendly at lunch," he said.

"I can't believe it," Matteson said. "That's what she told me you thought and I told her she was crazy. Because I held her hand across the table? For Christ's sakes, I hold my mother's hand when I take her out to eat. Don't you?"

"I don't. My mother's hand is as cold as her heart," Trace said.

"Listen, Tracy," the doctor said, "I don't care what you think about me and I don't care if you're miserable for the rest of your life, it's all no concern of mine. But Jeannie's my friend, so I care about her. If she had any sense, I think she'd walk around you like an open sore, as far as I'm concerned, but she seems to like you for some godawful unknown reason."

"I don't like Gilbert and Sullivan," Trace said. "I can't be all bad."

"Maybe not. All I want you to know is that nothing's

going **on.** Didn't go on. Won't go on. I don't like redheads, actually."

"Then I'm an idiot," Trace said.

"I thought that's what I was just telling you."

"You were kinder than that," Trace said.

"My bedside manner. You here to see Mr. Carey?"

"Yeah. Mrs. Carey's inside. And the kid."

"Kid?"

"That Melinda who's staying with them. Muffy. How's he doing?"

Matteson shook his head. "No change and not well. You know, three times a day, I have him respirated with pressurized oxygen. It's a totally new technique. At night, he sleeps in an oxygen tent. Shit, if he doesn't get better, he should at least stay the same. He shouldn't be going downhill."

"Maybe your oxygen theory doesn't work," Trace said.

"It works. It just doesn't work now on him and I don't know why. He's stabilized physically. There should be some improvement, but nothing. I don't understand it." Matteson got to his feet. "I have to check somebody else down the hall, then I'll be in."

Trace stubbed out his cigarette in the ashtray and went into the room. Should he have told Matteson that Carey had said that "they" were trying to kill him?

Maybe not. Not yet.

Mrs. Carey was still standing at the end of the bed, her lips moving gently. The pair of pajamas, gray-and-red-striped cotton, were lying on the bed, and they looked pathetic to Trace, like a Christmas-tree ornament abandoned in the middle of some dirty slum street.

"Do you want to come home, Mitchell? Oh, I wish you could answer me. Muffy's such a help. It's almost like having Buffy home again. I wish you could tell me if you want to come home . . . It's all right, I'm going to talk to Buffy tonight and I'm going to ask her. She'll tell me what's best to do."

She noticed Trace at the door and smiled to him, then turned back toward her husband.

At that moment, there was a gasp from Carey's lips. An eerie groaning sound, that ended in an explosive "No." And then his head fell to one side on the pillow.

Trace ran to the man's side, looked at him, and knew he was looking into the face of death. He remembered Matteson and barked, "Muffy, take care of Mrs. Carey." He ran out of the room and hurried down the hall, slamming open doors, looking inside. He found Matteson talking to a patient.

"Doc, a problem. Carey."

"I'll be right back," Matteson said to a nurse, and turned toward Trace.

"Hurry."

Trace held the door to Carey's room open for the doctor, who rushed by him and to the man's side. He felt in the throat for a pulse, then put his head to the man's chest.

He turned to Trace and said, "Tell the nurse I want ten ccs of epinephrine. Right now." Without waiting for a response, he turned back to the man. Mrs. Carey was still standing, alone, at the end of the bed, her moans a soft keening sound in the room.

Trace went back to the room where he had found Matteson.

"Ten ccs of epinephrine for Dr. Matteson. Room two-thirteen. On the double." She nodded and ran past him. When Trace went back ito Carey's room, the doctor was on the bed, kneeling, with his legs on both sides of the old man's body. He was pressing on his chest with steady thumping pressure, then releasing and starting again.

The striped pajamas had been thrown to the floor. Matteson repeated the chest pressure three times, then leaned forward, pinched Carey's nostrils with his right hand, and softly blew air into the man's mouth. He felt for the throat pulse again. He was mumbling under his breath.

"Breathe, goddammit, breathe. You're not dying on me. Not now. Breathe."

He straightened up and started pumping the chest again. He saw Trace at the door and yelled, "Where the hell's that nurse? Tell her to get her ass moving."

Trace went back into the hall. Behind him, he heard Matteson mumbling. "Oh, no. You're not going to die. Not on me. Breathe, godammit, pull in life. Breathe. Breathe. You've got to live."

The nurse was running down the hall toward Trace and he held the door open for her. She ran inside and handed Matteson a syringe. He ripped open Carey's hospital robe, felt his ribs, then stabbed the needle through the chest wall into the heart. He handed the hypodermic back to the nurse and said, "Get the defibrillator. Hurry it up now." His voice was hurried but gentle.

He pressed his left ear close to Carey's chest, then began the steady pressure rhythmically on the chest again. "Little bit there. It's coming, old-timer. Come on. Breathe with me. We've got that beat now. Pull in that air. Okay. Okay. Okay. You're going to live. Goddammit, you hear me, you're going to live. You're not quitting on me now."

Suddenly, Trace heard a big sip of air come through Mitchell Carey's mouth.

"Attaboy," Matteson said. "Keep it coming now." He growled to Trace, "Give me that oxygen."

Trace walked to the large light-green tank beside the bed, took the mask from atop it, and handed it to Matteson, who placed it over Carey's nose and mouth, then snapped, "Well, turn it on."

Trace shrugged in confusion, then saw the large back-yard faucet-type valve next to the pressure indicator and turned it on.

"How much should it go?"

"Turn till I tell you to stop."

Trace kept turning and Matteson said, "Okay, leave it there."

The doctor sat back on his haunches and looked down at Carey. Trace could see the old man's chest rising and falling slowly. Color seemed to be flooding back into his face. Matteson reached a finger for the throat and found the pulse, and as Trace watched him, he nodded. Mrs. Carey still stood at the foot of the bed, weeping softly, and Trace walked over and helped her to a chair.

"Everything's going to be all right," he said. He saw Muffy sitting in her chair, watching with interest. She had a cigarette in her mouth and was lifting a lighter toward it, and Trace slapped the cigarette away. "Leave that goddamn cigarette alone. There's oxygen in this room."

She looked at him, an annoyed expression on her face.

"You're a big goddamn help," Trace said, then walked back to the bed as George Matteson let out a long sigh and clambered down from the bed. He stood by Carey's side, taking the pulse in his wrist and feeling his chest. He made a slight adjustment on his oxygen valve, sighed again, and walked over to Mrs. Carey, who looked at him expectantly.

"It's okay, Mrs. Carey. I think he'll be all right."

Tears streamed down the old woman's cheeks. "Can I . . . can I look at him?"

"Sure. Of course." Matteson looked at Muffy and said sharply, "Help the lady."

Muffy rose slowly from the chair and walked Mrs. Carey over to the bed where they stood looking at Mitchell Carey. The nurse reentered, wheeling an electrical-shock unit, and Matteson said, "We don't need that now. Stay here and watch him."

"Yes, Doctor."

"I need a cigarette."

"I thought you didn't smoke," Trace said.

"I don't. That's why I need one," the doctor said, and Trace followed him into the hall and lit a cigarette for him.

Matteson took a long, slow, deep drag and Trace said, "Good job in there."

"Huh. Oh, yeah. Thanks. I—" He shook his head vigorously from side to side. "I can't stand people dying on me. Dammit, they don't have any right to." He was looking at the floor and he took another puff of his cigarette, then glanced over at Trace. "Anyway, now you know how sometimes people just have a heart attack and die."

"Yeah."

"I'm glad you were there and got me right away. A couple of seconds might have been the difference."

"He's out of the woods?" Trace asked.

"I don't know." Matteson shrugged. "Ask me in twenty-four hours. The first day is always touch and go 'cause so many things can go wrong. Heart attacks aren't always logical."

"No cause, no explanation?"

"Right. Anything. Nothing. It just happens. It's so hard to figure out what makes the body work, and with old people, well, it's not working good to start with and you just don't know. I hate medicine. You're supposed to be God and you're not God, you're just blundering around in the dark, trying to do the best you can, and you've got ladies like that one in there and they think you can do what you can't do. I mean, you're as powerless as anybody else is."

"You saved one life today."

"Yeah. That's today. I was lucky to be here. I was lucky you had the good sense to call me right away. You want a guarantee? I can't give you a guarantee. Maybe I won't be here the next time. Or you won't. I don't know. I don't know why I do this," Matteson said.

"Is this the way it was with Plesser?" Trace asked.

"Plesser? Oh. Yeah. But nobody was here and so nobody called me and he just died and nobody helped him.

Maybe we couldn't anyway. I'm getting out of this damned business."

"If you didn't want to deal with death, why'd you get involved with old folks?" Trace asked. "You know you're going to lose some of them." He noticed Matteson's hands were shaking, as if in rage.

"Because that's what I do. I don't know. You think it's for the money? You know what plastic surgeons make? You know, I could spend the rest of my life carving new noses and be a millionaire. You want fat out of your baggy eyes? Come to George Matteson. Service with a smile. I'll screw every third good-looking woman to help my reputation. Nobody calls you for an emergency nose job. Nobody wakes you up in the middle of the night because somebody you've been holding by your fingertips, just this side of death, slipped away because you closed your eyes to take a rest. Nobody— Ahhh, I'm sorry, Tracy, I'm just tired."

"You ought to get some rest, Doc."

"Later. I've got too much to do."

"Thanks for telling me about Jeannie," Trace said.

"Yeah," Matteson said. "Yeah."

A few minutes after Dr. Matteson went back into Carey's room, Muffy came out and leaned against the wall across from Trace and lit a cigarette.

"Still think he's trying to kill Mr. Carey?"

"Maybe not this time," she said. "We all were there."

"Come on. Park it, kid," Trace said.

"I never said it was him. Maybe somebody else around here. He sure isn't getting any better staying in this dump. He was better at the hospital." She took a long pull of her cigarette, then stepped close to Trace to snuff it out in the large ashtray. "I'm going to call our night nurse and have him come down early."

"A male nurse?" Trace said.

"Yeah. It's his night off, but I want him around."

"In case the crazed killers of Meadow Vista are prowling the corridors tonight?" Trace asked.

"Something like that," Muffy said.

21

When Trace got back to the country club, he had three messages waiting for him. One was from Jeannie Callahan and he realized she must have written it when leaving the club's restaurant at lunchtime. It read, "Please call. Jeannie," and left a telephone number. The number had a seven in it and she had drawn a line through the seven. The second message was from Chico and left a number for him to call. Another message left just a number, no name.

"No calls from Rome?"

"No, sir," Dexter said.

"These'll have to do, then."

Trace lay the messages on his bed, looked at them, and dialed Jeannie Callahan's number. It rang four times before a taped message clicked on.

He decided he even liked her voice as he listened to her very businesslike message, reporting the office's working hours and asking that name, phone number, time of call, and nature of business be described in the thirty seconds after the beep tone.

The beep tone sounded and he said, "Did anyone ever tell you you've got a very sexy voice? This is Trace and I'm still staying at the Golden Age Golf Club. I think it's rotten of you, cheating on me in public, but I've decided not to give you the beating you deserve and I'm going to forgive you instead. This offer's only good for an hour.

Call me. Unless I get you at your apartment instead. Then ignore this call.''

He hung up and looked in the local telephone book, but Jeannie's home number was not listed.

He called Chico. The telephone number was a Holiday Inn in Memphis and her voice seemed glum as she answered.

"This is Trace. What's up?"

"Hi, Trace. Just thinking of you.''

"That's a nice thing for you to do every third day.''

"Want some company?" she asked.

"Why? You tired of your sister already?''

She hesitated before answering. "Oh, come on, Trace, you know I wasn't here with my sister.''

"Yeah, I know," he said, and waited.

"You're not going to make this easy on me, are you?''

"You know me. I never make things easy for anybody,'' he said.

"All right. That guy I was seeing the last couple of nights in Vegas?''

"The sweating greaseball with the bald spot? The one who kept his hands in his pockets all the time?'' Trace said.

"You're making that up.''

"Just a guess," Trace said.

"He didn't look anything like that.''

"No? Was he the man of your dreams?''

"Trace, this is hard enough. Will you shut up and listen?''

"Go ahead.''

"Anyway, that guy I was with, he offered me a job with his company.''

"Entertaining clients from out of town?''

"Goddamn you, Trace, that's cruel.''

"Sorry," he said impassively.

"He said that he ran a business that specialized in providing tests for students. You know, things like SATs.

194

That's exactly my field. My degrees are in that. And he needed a new sales manager. That's what we talked about.''

"And you were going to leave my fireside in Las Vegas to go take a job in Memphis, Tennessee? Without talking to me?''

"I would have talked to you. I wanted to check it out first. Hey, I'm not twenty-one years old anymore.''

"No, you're twenty-six.''

"How come you can't remember that on my birthday? So I came down to talk to him about the job.''

"And you stayed with him for a couple of days and played house?'' Trace said.

"All right. If you want to call it that.''

"I could call it something else. And there wasn't a job, was there?''

"No, there wasn't. It was all a load of crap.''

"He's married too, right?'' Trace said.

"Yeah. And his wife was in England visiting relatives and I had to get out before she came back,'' Chico said.

"Is he paying the rent for the Holiday Inn?'' Trace asked.

"He offered, but I wouldn't let him.''

"Good girl. Preserve your shredded virtue. You know, for all your brainpower, you may be the dumbest hooker in the world,'' Trace said. "Part-time hooker. Excuse me.''

"Okay, Trace, you want to rub my nose in it, go ahead. Yes, I'm a part-time hooker. And, yes, I'm tired of dealing blackjack to guys who want to trick with me, and I'm kind of getting tired of figuring out that you and me just aren't going anywhere at all, and I thought this was a chance of making a good move for myself, and it just didn't work out.''

Trace said nothing, and after a pause she asked, "So I asked you, do you want company?''

"Actually, I don't think so. This whole case up here is pretty complicated.''

"I usually help out on the complicated ones," she said. "And I've got a few days."

"Naah. And, besides, the clerk here thinks I work for the Vatican. It'd blow everything if I had some woman booking in with me."

"Tell him I'm the head of the Church in the Far East. If he believes you're with the Vatican, he'll believe anything."

"It'd never work. You don't have the shifty eyes of a prelate."

"I could stay somewhere else," she said. He could almost hear her shrug over the phone and he could picture her perfect tiny body and her soft face with the well-deep dark eyes and he wondered for a moment why he was playing nasty games with her.

"If you want to come," he finally said, "there's probably motels in some of the other towns around here. You'll have to rent a car at Newark Airport and drive in yourself. I'm probably going to be busy. So call me after you get in and we'll see if we can get together."

"All right, Trace," she said.

He hung up and looked at the other message. It was a simple seven-digit number with no area-code prefix. If Dexter had gotten it right, that meant whoever called had called from New Jersey. And who did he still know in New Jersey?

He dialed the number.

"Hello," said a voice, and Trace nodded and slowly replaced the receiver, even as his ex-wife's voice continued to bark, "Hello, hello. Is anybody there? It's you, Devvie, isn't it? It's you, you bastard."

Click.

22

Trace's stomach hurt and he didn't know if it was from the previous night's pummeling or because he was hungry. He ate a bacon cheeseburger in the cocktail lounge and found out the pain was from the pummeling because he still hurt.

He tried Jeannie Callahan's telephone number again, but when it didn't answer after three rings, he hung up before the tape cut in on the fourth ring.

And because he didn't have anything else to do, he drove back to Meadow Vista Sanatorium.

As he was parking in the lot, he saw a dark-colored car pulling out of a spot. Inside the car were Dr. Barbara Darling and Nurse Thelma Simons. He waved warmly to them, but they either didn't see him or didn't care to have him ruin their night, because they ignored him. He noticed that Nurse was wearing her starched white uniform. Maybe she slept in her uniform, he thought. Standing up, so as not to ruin the creases.

Trace went into Mitchell Carey's room. A big young blond man wearing a white uniform was sitting in a chair next to the bed, reading *Hustler* magazine. A copy of a karate magazine was on the cabinet behind him and a gym bag was under the bed.

Carey's bed was covered with a clear plastic tent and Trace could hear oxygen hissing faintly inside the plastic.

"Who are you?" the young man said as Trace entered.

"Devlin Tracy, a friend of the family. How is he?"

"He's okay. I've got orders to call Dr. Matteson if anything changes." Trace didn't like the young man's face. He talked with his lips pulled down tightly over his teeth and he had too many muscles by half.

"He say anything?" Trace brushed by the young man and stood by Carey's bed, looking down at him.

"Him? Naah. I don't think he's likely to say much again. Maybe to you, not to me."

"You might be right," Trace said. "Then again, he might fool you." Trace did not like him talking as if Carey could not hear or understand. "What's your name?"

"Jack Ketch," the young man said.

"You the night nurse?"

"Yeah. The family told me to come in tonight."

Trace's foot hit the young man's gym bag and he felt somehow offended that there was a gym bag in a hospital room. He pushed it farther under the bed with his toe, but he had to push hard. The bag was heavy. Damned idiot probably carried his weight-lifting equipment around with him, Trace thought.

"I'll probably stop in to see you later," Trace said. "Don't get up. I can find my own way out."

"I wasn't planning to get up," Ketch said.

Trace walked to the telephone on the landing outside Three East and called Jeannie Callahan's number again, but there was no immediate answer and he hung up after three rings.

He drove out of town to her apartment building, but she did not answer the doorbell, and in disgust at the prospect of spending another night alone in Harmon Hills, he stopped at a tavern and watched the news and a few innings of a baseball game. He called Jeannie's number again, got no answer, and drove out to the Carey house.

He parked his car on the street behind a brown Volkswagen whose owner also had ignored the no-parking signs.

As he walked up the driveway to the house, he saw the

garage doors open and the two Cadillacs parked inside. But there were no lights on in the house. He walked onto the flagstone front porch, reached for the doorbell, then stayed his hand.

He listened for a few moments but heard no sound, and then he walked from the porch into the garage. The door leading into the house was unlocked.

He walked in quietly and paused. Down the long hall, he heard the faint hum of a voice talking softly.

The voice was coming from the study down the hall and it was low, hypnotically one-noted. He walked on the heavy sound-swallowing carpet and stopped outside the doorway. The door was partially open and he leaned to the side to look inside.

The room was illuminated only by a pair of black candles atop a small game table. Amanda Carey sat at one side of the table and Muffy on the other, their hands joined on the tabletop. Incense curled smokily from a saucer on the cabinet below the bookshelves.

The crystal ball was in the middle of the table, between the woman's hands.

It was Muffy's voice Trace had heard. Both women's eyes were closed and Muffy's head was thrown back so her neck muscles and tendons were stretched taut.

Trace saw her hands clench tightly around Mrs. Carey's.

"She's here," Muffy whispered. "I can feel it now. She's here."

"Oh," slipped from Mrs. Carey's lips.

"Buffy, we're here," Muffy said. "Your mother and me. Talk to us."

But there was only silence in the room and Muffy said again, "Talk to us. Please. We want to talk to you."

There was only silence again. Trace saw that the blinds were drawn on the big windows in the front of the house, but they were open on a side window, and as his eyes grew accustomed to the dark, he could see the clumps of dark bushes on the sprawling lawn beyond the window.

He heard Muffy whisper, "Ask her, Nana. Talk to her. She might answer you."

Haltingly, hesitant, Mrs. Carey said, "Buffy, are you here?"

Only silence answered and Mrs. Carey said again, "Buffy? Please?"

And then there was a sound. It was faint, but it seemed to come from all over the room as if it had no central source. It was the voice of a young woman, saying, "Nana, Nana I'm here, Nana."

Involuntarily, Mrs. Carey clamped a hand to her mouth.

Muffy reached across the table and took Mrs. Carey's hand again and replaced it on the table. Mrs. Carey's eyes had opened, but now she closed them again and said, "Buffy, I'm so happy you're here. Are you all right, darling?"

"Oh, Nana, I'm so cold. And scared."

Mrs. Carey was silent, and Muffy said quickly, "Why are you scared, Buffy?"

"Nana, I'm afraid for my father. He's so sick," the voice came back.

Trace looked around the room but could see no one else.

"What should we do?" Mrs. Carey said.

Trace saw the old woman screw her eyes tightly closed as if willing an answer, and Muffy tossed her head back with a snappy little jerk and the voice again responded. "Oh, it's so lonely in the house without him. So lonely." The voice was a mournful, pitiful wail.

There was silence again and Muffy said, "What should we do, Buffy?" Then she jerked her head back as if awaiting an answer and the voice came again.

"Nana, don't let them hurt Pop-pop. Bring him home, bring him home. Listen to Muffy and bring him home."

There was a flickering on the heavy dark drapes at the

front of the room. Muffy's eyes were still closed, her head back. Mrs. Carey's head was slumped forward on the table and Trace could hear her weeping. Suddenly, Muffy opened her eyes and she hissed, "See. Nana, look."

The old woman lifted her head and Muffy released her hands to point toward the drapes. On them appeared the lighted image of a young woman. It was vague and amorphous because of the folds of the drapes, but it was a young woman with long hair, and her arms were extended outward.

"It's her," Mrs. Carey said. "It's Buffy "

"She's calling you," Muffy said.

"I love you, Nana. I love you, Muffy Bring him home," the voice said.

Mrs. Carey jumped to her feet and stepped toward the drapes. The image vanished. One moment it was there and then it was just gone.

She looked about in confusion, then turned back to Muffy, who got up from her seat and walked to the old woman and put an arm around her.

"It's all right," she said soothingly. "It's all right. She's here in the house. She'll always be here with us."

Trace quietly ran back through the house. In the kitchen was a door leading outside, and he let himself out onto the paved patio and ran around the back of the house.

He moved silently toward the windows of the study, but there was no one there. He knelt down to feel with his fingers. The soft earth was mashed with footprints, but he could not tell if they were ten minutes or ten days old.

He looked in through the window and saw Muffy still comforting Mrs. Carey. The window was streaked and dusty, but in the lower right-hand corner, there was a precise three-inch circle where the glass shone clear, as if it had been washed recently.

He looked around on the ground to see if anything had been dropped, but saw nothing.

When he returned to his car, he noticed that the brown Volkswagen that had been parked in front of his was gone also.

Trace looked up and saw Police Officer Lauren Wilcox entering the country club's cocktail lounge.

She looked around the almost-empty lounge, saw Trace, smiled, and started toward him.

Trace noticed Hughie watching the woman as she came near. Even in her uniform blues, she was very trim and moved smoothly, and Trace said, "Hi, officer. How's the law's most beautiful minion?"

"Hello, Trace," she said. She looked around to make sure no one was able to hear them, then said softly, "You've got to come with me."

"Why?"

"My husband wants to talk to you."

"Oh, Christ, I knew it was going to happen. I fool around just once in my life and now a husband is after me."

"Not about that, you idiot. That's our secret. Come on, we've got to hurry."

"Okay." Trace followed her outside.

"We'll take my car," she said, and Trace got into the front seat of the squad car.

"What's going on?" he asked as she drove away.

"You don't know?"

"I wouldn't ask," he said.

"Last night, at that apartment, you were visiting a friend?"

"Yeah."

"That was Jeannie Callahan, wasn't it?"

"Okay. If you know anyway, yes."

"Did you see her tonight?"

"No."

"Somebody did."

"What's that supposed to mean?" Trace snapped. "Dammit, what are you talking about?"

"Somebody beat her up."

"Oh, for Christ's sakes. Is she all right?"

"Yeah, I think so. Frank just asked me to bring you in. Were you there?"

"Where?"

"At her office."

"No," Trace said. "Where is she now?"

"At the sanatorium. It's the closest emergency room."

"Take me there, will you?"

"After you talk to Frank," she said.

"Why me?"

"Damned if I know," she said. "He didn't tell me." She paused a moment, then reached out and touched his leg. "Don't worry," she said. "I don't think you're the lady-beating type either. You know, if I knew I was going to be bringing you in, well, last night . . ."

"Don't worry," Trace said. "My lips are sealed."

"I didn't fill out a report about the vandalism or anything," she said.

"I won't mention it," Trace said.

The door to Jeannie Callahan's office was open, and Lt. Wilcox, his back to them, was looking at the file cabinet when Trace and the policewoman walked inside.

"I've got him, Frank," the woman said.

Wilcox turned around, looked at Trace in disgust, and said, "Okay, Tracy. Sit over there."

His wife lingered in the doorway and the lieutenant said, "You can go back now, Lauren. I'll call you when we're through."

"All right."

Trace noticed that the second drawer of the four-drawer file cabinet was open, and the metal rim of the drawer was twisted, as if it had been bent.

Wilcox leaned on the file cabinet and said, "My wife tell you what happened?"

"Yes. How bad was it?"

"Not too serious. Where were you tonight?"

"I was at the country club just now and earlier. I stopped at the sanatorium and at Mitchell Carey's house. Lieutenant, what's going on?"

"Where were you about nine-thirty or so?"

"At the Carey house."

"They vouch for you?"

"I didn't see them. The house was dark, so I went back to the country club. Why are you questioning me?"

"All right, why were you angry with Miss Callahan?"

"Who said I was?"

"You said you were," Wilcox snapped. "Dammit, Tracy, I want some answers out of you." In the harsh light of the desk lamp, his pitted face looked like a lunar landscape.

"Listen, Lieutenant—"

"No, you listen. I think you were ticked off at Miss Callahan and you busted in here to steal something. When she surprised you, you clocked her and then you beat it. What do you think of that?"

"I think it, and you, are both full of shit," Trace said evenly. "Are you going to charge me?"

"I don't know yet."

"You better make up your mind real fast. Charge me now or I go out that goddamn door. Charge me now and do it wrong, and I'll have your ass for lunch." He stood up.

Trace had to admire Wilcox. The bluff didn't work and the policeman didn't blanch. Instead, he said, "Then I guess I'm going to have to charge you."

"Fine," Trace said. He sat back down. "Ask away. I'll wait a couple of minutes to make my phone call."

"Why did you threaten Miss Callahan?"

"I didn't."

Wilcox walked behind the lawyer's desk and fiddled with an oblong gray box. Then he pressed a button and Trace's voice filled the room.

"This is Trace and I'm still staying at the Golden Age Golf Club. I think it's rotten of you, cheating on me in public, but I've decided not to give you the beating you deserve and I'm going to forgive you instead. This offer's only good for an hour. Call me . . ."

"What's that all about?" Wilcox said. "What the hell are you laughing about?"

"Hoist by my own petard," Trace said.

"What?"

"Never mind. Do you think that's a threat on that tape? Tell me, Lieutenant, do you get many muggings where the muggers call first and leave their ID so you can be sure to pick them up later? Dammit, the call I made was a joke. She was having lunch with some other guy today and I was joking."

"That's all?"

"That's all."

"What other guy?"

"She was having lunch with Dr. Matteson at the golf club."

"Matteson, huh?"

"He's a client of hers," Trace said.

"Well, if you didn't bop her, who did?" Wilcox said.

"What happened?" Trace asked. "Maybe I can help."

"Miss Callahan came to the office at half-past nine. She was specific about the time. She let herself in and then she realized someone was here. She headed for the door, but whoever it was grabbed her, spun her around, and punched her. It knocked her out. When she woke up a couple of minutes later, she called us. She said that whoever it was must have been rifling her files, but she couldn't see anything missing. So now, help. You add anything to that?"

"No," Trace said.

"You're a big help. What are you in town for anyway?"

"I told you the other day, I'm checking on that Plesser insurance thing."

"The Careys have anything to do with that?"

"Mr. Carey's a friend of my boss. He asked me to check in with the family." Trace hesitated and Wilcox said, "And nothing but the truth."

"And my boss wanted me to make sure that nothing happened to Mr. Carey like it happened to Plesser."

"Why should your boss be worried about a thing like that?"

"Because that girl who's living with the Careys filled his head with shit."

"Oh. What's Miss Callahan's connection with all this?"

"I ran into her because she's the Careys' lawyer. And she's Dr. Matteson's lawyer. The Plessers are suing him."

"That wouldn't give Matteson any reason to come here and hit her, I guess. Are they going out together?"

"Matteson told me no," Trace said.

Wilcox sighed. "Okay. I don't have anything to book you on. You know that. We can go, I guess. My photographer's already been here."

"Will he get prints?"

"It's always a guess. He pulled up some with tape, but the way he works, the asshole, they'll probably be his own."

Trace waited in the hallway for Wilcox to close up the office. At the head of the stairs was a large ashtray, and Trace saw in it an apple with only one bite taken from it.

He thought for a moment, then picked up the apple, shook the sand from it, and stuck it in his jacket pocket. Wilcox was fumbling with the office lock.

"Just a minute, Lieutenant," Trace said, "I left my cigarettes inside."

"Oh, for Christ's sake, hurry up."

Trace went into the office, pretended to take his cigarettes off the desk, and before leaving, glanced inside the small refrigerator near the office door.

"What are you doing in there?" Wilcox said.

"I was thirsty. I thought Jeannie might have a bottle of beer around."

"Does she?"

"No."

"Some days nothing goes right. I should have booked you."

"It wouldn't have held up," Trace said.

"Why not?"

"You forgot to read me my rights."

"In Harmon Hills, you don't have any rights."

Wilcox dropped Trace off at the country club and the insurance investigator went into the cocktail lounge, where he found Hughie getting ready to close the empty bar.

"You have a small plastic bag or a piece of Saran wrap?" Trace asked.

"Let me look." Hughie came back out of the storeroom with a piece of wrap that looked as if it had held a tuna-fish sandwich. Meanwhile, Trace looked at the apple in his pocket. He didn't know what he was doing, but he had read somewhere that toothmarks were as almost as individual as fingerprints, and where the bite had been taken from the apple was a clear set of toothmarks. Trace wondered why he hadn't just given the apple to Lt. Wilcox and decided it was because Wilcox would probably have eaten it. He wrapped the apple in the piece of plastic wrap and handed it back to the bartender.

"Hughie, I want you to put this in the freezer."

"What for?"

"I want to save it."

"If you want, you can throw this one away and I'll

bring you a new apple tomorrow. No charge. It's apple season."

"I need this apple, Hughie. It's evidence."

"George Washington's dead."

"That was a cherry tree, not an apple tree. Please, just put this in the back of the freezer. It's important. And don't let anybody throw it out."

"I'll put a sign on it that says it's a disguised Nazi hand grenade. That should do it," Hughie said.

"Wonderful."

"How long do you think I'll have to keep it?"

"Just till tomorrow," Trace said.

"Good. Just don't tell anybody I'm doing this. It might start a fad and I've only got a small freezer."

There was a young nurse on duty in the emergency room in the East Building at Meadow Vista and Trace said, "I'm Dr. Wasserman. Is Miss Callahan ready to go yet? I've come to pick her up."

The woman looked at a sheet in front of her. "Miss Callahan's been admitted to Room Two-twenty-two. She won't be leaving right away. Dr. Matteson's taking care of her."

"She just called. Is Doctor still with her?"

"I think so."

"Thank you. I'll confer with him. It's okay, I know my way."

When Trace walked into the room, Jeannie was sitting up in bed and Matteson was leaning against the small nightstand next to her bed. He was wearing a raincoat over his pajamas.

"If I were the jealous type," Trace said, "this'd bust it."

"Trace," she cried out happily. "Tell this idiot to let me out of here."

"Not a chance," Matteson said.

Trace looked at the young lawyer. She had a bruise on one cheek and the flesh was turning an ugly eggplant color. Trace knew, from his own experience, that in another twelve hours or so she would have a rip-roaring shiner.

He stood at the side of the bed, looking at her, before he leaned over, kissed her, and said to Matteson, "She is one ugly-looking thing, isn't she, Doc?"

"That's why I won't let her out. She might frighten people on the street ."

"Will I be able to play piano, Doctor? That's all that's important," Jeannie said.

"Sure," Matteson said.

"That's funny. I couldn't play before."

"Jokes. Jokes she makes already. I've brought her back from death's door and she makes jokes," Matteson said.

"Who did it, Jeannie? Any ideas?"

Matteson said, "I'll leave you two alone. As long as I'm here, I'll look at some patients. They don't wake me up and make jokes."

"Just a minute, Jeannie," Trace said, and walked into the hall with the doctor. "What's the story?"

"She's just got a bad bruise. Nothing fractured and no danger that I can see. But I'm keeping her overnight just to be sure. Sometimes head injuries are sneaky."

"Okay. I won't let her leave. Thanks, Doc."

"I'll have the nurse give her a sedative," Matteson said, then shuffled away.

Trace said, "If you hear from the girl downstairs about a Dr. Wasserman?"

"Yeah?"

"That's me."

Matteson looked puzzled, then shrugged. "Okay, if you say so."

Trace went back to Jeannie's bed.

"How do you feel, kid?"

"Like I got run over by a freight train."

"Matteson says you'll be all right. He just wants you to stay around for one night."

"I know, and I guess he's right. It's just, well, being in a hospital's depressing."

"If I tap-dance on your face, will that cheer you up?" Trace asked.

"Sorry. Somebody already tried that tonight. It left me cold."

"Very funny. Tell me what happened."

"I had a late meeting out of the office and I was driving—"

"A meeting with who?" Trace interrupted. "Don't leave anything out."

"With Wilber Winfield. I left the plant and I was driving home and I decided to stop at my office to pick up some files. When I went in, I got this sense that somebody was in my office."

"Did you turn on the light when you went in?"

"No."

"Why not?"

"Force of habit. The hall light shines right in my office when the door's open and I was just going to walk across the office and open the cabinet and take out what I wanted. It's what I guess I always do when I come in at night to pick up a file."

"And what happened?"

"I told you, I got the feeling there was somebody there. Then I noticed my file cabinet was already open. I turned and started back for the door. Then I saw somebody jump in front of it and slam the door closed. I told this all to the cops."

"Did you recognize him?"

"No. He was big, was all. I could only see his outline against the light."

"What happened then?"

"I was going to scream, but before I did, he slugged me and put my lights out."

"Did he say anything?"

"Like excuse me? No, nothing like that. He just grunted when he hit me."

"Grunted?"

"Yeah. Grunted. You know, like pigs do. Big exhale and grunt."

"What then?"

"What else, then? I went out like a light. Was I supposed to take notes?"

"I'm asking the questions, Counselor. You just answer."

"I was out. What do you want from me?"

"What'd you do when you woke up?"

"I called the cops."

"Not so fast. Were the lights still out?"

"Uhhh, no. The lights were on."

"How about the file cabinet? Open or closed?"

"Closed, I think. Wait. The one drawer was open."

"What, then?" Trace asked.

"I told you, I called the cops."

"Did you check the files?"

"Yeah. I couldn't see anything missing."

"Did you eat an apple?" Trace asked.

She looked at him in bewilderment. "No, actually I sent out for some avocado pizza. I thought it would look good with my bruises. What are you talking about?"

"Yesterday, you had an apple in your refrigerator. It's not there now. Did you eat it?"

"I don't know. No. I always keep bringing in apples 'cause they'll make me healthy or something, and then I forget to eat them. I hate apples. I didn't eat that one either. It's gone?"

"Yeah. I think the burglar ate it."

"That makes it easy," she said. "Let's just pump the stomach of everybody in New Jersey and arrest anybody

211

who upchucks apple. I think it was a McIntosh. You want me to write down a description? That should narrow it down a lot."

"Are you always so nasty?"

"Only when I get dopey questions. Apples."

"Remember you said that. I just hope that when you find out how brilliant I am, you'll be big enough to apologize."

"Let's wait and see."

"There was only one guy?" Trace asked.

"I already said there was. You're worse than the cops. One guy. A big guy."

"No sign of any little guy hanging around? Maybe when you parked and came in, did you see anybody sitting in a car? A green Pontiac or something with a slope back, maybe?"

"No. Why?"

"When I left your house last night, I had my bell rung by two guys. A big one and a little one in a green car."

"Why? Why you, for God's sake?"

"I don't know. I think somebody's trying to keep us apart, Jeannie."

"Whatever happened to anonymous letters? Threatening to tell your wife about the whole sordid affair? I could deal with heavy breathers on the phone even. Not getting beat up."

"The phone," Trace said. "Did you listen to your messages?"

"Yes. I got yours, you chowder head."

"Don't knock it. It made me the prime suspect in your whupping. Were there any others?"

"Just one."

"Who was it?"

"I don't know. He hung up without leaving a message."

"It was probably the burglar checking to make sure you were out," Trace said.

212

"Maybe. I liked getting your message. I'm glad you're off the snot."

A nurse bustled into the room, nodded at Trace impersonally, and said, "Time for a pill, Miss Callahan."

"I don't want it."

"Doctor's orders," the nurse said.

"Take it," Trace said. "It's to make you sleep. Once you fall off, I'll sneak back in and work my wicked will on your body."

"I'll take two," Jeannie said. She washed down the pill with water, and the nurse left.

Trace said, "Your meeting with Winfield tonight. What went on? Was there anything that made him upset?"

Jeannie shrugged. "I don't think so. He wasn't there. He had some other appointment or something. I met with the controller and the accountant. There wasn't anything wrong. All routine work."

"You didn't see Winfield at all?"

"No."

"Okay. Go to sleep now. When you wake up in the morning, you won't recognize yourself."

"Oh, God, I'm going to be ugly. Who'd want to be seen with me?"

"I'll keep you hidden under the sheets until you heal," Trace said gallantly.

"Good."

Trace turned off his tape recorder and waited fifteen minutes until she was asleep. As he closed the door, he heard her breathing heavily behind him.

He walked down the hallway toward Mitchell Carey's room and saw Matteson coming out of Room 213.

"How is he?"

"Everything looks all right," Matteson said. "I just talked to the nurse and she said that he's been resting quietly."

Trace nodded and Matteson said, "I think I'll probably find a bed and sleep up here tonight."

"Okay. If you need me for anything, I'll be at Sylvan Glade," Trace said.

Back at the hotel, Trace went behind the desk to take a message from his mailbox.

It read simply "Chico" and gave a New Jersey phone number.

Trace called her from his room, and when she answered, he got the rush he always got when he heard her voice. It seemed to have a smile built into it and it warmed him. Until he remembered where she had been and why.

"This is Trace."

"Hi, Trace. Listen, I'm in this motel and it's real scuzzy. You looking for a roommate?"

"Did you have any trouble finding a place?"

"No. I got a car at the airport and this was the first place around, but it's the pits. No wonder you moved out of New Jersey if the motels are all like this. What do you say?"

"Well, I'm kind of busy right now," Trace said, still avoiding her question and invitation.

"This late?" she asked.

"Yeah. Things are complicated."

"You want to talk about it?" Chico asked.

He paused a moment as he realized he wanted to. He wanted to discuss it with her and let her fine brain chew it over, and yet he didn't want to see her.

"Maybe tomorrow," he said.

Her answer was chilly. "All right. If that's the way you want it."

"We'll talk tomorrow," Trace said.

23

Trace's Log:

Another long day's journey into night and I'm tired. Tape Recording Number Five, one A.M., Friday, in the matter of Mitchell Carey. This has been our usual sweet, let's-stick-it-to-the-cranky-bastard kind of day, hasn't it? First I thought I was cuckolded by another woman, but I wasn't. Then I was at the bedside of a dying man who lived. I got arrested for assault, but the cop changed his mind. I went to a séance. It's all been wonderful.

But what do you expect from a day that starts with the ex-wife calling? God, I'd almost forgotten about that. I've got to get out of this town. Bruno, What's-his-name and the girl could be galloping here right now. And they know where I'm staying.

And I've got to find a faster way to make these tapes. First I have to live them and then I have to replay them before I can figure them out. That's not bad if I make a tape when I'm getting laid or something, because I don't mind reliving that. But if it's dull or depressing or dangerous, then I have to live it first, which is lousy, and then hear all about it again when I play the tape. This is no fun.

I've heard there's a new recorder on the market that plays things back at double speed without turning everybody into a chipmunk. Maybe I'll get Groucho to spring for one of those.

Chico . . . scratch Chico, I've got work to do.

There are three more tapes in the Master File. I've got to buy more tapes. Maybe I can tell the office that they don't sell tapes in New Jersey and I had to go back to Las Vegas for them. Think about that for a while, Trace.

All right, so I told you that Cora called, trying to palm off Spazz and Tard on me. Not a chance. She birthed them; she keeps them.

That was one sweet call. And then we had Nick Yule call. My stomach is hurting from getting beaten up and he is snooping around, seeing if we're going to settle. I told him no. I like to tell lawyers no. He turned Jeannie down and he wants to deal with me, which means he's trying to whipsaw us. Let him sweat awhile.

So I've got Wilber Winfield on tape. He's got everything. The motive, the opportunity, everything I need to pin a murder plot on him. Except nobody's trying to murder Mitchell Carey. Least of all Wilber Winfield. Sorry, but you've got to like a man who wears lace-up shoes and knows all about how peanut butter falls and at age 212 still has an eye for titty little blondes. But natural charm aside, he had, make that *has*, a reason for being ticked off at Mitchell Carey. Winfield now owns less than half the company so Carey can do anything he wants. And what he wanted before he got sick was to sell, and so Winfield's going to be put out to pasture whether he likes it or not. Of course, he's going to take twenty or thirty million out to pasture and that makes pasture pretty nice. But if he doesn't want to go? And if Carey dies, he gets back a big piece of Carey's share and control of the company. He's got all the motive in the world, dammit, but he's not the type. I think he'd challenge Carey to a hand of showdown poker for the whole business. I don't think he'd try to kill him.

And he wasn't much help while I was trying to get other suspects. Matteson, he says, would look pretty suspicious collecting on another insurance policy. Muffy's not an heir and Amanda's not the sort. If it was Jeannie, Carey'd be dead by now. Okay, so it's nobody. Good, Trace, go home before the Mongols descend on you.

So much for Winfield, and then there was my noontime running into Matteson and Jeannie, playing squeezie fingers at the golf club, and I acted like an imbecile, so let's forget about that. Especially since it all worked out later.

Then on to the Careys' for my first burglary of the day. Muffy's skin-diving and Mrs. Carey's watching and I'm going through the upstairs bedrooms, and what do I find out? That Muffy's changed her hairstyle. That she's got a big green tank of air up there to fill her little scuba tanks, I guess. And that she's got a photo album and all the pictures of Petey are gone. So who's Petey?

I've got to ask her that.

She wasn't very happy when I joined them at the sanatorium, but then neither was Nurse Simons and who cares?

I don't like that hospital. I don't like thinking about that old woman standing there, holding those sad pajamas, and talking to that man, who can't do anything except lie there.

So out I go, into the hall, and Matteson patches up everything about Jeannie, so that was okay, and I believe him. Maybe I'm just getting gullible, it occurs to me. I seem to be believing everybody. And Matteson anyway doesn't understand why Mr. Carey's not getting any better.

It was on my mind, somehow, all day. I guess that's why I busted back into the Careys' again tonight. When Mrs. Carey was talking to her husband, she said that she was going to talk to Buffy tonight about what to do. That's when her husband woke up and shouted "no" and died.

She said Buffy, not Muffy. And Buffy's dead. It had been on my mind all day, and I didn't know it.

Good thing Matteson was there, or Mr. Carey, I know, would have died. Somehow Matteson worked too hard to save him for me to credit him with wanting the old man dead. And Muffy, that little bitch, getting ready to smoke with oxygen in the room, and talking about the old man like he's some kind of house plant. Well, at least she had the sense to call the night nurse in.

I'll tell you, maybe Matteson is and maybe he isn't running around with Jeannie Callahan, but if I got sick, I wouldn't mind having him around. He could just have gone through the motions today if he wanted, and none of us would have known any better.

It's confusing and getting confusinger. I don't know what I'm doing here.

So Chico wants to come back. The sweet little hooker who swallows a hook about a job. Well, whatever she wants to do. Lying to me just kind of busted it all.

Back to the sanatorium and see Dr. Darling and Nurse Simons leaving together. Great. I hope they're lesbians. And they poison each other.

What's the night nurse's name? Jack Ketch. Yes indeed, he is one big plug-ugly. Weight lifter's muscles and probably dumbbell brains.

So what is the scam being pulled on Mrs. Carey by Muffy the Magnificent? Oh, Nana, I'm so cold and scared. Oh, Nana, don't let them hurt Pop-pop. Bring him home, bring him home.

Yes, world, I don't think it's a scam; I know it's a scam because I don't believe in ghosts and séances and spiritualists and any such bullshit, and if the truth be known, I don't much believe in hypnosis either, even though I've seen firsthand that sometimes it works.

Ghosts don't leave neat clean little three-inch circles on the outside of window glass. I've been sitting here, with my eyes closed, listening to that tape, trying to remember just how it all happened and I know how it worked. Everytime the ghost was supposed to give an answer, Muffy nodded her head. That was her signal for the accomplice to give the next answer. I don't know if he— Hell, maybe she was imitating the voice or using a recorder or what, but that's the way it worked, and Mrs. Carey couldn't see anything because her back was to the window.

No, wait. They were using a recorder, 'cause sometimes Muffy'd ask a question and the voice would answer Nana. Good thinking, Trace.

So it's Muffy's scam, but why does she want Mr. Carey home? She want him dead? He's dying just fine in the hospital, it seems. He came close today and I could tell her rooting was all for the grim reaper, for all the help she was to me and Matteson.

Chico'd figure that out.

To hell with Chico. Let her go run an educational testing center. She can trick with every other applicant. They won't pass the tests, but most of them won't care.

Remind me never to leave taped telephone messages. From now on, I just hang up in the middle of the "I'm out but I'll get back to you" routine, just like everybody else does. I made the mistake of leaving a message for Jeannie Callahan and it nearly got my ass in jail.

I don't mind getting kicked around once in a while. Hell, I've been married, I'm used to abuse and assault, but for somebody to clock Jeannie Callahan is a no-no and I want to find that guy. I think he's the guy whose teeth fit in that apple downstairs in Hughie's freezer, and I want to know who he is. His teeth won't fit in any more apples. Unless he's real big and then I'll hit him from behind with a stick.

He's probably old. He grunted when he hit her. A real sweetheart.

And what was he doing in Jeannie's files? Does this somehow have something to do with whatever she's working on? The Plesser problem? Dissolving Carey's company?

I don't know. She doesn't either. A long interview with

her on tape and she doesn't know anything about who hit her or why.

I just don't understand what's going on.

Anyway, Mr. Carey's all right. I feel better for the time being knowing that Matteson's staying there tonight. I don't like that goon nurse talking about Carey as if he's already dead, him with his gym bag and his *Hustler* and his karate magazines, screw him. I don't know anything about it, but I just think that maybe Mr. Carey is lying there in bed, able to hear everything that's going on and just not able to say a word. I don't know and it's kind of a rotten thought, but maybe it's so.

Oh, world, I'm tired. I like Jeannie Callahan. I like her very much. Do I like her enough to hang around New Jersey for? I don't know.

I don't want to talk to Chico anymore. Even if she is my roommate. Even if she is a lot of help on things like this.

Never mind it. I'm fed up with her.

My expenses for the day are the usual, whatever you decide on, Groucho.

I'm tired.

I don't want to talk to Chico anymore.

Good night.

24

"Who's there, for weeping out loud?"

"It's me, Trace. Open up."

Chico opened the motel-room door partially, hid behind it, then pulled him into the room and closed the door. She was naked.

"I expected you," she said, "but then I got tired of waiting and I thought you really weren't coming, so I went to bed."

"I hate being predictable," he said.

Here he was with her, she naked, and he didn't know what to do. Should he kiss her hello? Maybe he should wait and see first what she did?

"Why didn't you wear a bathrobe?"

"What?"

"You didn't know who was at the door, why didn't you wear a bathrobe? I don't know what to do. I'm mad at you. How can you be mad at a woman who doesn't have any clothes on?"

"If that's getting to you, wait until I try this," she said. She reached her arms up and clasped her hands behind his head and pulled it down to hers. She kissed him, wetly and warmly, and slid her hands down his back, clasped his buttocks, and pulled him tightly against her.

Trace dropped the plastic laundry bag holding his tapes, then caressed her smooth flanks. She smelled as fresh as a breeze.

"Why didn't you invite me to stay with you?" she said.

" 'Cause my life is orderly now. I've got one tooth-brush in the bathroom. I have you come over and the next day there's four toothbrushes in the bathroom. After two days, six. Toothbrushes multiply like rabbits and paper clips. Then I don't know which one's mine and I fall behind in brushing my tongue."

He was pulling her close to him.

"You going to rape me?" she said. The corners of her large black eyes crinkled with a smile.

"After driving all this way, I ought to do something."

"Wanna tie me down? The towels here are as thin as paper. You can rip them up and tie me down. Then when you savage my body, I won't be able to get away."

"You won't try to get away," he said. "Where would you go anyway?" And he thought, To Memphis, Tennessee.

And he pushed her back from him and looked at her flawless young body, and he thought, So what, and he pushed her onto the bed.

Later they lay in bed and Trace told her what had been happening in Harmon Hills. She grunted assent a lot but was mostly content to listen.

"Any ideas?" he finally asked her.

"Not right now. I like to let them sneak up on me."

"Okay," Trace said. "Turn out the light. This is my last cigarette of the night."

"I know, no talking to you on your last cigarette."

"Right."

"One thing, Trace."

"What?"

"You didn't say you were glad to see me."

"I don't know if I am."

Trace woke in the morning with a bright spear of sunlight in his face. Chico was not in the bed and his tapes were stacked neatly on the small table in the room. There was a note on the table.

Trace:
Where was Wilber Winfield when he was supposed to meet the lawyer?
Where has Nicholas Yule been while everything's been going on?
What was in the file drawer that got looted?
Did the guy that hit you grunt?
When did the Plesser family announce its lawsuit?
She must be some kind of lady. Did you have to fall in love with her?

The note was unsigned.

Trace thought about showering, then changed his mind, packed his tapes, and drove back to the country club, where he showered, then called Meadow Vista Sanatorium and asked for Jeannie Callahan's room.

"I'm sorry," the operator said after a wait. "Miss Callahan's been released."

"Thank you," Trace said. He called the lawyer's office and got her home phone number from her secretary. She answered on the first ring.

"This is Trace. How do you feel?"

"All the pain of a hangover but none of the fond memories. And my eye's turning black."

"You must be a fine figure of a woman."

"It's no joke," she said.

"Wear sunglasses."

"I'll need glasses as big as saucers, as dense as manhole covers, to hide my stomping. It'll give my goddamn clients ideas, think they can arm-wrestle me for my fee or something. I hate this. Do you know I was voted Miss Equitable Settlement in my law class? Now I look like a battered wife."

"Did you hear from the cops?" Trace asked.

"No. Not a word."

"I'll call them. Are you staying home today?"

"Unless somebody invents a makeup for mugging victims. Today's Friday. Maybe with that and the weekend off, I'll look human on Monday."

"I'll be over later if you want."

"I want. And if you laugh at me, I'll kill you."

"Want me to bring anything?"

"Just your own beautiful self," she said.

"There's a slight charge for delivery."

"I'll have your payment ready when you get here."

Trace called the police department, but Lt. Wilcox said they had found out nothing yet. "I checked the neighborhood. Nobody noticed a suspicious car parked or saw anybody leaving the place."

"What happened with the fingerprints?" Trace asked.

"A lot of smears and a lot of sets of the lawyer's. You got anything for us?" Wilcox asked.

"No." Trace decided not to mention the apple. And how could he mention it even if he wanted to? Could he say, "Lieutenant, I've got an apple with a bite taken out of it."

And Wilcox could say, "My God, Tracy, that's just the kind of break we've been looking for. This will nail the perpetrator to the wall. Where did you get that apple?"

And Trace could say, "I stole it from an ashtray. It's got sand on it."

And Wilcox could say, "Don't disturb the sand. In the hands of a forensic genius, even sand has something to say."

No, Trace thought. Best, all in all, not to mention the apple.

Wilcox was saying, "I'll want a statement from you."

"I'll stop by and give one."

"If I'm not here, give it to my wife."

And fifteen answers jumped into Trace's mind, but he

224

decided that all of them would get him shot, so **he said** simply, "I will, Lieutenant," and hung up.

The phone rang a moment later and Dexter told him that a Mr. Marks had called and said it was very important that Tracy call him right back.

"Groucho or Karl?" Trace asked.

"He didn't say, sir. He seemed to think you'd know the name."

"Must be Groucho," Trace said. "Karl hardly calls anymore."

"What's up, Groucho?" Trace said after finally getting through the secretarial wall at Garrison Fidelity.

"Nicholas Yule. Did you tell him we wouldn't deal?"

"I don't remember," Trace said honestly.

"Well, he called yesterday. He said he told you his clients might be interested in settling and he said that you told him our company wouldn't be. Did you tell him that?"

"If he says so, I probably did. Would a lawyer lie?"

"You didn't have any right to tell him that. Maybe we will settle. Maybe it's the best thing to do."

"Is this what you called me about?"

"Of course it is."

"I'm not interested in this insurance bullshit," Trace said.

"Hold on. You're working for us. What do you mean, insurance bullshit?"

"I prefer dealing with the big questions of life and death," Trace said. "Office details bore me."

"Then stay the hell out of them," Marks yelled. "Don't commit the company to things it shouldn't be committed to."

"Are you going to meet with Yule?" Trace asked.

"Probably. Or have the lawyers do it."

"All right. I'll give you two good tips for the company."

"Go ahead."

Trace said, "One. Before you do anything, have our legal beagles talk to Jeannie Callahan. She's the doctor's lawyer and she's smarter than Yule and smarter than you, for that matter. She'll know how to deal with Yule best."

"All right. That's one," Marks said.

"Two. If anybody meets with Yule, tell them not to hire his band. He's a lousy trombone player."

Trace dressed and went down to the cocktail lounge to wait for Chico. It was pushing toward noon and the lunchroom was filling up.

Trace asked Hughie, "Don't you ever get any time off?"

"I don't need any, except weekends," Hughie said. "Bar opens near noon and I open it and generally I close it by eight or nine o'clock, except when I get a live one like you staying here. Whatever hours I work, I get paid for."

"Still terrible hours."

"Look at the bright side. It keeps me away from the racetrack. Finlandia?"

"Yeah."

"Nice assistant you got," Hughie said as he poured the vodka.

"Oh? Which one?"

"The little girl with the slanty eyes. Mako or something."

"Chico. What'd she want?"

"She came in early and collected your apple. Hey, was it all right to give it to her? Should I have asked her for a password or something? You didn't tell me not to give it to anybody."

"It was all right. She's got enough sense to do something with it."

"Eat it," Hughie said as he put the drink on the bar.

"Huh?"

"Eat it. That's what most people do with apples."

"Can't eat that one. It's evidence. Chico might eat it,

though. That girl would eat a dog-food billboard if she missed a meal. She ought to weight five hundred pounds."

"Some things are better left alone," Hughie said, and strolled off to the other end of the bar where two golfers, wearing outfits whose colors would shame a baboon's backside, plopped themselves down.

Trace wondered where Chico had gone with his apple. It would be like her to eat his apple. The woman would eat anything.

She must have been up all night listening to his tapes, and he realized, with a pang, that it must have been painful because he had been abusive to her on the tapes. He tried to remember what he had said on the tapes, but each time memory prodded him, he told himself, No, I didn't say that, I wouldn't have said anything that harsh. But he had, and he knew it.

He asked for the bar telephone and called Dr. Matteson at Meadow Vista.

"How's your star patient?" Trace asked.

"Which one. They're all stars."

"Lady Lawyer Callahan. You sent her home?"

"Yeah. She was fine. Slept through the night like a baby."

"No chance of complications?" Trace asked.

"No. Maybe she'll get a pimple."

"How about Mr. Carey?"

"Stable today. He had a good night." Matteson hesitated and said, "Mrs. Carey called this morning. She said she wanted to talk to me about his treatment. It sounded important. Do you know what that's about?"

"I think so," Trace said. "I think she's going to tell you that she wants to bring her husband home."

"She can't do that," Matteson snapped. "The man just had a heart attack. He could go any minute."

"It's not my idea, Doc."

"Who the hell's idea is it?"

"A voice from beyond," Trace said.

"What are you talking about?"

"Never mind. I think that Muffy is putting Mrs. Carey up to it."

"I'll talk her out of it."

"Good luck," Trace said. "I'm going to look in on Jeannie today."

"Good. Save me a call. Thanks, Tracy, for the tip."

When Chico came in, she was carrying a shopping bag.

"Want a drink, bag lady?" Trace said.

"Don't knock the bag. There's all kinds of goodies in there. How do you deal with that desk clerk?"

"Dexter? What'd he do?"

"His name would be Dexter. He grilled me when I came in."

"What'd you tell him?"

"I told him I was looking for you. He wanted to know who I was, so he annoyed me and I told him it was your birthday and I was from Strip-O-Gram and I had my beaded costume in the bag. Come on, I don't want a drink. Let's go to your room. We'll really give Dexter something to talk about."

Hughie said, "That's her. That's the woman who stole your apple. Should I call the police?"

"Hughie, this is Chico. Don't call the cops on her just yet. Not until you see her stealing food from other people's plates."

In his room, Trace sprawled on his bed while Chico pulled the drapes, darkening the room.

"Is this business or pleasure?" he said.

"Sit up, you slug. I don't like talking to a prone figure."

"You could have fooled me," he said, but hunkered himself up into a sitting position.

"Presto, flasho," Chico said. She stood at the foot of

228

the bed, reached into the bag, and pulled out a black plastic flashlight.

"If you use Eveready batteries," Trace said, "you can scare away grizzly bears."

"What are you talking about?"

"Sorry. It's a dated reference, too old for you. So you've got a flashlight. What about it?"

"Not just any flashlight," Chico said. She flicked the switch and Trace saw projected on the room's white wall a message:

BOFFA'S MAGIC SHOPPE
WHERE EVERY TRICK'S A TREAT

The legend was slightly out of focus, but Chico twisted the top lens cap and the letters grew sharp.

She reopened the room's drapes.

"It's a magician's projection light," she said. "I found this magic shop over in the next town. Magicians use this one for phony spirit appearances. That's how little Buffy showed up on the drapes last night."

"How does it work?"

"You just use any kind of slide or positive transparency. For a message, you can write or print anything on a piece of clear plastic and you stick it in this slot at the top and then just turn the light on."

"Chico, you're a wonder," Trace said. "When I was snooping in Muffy's room, I found a bill from a photo shop for a transparency. That's what she used. She copied one of the dead kid's pictures."

"Elementary, my dear imbecile. And if you liked that, you'll love this." She reached into the bag, pulled out a greenish lump, and tossed it to Trace. He turned it over in his hand before realizing it was a mold of teeth.

"From the apple?"

"Right. I dropped it off at a dentist in town and he made this mold for me."

"How close is it?"

"It's not perfect, but he said it's pretty close. He said you can see the spaces between the teeth and one incisor is kind of splayed outward." She paused for a moment and hitched her thumbs in her belt. "Got to be one ugly Chiclet-toothed critter made them marks, pard."

"They weren't the marks of a human being; they were made by a giant wolf," Trace said.

Chico grabbed a towel and wrapped it around her head like a kerchief. In a thick Russian accent, she said, "Even a man who is pure of heart and says his prayers by night can become a wolf when the wolfbane blooms and the autumn moon is bright."

"Higher and higher with Maria Ouspenskaya," Trace said. "Or was it Bela Lugosi?"

"Would you do the polka with Oscar Homolka?" Chico said.

"Don't get started on your old-movie routines. You're wandering."

"All right. Give me those teeth back. You get your sweaty hands all over it and you'll melt it or something and it won't match anybody."

"How'd you get a dentist to make a mold for you like that? Usually, you couldn't get a dentist to hurry if your jaw fell off."

"You really want to know?" Chico asked.

"Probably not. Not if it involves your having a cavity filled."

For a split second, Chico looked pained, but she smiled. "I talked him into it," she said.

Trace tossed the mold back to her and she caught it and replaced it in the bag.

She brought out a box. "The *pièce de résistance*," she said.

She opened the box and took out a rubber suction cup with a long wire hanging from it.

"What's that?"

"It's a loudspeaker," Chico said. "You can find it in some specialty sound shops. You plug that wire into your radio or your tape recorder and attach the cup to a wall and it gives a vibrating sound that seems to come from all over."

"Or to a window," Trace said.

"Exactly. That's where the sound came from last night. It explains that circle on the window. It's where the speaker was attached."

"With this five-dollar kit, you too can be a spiritualist medium. Run your own séances. Mystify your friends. Scare the crap out of old people," Trace said.

"Yeah, but it's not five dollars either. All this cost me a small fortune."

"Write it down for me and boost the prices. Then we'll tell Groucho we lost the receipts," Trace said.

"I'll settle for breaking even."

"You do what I say. Marks has been cutting my expenses again. I start giving him honest bills and I lose money, 'cause he cuts everything in half. We've got to triple everything just to stay even with that man. I swear he's the most mistrustful man I ever met."

"Maybe if your name wasn't on it, he'd just pay me back the money I laid out," she said hopefully.

"Don't count on it. I know Groucho," Trace said. "Anything else in that bag?"

"No. But I've got more coming. I lucked up and got hold of this newspaper reporter in Muffy's hometown."

"Wait a minute. How'd you find out her hometown?"

"A snap. I called the college and told the registrar I was thinking of hiring her for a job and they verified that she had a degree from them. And I told them I spilled coffee on her application, what was the name of her high school, and they gave it to me."

231

"I never fail to be overwhelmed by the devious Oriental mind."

"You think my people were shoguns because they were good with those swords? Of course we're devious. Anyway, it's a little town in upstate New York, near Ithaca, and I found out the name of the newspaper in that town." She hesitated. "You want to know how I found out the name of the newspaper?"

"Yes. I want to know every trick you use."

"I called Information. And I found this small daily newspaper and talked to a reporter and I charmed him a little bit. Well, like most newspapers, they keep the high-school yearbooks around."

"I didn't know that," Trace said.

"Sure. Young kids are always wrapping their cars around trees and things or getting lost in boating accidents, and if the newspaper's got a yearbook, then they've always got pictures of the victims without pestering the family."

"Live and learn."

"So as luck would have it, this reporter is coming down to New York City today. And he promised to drop off the yearbook for me."

"You must really have charmed him," Trace said sourly.

"I think the hundred dollars I promised him charmed him more," Chico said. "Isn't that terrific?"

"What do we need a yearbook for?"

Chico shrugged. "Maybe nothing. But maybe it'll tell you something you ought to know about Muffy."

"I hope so. I don't see how I can get Groucho to go for three hundred dollars for a yearbook without there being something good in it," Trace said.

"A hundred," she corrected.

"That's our cost. We'll ask for three hundred and negoti-ate down," Trace said. "Trust me. I've been through these negotiations dozens of times."

"You've never won one," she said.

"No. But I know all Groucho's tricks and I'm overdue."

Chico went to the bathroom and Trace took the green tooth molding out of the bag and held it in his hand, looking at it. When the young woman came back, he had his jacket on.

"I'll be back in a while," he said. "If you want to wait."

"Where you going?"

"I want to ask Jeannie if she recognizes whoever might belong to these teeth. In case it was a friend waiting for her."

"You want me to go with you?" Chico asked.

"No. You must be starved. Why don't you go feed yourself and I'll meet you back here later?"

"How much later?"

"I don't know," Trace said.

"Maybe I'll be here and maybe I'll go back to my place," she said.

"Okay," Trace said. "Leave me a note if you go."

"Don't worry. I'll be gone," she said.

25

"Hi, son. Come to talk about peanut butter?"

"No, business."

"Sounds serious."

"It is. Last night somebody broke into Jeannie Callahan's office, just about the time you were supposed to be meeting with her."

"Damn, that's too bad."

"Why'd you miss the meeting?"

"I'm a suspect in the burglary?"

"In my eyes you are. Why didn't you make the meeting with her?"

"Gentlemen don't generally talk about things like that."

"Make an exception in this case."

"Oh, hell, why not? If I don't talk about it to somebody, I'll go crazy. Remember that little blonde I showed you?"

"In the pink sweater?"

"Yeah, that's her. Well, yesterday, after you left, she came into the office here and she started, what do you young folks say, coming in to me."

"Coming on."

"Yeah, that's right. She was coming on to me. So one thing led to another and I took her to dinner and then we stopped someplace and spent the night."

"You missed a business meeting so you could get laid?"

"Sure. Wouldn't you?"

"I guess I would."

"If you were my age, I know you would."

"Thanks, Mr. Winfield."

"Anytime, Mr. Tracy."

26

"Well, what do I look like?"

"Let's see," Trace said. He stood in the doorway of Jeannie Callahan's apartment, sizing her up. "The body is lissome and exquisite. Very nice. The right side of your face is an absolute joy to behold. I love your eyes and lashes. Your teeth are marvelous. Your smile warms my days."

"Keep going," she said suspiciously.

"And the left side of your face looks like a slab of liver that got tenderized by a tank tread."

"Naff off," she said, and swung the door closed in his face.

He caught it and pushed it back open. "But I'm willing to forget it," he said. "Just keep your good side to me."

"Okay. Since you're partially nice, you can come in and get partially drunk with me."

Trace helped himself to a drink in the kitchen and was pleased to note that Jeannie had already started to learn: the vodka was chilled and thick in the refrigerator's freezer compartment, the way he liked it best.

Jeannie had a brandy in her hand, a large snifter almost full, when Trace joined her on the couch.

"How are you feeling?"

"Fine. Brandy wounds all numbs."

"It numbs all wounds too. Any second thoughts about

what happened in your office last night? Any flashes of memory?''

"No. Just a big fist coming out of the dark. And a grunt. Dammit, I wish I had been you. I would have clubbed that bastard."

"It's obvious you're talking about my size and not my fighting heart," Trace said. "What kind of stuff do you keep in that file cabinet?"

"Documents mostly. Betsy keeps most of the real records out in the computer room."

"Yours filed alphabetically?"

"Is there any other way to file things? Drink up, you're slowing me down," she said.

"How many drawers in that file cabinet? I forget."

"Four," she said. She reached down and lifted Trace's glass to his lips. He took a long sip before putting it back down.

"So that'd be like A to F, G to M, N to S, and T to Z in the four drawers."

"How'd you do that so fast?"

"I was an accountant in an earlier life," Trace said.

"I hate accountants."

"Now I'm a drunk."

"I love drunks," she said.

"I noticed. So he broke into the second drawer, that's G to M. What's in that drawer that's so important?"

"Ask him," she said. "Catch him and ask him, and after he tells you, kick him in the nuts for me. I'm going to put a head on this. You ready?"

"Not yet," Trace said. He noticed that she lurched a little as she walked toward the kitchen. She came back, put her glass down, and leaned back on the couch with her head on Trace's shoulder. They sat quietly for a while.

"It wasn't G to M," she said abruptly.

"Why not?" he said.

"Top drawer doesn't count. I keep my checkbooks and

stuff in there. The files start with the second drawer, maybe like A to H.''

"Good. Now we're getting somewhere. A to H.''

"Talk about it later,'' she said. "Kiss me now.''

"That purple stuff on your face might be catching.''

"Them's bruises, son. Honestly won on the field of battle. 'We few, we ancient few, we band of brothers,' how's it go?''

"Happy few,'' Trace said, " 'We few, we happy few, we band of brothers, for he today that sheds his blood with me shall be my brother.' ''

"Very good,'' she said. "I'm impressed.''

"The perils of a Jesuit education. I remember everything and understand nothing.''

"Kiss me anyway,'' she said, and he did.

"It was Carey's file they were looking for,'' he said. "That'd be in that drawer.''

She nuzzled her face into the hollow between Trace's arm and chest. "Wanna make love?''

"Not just now.''

"Another drink?'' she asked.

"You just poured that one.''

"Somebody musta stolen it while my back was turned.''

Her glass was almost empty and he hadn't even seen her drink it.

"No, I'll pass this round,'' he said. "Hold on. I want to show you something.''

He fetched from his pocket the green wax mold of teeth.

"Recognize that?'' he asked.

"Obviously somebody who didn't brush after every meal,'' she said.

"I think that's the guy who cold-cocked you,'' Trace said.

"I didn't get a chance to look into his mouth.''

"Recognize it, though? You know anybody with a big ugly mouth like that?''

"No. I only hang out with people with perfect teeth. I'm very prejudiced against bad teeth. Against empty glasses too."

She got up and teetered out to the kitchen. He heard the bottle cap fall on the floor. When she came back holding a glass, her hand was wet.

"Only half full," she said. "I'm tapering off."

As she set the glass down, the telephone rang and Trace watched her go to the phone and stand there, swaying gently in her shoeless feet.

"Hello, George," she said thickly. "No, I'm all right. Really, I'm feeling fine. Trace is here. Devlin Tracy. Right. Yeah. I'll be okay. Thanks for calling. Oh. Okay."

She turned and held the phone out to him. "It's George. He wants to talk to you." She carried the phone to him.

"Hello, Doc."

Jeannie took a sip of her drink, then curled up on the couch and put her head in Trace's lap.

"I met with Mrs. Carey and Muffy today. Dammit, they want to move Mr. Carey tomorrow. I couldn't talk them out of it. I may have to get a court order to stop them."

"Did you warn them?"

"I wouldn't talk to that snotty broad. I don't like her. But I told Mrs. Carey that her husband might die if she moved him."

"What'd she say to that?"

"She said she wanted him home. She said her daughter would want that too."

"Sorry, Doc."

"Not as sorry as I am. I don't even know if he'll survive a trip home in an ambulance. Are you going to see Mrs. Carey?"

Trace thought a moment and said, "Yes, I am. Tonight."

"Try to talk her out of it," Matteson said.

"I just might be able to."

"I owe you a big one if you can."

"Okay."

When he leaned forward to hang up the phone, Trace saw that Jeannie Callahan was sound asleep on his lap. He shook her shoulder. "Jeannie?"

"Yes," she said softly, her eyes still closed.

"Did Mitchell Carey make out a new will in the hospital?"

"Carey? New will?"

"Did he make a new will out in the hospital?" Trace snapped the words to try to penetrate her drunken fog.

"New will? New will? No. He can't even talk, how's make will?"

He sat quietly for a moment and she was again asleep. When she was breathing deeply, he moved out from under her and gently placed a pillow under her head.

He emptied their two drinks into the sink, then unplugged the telephone so its ringing wouldn't wake her. He put on his jacket and walked toward the door, then came back and kissed her on the cheek.

"I think I love you a little bit," he said. "Maybe a whole lot. But what we've got here isn't companionship, it's two compulsions. Six months together and we'd both be dead, or our brains so pickled that we wouldn't know if we were alive or dead. So long, little girl."

When he left, he locked the door tightly behind him.

27

Chico had gone back to her own motel and Trace talked with her for an hour on the telephone before he drove to Mrs. Carey's home.

The old woman seemed pleased to see him when she answered the door. "Come in, Mr. Tracy. Have you heard the good news?"

"What news is that?" Trace said. He closed the door behind him but was careful that it did not click locked.

"Mitchell's coming home from the sanatorium. Tomorrow."

"That's what I wanted to talk to you about," Trace said.

"Why don't you go into the study and make yourself a drink? My tea is steeping, I'll be right in."

In the study, Trace looked out the side window toward the bristling hedges jutting up from the rolling trimmed lawn like ghostly black apparitions. He shook his head and poured himself a drink from the liquor cabinet and was standing there when Muffy steamed into the room.

"What are you doing here?"

"I've come to talk to Mrs. Carey."

"If you've come to talk about Mr. Carey, forget it. Her mind is made up."

"Who made it up for her?"

"She makes up her own mind."

"Good. Then she can change her own mind," Trace said.

"Listen, you—" she started.

"No, *you* listen. I don't like you. As far as I'm concerned, you're a Svengalian little shit who's got her hooks out for the Carey money, and you best back off or I'll spend some time proving it. Now, go haunt a house. Or look in your crystal ball or something. If I want to hear from you, I'll rattle your chain."

Muffy looked at him, then curled her lips back, baring her teeth. It was a feline gesture, the thing a cornered cat might do, Trace thought. Wordlessly, she walked from the room, and Trace again glanced toward the window but still saw nothing except the blackness of the night.

Trace was sitting at the small table in the center of the room when Mrs. Carey returned with her tea on a tray.

"Would you rather sit over here?" she said.

"I wanted to talk business with you and I thought this was more businesslike," he said.

She joined him at the table, and while she poured tea and spooned honey into it, he looked past her toward the side window, but still saw nothing there that he wanted to see.

She looked up at him expectantly and he said, "I'm here as Bob Swenson's friend and a friend of yours, Mrs. Carey."

"Thank you. I've always sort of felt that," she said.

"You saw Dr. Matteson today?" he said, in a gentle question that needed no answer, but the woman nodded.

"A nice man," she said. "Very nice. And so caring."

"Then why don't you listen to him? He told you it might be killing your husband to bring him home now."

She visibly winced when Trace said "killing," but she sipped her tea, pursed her lips, and said, "I'm sorry, Mr. Tracy. Muffy just said you'd probably try to talk me out of it, but I have my reasons."

"What kind of reasons?"

242

"I can't tell you about them, but they're very good reasons. We're going to be a family again. A real family."

"I think I know your reasons, Mrs. Carey. You remember Houdini, the magician?"

"Of course."

"Do you know he spent most of his adult life looking for a spiritualist, a medium, who wasn't a fake? And he never found one?"

She had a small smile on her lips, as if to say she had heard it all before. If she was surprised that Trace knew about her reasons for wanting her husband moved, she did not show it.

"All the so-called spiritualists, the fancy mediums, the spoon-benders, the watch-starters, today, they're all fakes," Trace said. "Magicians' tricks."

"Some people never believe," she said gently.

Trace saw a motion over her shoulder and he nodded his head. "All right, Mrs. Carey, I didn't want to do this, but let me show you just what you believe in, enough to maybe kill your husband."

He walked to the light switch by the door and turned it off. The room was lit only by the hall light shining through the partially opened door.

He sat back down and said, "Close your eyes, Mrs. Carey, and hold my hands."

"This is—"

"Please. Just do it."

Grudgingly, slowly, the woman complied, and a moment later, a soft eerie female voice filled the room.

"Devlin, are you there? Are you there?"

It was a soft and haunting voice, and Mrs. Carey's eyes opened wide with shock.

"Please, Mrs. Carey. Just listen. Yes, I am here," he called out.

"Devlin, this is your mother."

"Yes, Mother."

"It's cold where I am." As the voice spoke, Trace kept his eyes on Mrs. Carey. The shock on her face had seemed to give way to confusion, then annoyance.

"Turn up the heat, Mother," Trace said.

"But they won't let me, Devlin. They said I didn't pay my bill. Come and get me, Devlin. In the great beyond. Come and get me, come and . . ." As the voice began to trail off, Trace said to the woman, "It's a hoax, Mrs. Carey, don't you see?"

"How do you know? How can you be so sure?"

"Because my mother's not in any great beyond. She's in the Bronx, busting my father's chops."

"But—"

"No buts. You want more? Here." He nodded again and suddenly an apparition began to appear on the drapes at the far end of the room.

"Look," Trace said. He pointed toward the drapes, and Mrs. Carey followed his hand with her eyes. "A spirit picture," he said.

The image on the drapes danced a moment, then stopped. It was fuzzy and dull and unrecognizable, and as Trace watched, it began to slowly grind its way into focus.

Finally the picture on the drapes was clear.

It was a cartoon of Porky Pig.

"Oh," said Mrs. Carey with pain in her voice.

The ghostly voice filled the room again. "Th-th-th-that's all, folks," it said.

"You want more, Mrs. Carey?" Trace snapped. "I can give you Goofy or Donald Duck. Maybe Clarabelle Cow? Or Buffy, if you want."

"Stop, stop," the woman cried. She covered her eyes with her hands.

Trace went to the light switch. The door to the room was now wide open. He turned on the light and waved toward the window for Chico to come in.

When he went back to the table, Mrs. Carey had tears in

her eyes and he felt a pain in the pit of his stomach at having been forced to hurt her.

"I'm sorry, Mrs. Carey. But all this spook nonsense around here, the crystal ball, the incense, the voices, they're all magic tricks, all part of a swindle."

The woman took a deep breath as if to compose herself. "I'm sorry, Mr. Tracy, but I saw Buffy's face the other night. And I heard her voice."

Chico came into the room, carrying a tape recorder with the suction-cup mike and the image-projection light.

"Mrs. Carey, this is my assistant, Miss Mangini. That was her voice you just heard."

The old woman turned toward Chico and for a moment her face showed anger at the young woman's participation in the scheme. Then her good manners reasserted themselves and she just nodded.

"I was wondering about that face, Mrs. Carey," Trace said. "But remember, the other day, the picture of Buffy was missing from the mantel there. Look over there. It's back. I think Muffy had a projection transparency made of it. I found the receipt in her room."

"Trace," said Chico.

"You were late."

"I know. I was meeting that reporter. He gave me this." She held out a high-school yearbook. "You ought to look at it."

She put it on the table and opened it. Even with a different hairdo, the girl in the lower right-hand corner of the page was Muffy. The legend under the photograph read:

> Melinda Belknap, AKA Bucky. A twin and already a veteran at being cut in half onstage. This talented mimic will go far in show business. Drama Club, Class Night.

Trace glanced at the picture, then turned the book around so Mrs. Carey could see it.

"There's your daughter's voice, Mrs. Carey. From our talented mimic, Muffy."

The gray-haired woman looked at the picture blankly, as if she could not comprehend what was being said.

"There's more, Trace," Chico said. "Turn another page."

He did, and at the top left-hand corner was a picture of a young man with a big gap-toothed smile. "Peter Belknap," said the caption. "Class magician. He and twin Bucky (Melinda) continually captivate the class with their illusions. A show-business career looms for Petey."

"The accomplice," Chico said.

"More than that," Trace said, and he looked down at the picture again. He had seen the face before, but it hadn't belonged to anyone named Peter Belknap.

"That's Jack Ketch," Trace said. "The night nurse in Mr. Carey's room."

"What name?" said Chico.

"Jack Ketch."

"Oh, Trace," she said with a keening sound.

"What's the matter?"

"Jack Ketch. It's an old British slang name. It means hangman."

28

The door to Mitchell Carey's hospital room was locked. Trace kicked it open. The flimsy lock splintered through the dried old wood of the frame and the door swung wide.

Jack Ketch was leaning over Carey's bed. He swung around as the door flew open.

"Hey, what the hell—"

Trace interrupted him. "Just came to check on Mr. Carey." He walked casually toward the side of the bed, but as he neared Ketch, he balled his fist and buried it deep in the young man's stomach. The air went out of him with a rush and he sank to his knees, groaning and holding his stomach.

Trace looked through the oxygen tent at Carey and saw the old man's face had a faint bluish pallor. He reached out his hand for the oxygen tank and found the valve had been turned off.

He opened the valve, and the oxygen began hissing into the clear plastic tent over the old man's bed. Trace lifted an edge of the tent to help clear away the carbon dioxide that might have built up underneath it.

Ketch was struggling to his feet. Without a word Trace leaned over and punched him in the face. The nurse fell backward onto his back, groaning.

There was no telephone in the room, so Trace walked to the open door and bellowed down the hall. "Nurse, Nurse."

A nurse came running around the corner into the corridor and Trace motioned for her to follow him into the room.

"Mr. Carey," he said. "Check his pulse. Make sure he's breathing."

The nurse looked worriedly at the male nurse lying on the floor, then again at Trace.

"Just do what I say," he snapped.

"Pulse seems strong," she said after a moment.

"All right. Now go get Dr. Matteson right away. Tell him that Tracy, that's me, wants him up here right away. Tell him that Mr. Carey's oxygen had been turned off and his body may be flooded with carbon dioxide. Got that?"

She hesitated, then nodded yes.

"Snap to it."

The nurse ran from the room.

Ketch was stirring and Trace punched him again in the face, but not hard enough this time to put him out. He reached down, grabbed the young man's long hair, and jerked him upward to his feet, then twisted an arm up behind him. He could feel the weight as the man sagged against him.

"What . . . where . . . ?"

"Just move, hero," Trace said, and pushed him toward the open door to the corridor.

When Ketch came to, he was lying in a bed, strapped down by canvas bands across his legs and another across his chest and arms.

His eyes registered shock when he realized he was under the plastic dome of an oxygen tent and he could hear the faint hissing of the oxygen and feel the chill of the gas surrounding him.

He breathed deeply and turned his head to look around the room.

Trace was leaning against the doorway, staring at him.

"Game's over, Florence Nightingale," Trace said. "Start talking."

"Where are we?"

"Don't worry, sweetheart. You're in Three East. Nobody's going to find you here. Not until I'm done with you."

"The guard," Ketch started.

"I sent him off on a wild-goose chase. Nobody knows you're here. Except me. Just the two of us, isn't that cozy? Now you're going to tell me what's been going on."

"Wait and read it in my memoirs," Ketch said.

"Yours. Or sweet little sister Muffy's?" Trace paused as the man in the bed gaped at him. "That's right. I know about you and your sister and your whole traveling medicine show."

"Then I don't have to tell you anything."

"You don't have to, but you will," Trace said. "Are you really a nurse?"

"Of course I'm a nurse."

"Then you know how dangerous oxygen can be, don't you?"

Ketch hesitated. "Yeah . . ."

Trace took his cigarettes from his pocket and lit one. "You ever seen an oxygen fire?" he asked.

"Just pictures." The young man squirmed against the bonds around his legs and chest.

"Then you got the idea. You know what you're going to look like after I puff this cigarette up and then toss it on that plastic tent of yours, don't you?"

"Now, wait . . ."

"No, pal. I'm tired of waiting. You're going to be incinerated, Ketch. I'll tell you what it'll be like. First, the cigarette's going to be on the top of the plastic for a minute before it burns through. You'll be able to watch the plastic starting to melt. Then the oxygen is going to flare up and you're going to be swimming in fire. Fire's a bloodsucker. It'll burn out the oxygen in the tent, then it'll burn down your nose and mouth, looking for more oxygen. In the meantime, your clothes will be burning. Your flesh will start to melt. It's mostly fat, you know, and it burns good. When it gets burning, it'll keep going because the tent'll be gone and the oxygen from the room will keep feeding the fire. Oh, yeah. Maybe the hose from the tank will ignite too. That'll be like a blowtorch aiming at your face. Nice way to die, Ketch.''

Trace puffed hard on his cigarette, shook off the ash, and puffed it again into a bright red glow. He held the cigarette between his thumb and curled middle finger, ready to flip across the room at the oxygen tent.

"So long, Ketch," he said.

"No, wait. I'll talk. I'll talk."

Trace put the cigarette back in his mouth, reached behind him, and pressed the on button of his tape recorder.

"You're going to talk of your own free will, isn't that right?" he said.

"Sure, sure, anything you say."

"Start at the beginning," Trace said.

But before Ketch had a chance to speak, something in the back of Trace's head exploded and his eyes rolled up into his head as everything went black and he pitched to the floor.

29

Jack Ketch had gone. Trace dragged himself to a sitting position on the floor and a starburst of pain flashed between his eyes.

He felt the back of his skull, gingerly, then looked at his fingers. No blood. He shook his head to try to clear it, and slowly, holding on to the doorknob, he pulled himself to his feet.

How long had he been unconscious? He didn't know. He seemed able to walk, and he started down the corridor toward the exit of Three East.

The guard was back at his desk.

"Who are you?"

"Later," Trace said. He pushed past the guard out into the hallway to the steps leading downstairs.

On the first step he stopped.

His tape recorder.

He could feel it vibrating gently against his right hip; he reached back, pressed the rewind button, and then pressed the button to play the tape.

Muffy's voice: "You idiot, Petey. You all right?"

Jack Ketch's voice: "Get me out of here."

Muffy: "Did you tell him anything?"

Ketch: "Jesus, that was tight. No. I didn't tell him anything. What does he know?"

Muffy: "There's nothing for him to know. We haven't done anything wrong."

Ketch: "Hurry up. My legs are killing me. I don't know. He acted like he was onto us about something."

Muffy: "I tell you. There's nothing for him to know. What'd we do? There."

Ketch: "Thanks. It feels like my blood stopped."

Muffy: "All we did is I befriended an old lady. And you've been working as a nurse at night. We haven't done anything wrong."

Ketch: "Muffy, you got balls, I'll tell you."

Muffy: "Hell with him. He wants to cause trouble, we'll give him trouble. Him tying you up. Threatening your life. We'll have his ass in jail."

Ketch: "I don't know. I think we ought to just get out of here. He caught me with Carey's oxygen off."

Muffy: "Nonsense. I was just down there and Carey's all right. So it's your word against this creep's. A million things. You wanted to see if the oxygen was working right. You were just checking inside the tent to see if Carey was all right. A million things. Come on, let's go. (Giggle.) Dear old Nana is probably worried about me."

(Sound of bed creaking. Footsteps. A loud crunch as if something hit the microphone.)

Muffy: "Leave him be. He doesn't mean anything. We're too close now to let go."

Ketch: "I'd like to kill him."

Muffy: "After we're rich."

(Sound of door closing.)

Trace saw the telephone on the wall next to the stairs and dialed the Careys' number.

Chico answered. "Carey home."

"This is Trace."

"What's the matter? You sound terrible. Where are you?"

"Actually, I'm about two steps from Three East."

"What's Three East?"

"It's the nut factory at the sanatorium."

"Trace, you've always been two steps from Three East."

"Is Mrs. Carey all right?"

"Yeah," Chico said. "She's shook but okay."

"All right. I think Muffy and her brother are on their way there. You get out of there with Mrs. Carey right now."

"Okay. What are you going to do?"

"I don't know yet. I think I'm coming there," Trace said.

"You sure you're all right?"

"I'm fine," he said. "Get moving."

He hung up, remembered Mitchell Carey, and hurried down the steps to Room 213.

Dr Matteson was at Carey's bedside.

"How is he, Doc?"

"He's alive. Are you leaving town soon?"

"Why?" Trace asked.

"Since you've been here, there's nothing but chaos. What the hell's been going on here?"

"I don't know. I think that night nurse has been cutting off the oxygen, letting him rebreathe his own carbon dioxide. Would that explain why your therapy wasn't working?"

"It could. His brain would be starving. Cells dying. He wouldn't have a chance."

"What's the chances now?"

"I don't know," Matteson said. "Time'll tell. Hey, where you going? You look like hell. I think you ought to stay here, let me look at you."

"Hospitals don't agree with me," Trace said.

"Well, well, the overbite twins. Bucky and Cluck," Trace said.

Muffy wheeled and glared at him in the study door. "Where's Amanda?" she snapped. Her brother was sitting

253

on the couch, a bottle of beer on the table before him. He rose to his feet.

"I thought it was best to get her out of here for a while," Trace said. "And shouldn't you be calling her Nana?"

Muffy paused, then said confidently, "It's all right. She'll be back. This is her home. And mine."

"That simple, is it?" Trace said. He stepped into the study, closing the door behind him.

"Actually, it is," Muffy said. "Make you a drink?"

"You're a cool one. I'll say that for you. I'll pass on the drink."

"Why not cool?" Muffy said. "I haven't done anything wrong."

"That's where you're mistaken. You've done a lot wrong." He turned to Ketch. "Sit down."

"Why don't you make me?"

"Nothing would give me more pleasure," Trace said.

"Petey, sit down. Let's let our guest talk. He seems to want to. And I do want him out of here before Amanda, Nana, comes home. He does have a way of disturbing her."

She had mixed herself a highball and she joined her brother on the couch. She sipped her drink, looked at Trace, and said coolly, "So?"

"You had me going for a long time," Trace said. "I couldn't really figure your game out."

"And now you have?" Muffy said.

"Yeah, pretty much. You, dummy, pay attention 'cause I'll ask questions later."

"I'm going to have fun taking you apart," Jack Ketch said.

"Not on your best day, Junior," Trace said. He leaned back against the study door. "The trouble with a pair like you is that you're stupid. And when you try to be smart, you're even more stupid and you get into trouble. Fish shouldn't try to fly."

"Sis, why are we listening to this? Why don't I just throw him out?"

"Aaah, let him talk. Maybe he can tell us how we went wrong." She smiled, as if sharing a private joke.

"I didn't like you, Bucky, right from the start," Trace said.

"Don't call me Bucky. That name's dead," Muffy said.

"You left a whole lot of pieces around for me to pick up," Trace said. "Coming back here after Buffy's death. What was it you saw? That Mrs. Carey was shaky and on the edge? So you started combing your hair the way Buffy used to. You started calling her Nana the way Buffy did. There was an old lady whose husband was near death and you were worming your way into her life like a second daughter."

"She's my friend's mother. I came here to help," Muffy said.

"But I couldn't figure out why you had Mrs. Carey talk to Bob Swenson. If you were figuring on killing off Mr. Carey, why have some insurance snoop looking into it?"

"Why indeed?" she said.

"That threw me for a while. I've been dealing with smart devious people so long I wasn't used to something that was dumb and obvious. You were afraid that Doc Matteson or his people might really get Mr. Carey to change his will or his insurance or whatever. Before you had a chance to get yourself cut in for a piece of the pie. You couldn't take a chance that he had already done that. If you planned to kill him, that put a stop to it. Maybe I will have that drink." Trace poured some vodka into a glass and sipped at it.

"Mr. Carey steered me wrong there. When I first came to town, he said that 'they' were trying to kill him. But he was wrong. You weren't trying to kill him. Not then. You were just trying to make sure that he didn't recover. That's why you had Earthquake McGoon here cutting off his oxygen at night, letting him breathe back his own carbon dioxide. Just to make sure that Matteson's oxygen therapy didn't have a chance to work. The lawyer told me about your checking into wills. It wasn't hard to figure out that you were nervous about Mr. Carey's. Even if you wanted to kill him, you couldn't. Not until you were sure that he hadn't made sure that you were written out somehow. What was it? When he was at the first hospital, did he catch onto your game. Is that what it was?"

"Maybe he didn't like my hairdo," Muffy said.

"And maybe he recognized it for what it was, an attempt to swindle your way into an old woman's confidence."

"Interesting story."

"It gets better. But you had to know if Mr. Carey had done anything about his will and Jeannie Callahan wouldn't tell you. That's when you had little brother here break into her office and rifle her files to find out. He hadn't counted on her coming back, and when she did, he knocked her out."

"What a lot of crap," Muffy's brother said.

"Not so much, dirtbag," Trace said. "Jeannie remembered that the guy who hit her grunted when he punched. I should have tied that together with you being a karate freak. That's the way you guys punch."

"A lot of guys do that," Ketch said.

"But not a lot of them are dumb enough to steal an apple from the lawyer's refrigerator, take one bite, and leave it where it can be found."

Muffy snapped her head to look at her brother; the young man looked shocked.

"Remember? You dropped it in the ashtray out in the hall. We had a dentist make a mold of it. It'll match your teeth exactly. Muffy, you both had beaver teeth when you were kids. Why'd you get yours fixed and not him?"

"We could afford only one. Petey's next."

"Maybe the state prison'll do it for him for free."

"Not on the basis of that cock-and-bull story," she said.

"Now this is just a guess," Trace said, "but the cops figure a pinch bar or a tire iron was used to bust into Jeannie's file cabinet. I wouldn't be surprised that they find that pinch bar in the trunk of Petey's VW outside. Probably with some little paint smears from the file cabinet still on it. But that's just a maybe.

"So there's no new will in the Carey file. That's last night, when you did your séance bit with Mrs. Carey. Very cute and very easy for two stage magicians like you two."

"You've done your homework, haven't you?" Muffy said.

"I try. That's why Buffy's picture was missing the first day I was here. You were having a transparency copy made at the photo shop in town. I saw the receipt the first day I broke into the house here."

"You what?"

"You heard me. That's when I saw the big green tank in your bedroom. I figured it was to fill your scuba tanks from. But scuba tanks take compressed air. Green tanks are a universal symbol. They mean oxygen. You had that here just for show, for when you got Mr. Carey home, maybe you could convince Dr. Matteson that you were continuing the oxygen treatments."

Trace put down his vodka glass.

"There was something Matteson said last night at the sanatorium. I went there to see Jeannie, but I bumped into him and asked him how Mr. Carey was. He said that he was fine and that the nurse said he was resting comfortably. But he called the nurse 'she.' And Petey was supposed to be on duty last night. I saw him there. But he had to sneak out to come play ghost here with you and then break into Jeannie's office."

"*And* eat an apple," Muffy said.

"Right. And eat an apple. I still couldn't figure it all out, though. This was a crime without a crime. Why didn't you just kill Mr. Carey? Okay, you had to wait until you were sure he didn't change his will. So now you know that. You could just have put a pillow over his face and that'd be that. Why not?"

"Tell me why," Muffy said.

"Yeah," Petey said.

"I kept thinking you were worried just about Mr. Carey's will. But you weren't. It wasn't just that. That book upstairs in your room about making wills. That didn't have anything to do with Mr. Carey. It was Mrs. Carey. You know, I'd like to take credit for figuring it out, but I missed it entirely. You went to talk to Jeannie Callahan right after you got into town, and you were talking about wills then. That's before the Plesser case, before you had any reason to worry about Mr. Carey changing his will to benefit the sanatorium. It was Mrs. Carey all along. You were planning to get her to leave everything to you, weren't you?"

"What do you think?" the girl said. Trace noticed that she had stopped sipping from her drink.

"I think you wanted to keep Mr. Carey a vegetable until you got Mrs. Carey to really start thinking of you as her own daughter and leave you everything. Then I think you planned to get rid of Mr. Carey. And then Mrs. Carey. So many ways to do it. An accident down at the pond. Heartbroken, she takes an overdose of sleeping pills. Maybe she falls in the pond and drowns. Or she just gets old and dies. That's what I think. It's no fun if you don't tell me if I'm right or wrong."

"You're absolutely right," Muffy said.

"Muffy," said her brother, "stop."

"It's all right, Petey. Nobody's here to hear anything. You've got it just about right, Mr. Tracy. One thing you didn't know is Mrs. Carey signed a new will today, leaving everything to me. You forget that Buffy herself told the old lady to trust me. I brought Buffy back here once and I can bring her back here again."

"That dog won't hunt," Trace said. "I showed Mrs. Carey how that dodge works."

Muffy shook her head. "You really don't know a great deal about it, do you? People who believe in spooks, they want to believe. Petey and I are good. We've got a whole bag of tricks, spirit photos, messages inside sealed envelopes, a whole list of things that'll keep Mrs. Carey believing until she dies."

"Which won't be long," Trace said.

Muffy shrugged. "You never know. She's very old and she's going to be crushed when her husband dies."

"Nice little swindle," Trace said.

"Swindle? You ought to know something. Buffy was my friend, but she couldn't come ·in out of the rain without help. Anything she did in school, I did for her. I got her her degree. It was my work. We lived together and that room was clean because I made it clean. I nursemaided her for four years. All that girl knew how to do was spend money. She had plenty of that and I didn't have a penny. You know, there's some poetic justice, Mr. Tracy. She got hit by a car while she was out shopping. That's all that girl was good at. Do you know I wrote her letters home for her? She was too lazy to even do that?"

"Did you kill her?" Trace asked.

"No. I thought about it a lot. Every time I thought how rich she was. But I didn't."

"You decided to kill her parents instead," Trace said.

"That's your story. Nobody's going to believe it. Least of all Mrs. Carey."

"No, Muffy, it's your story. Yours and Petey's. And I've got it all here on tape."

He patted his right hip. For a moment, the girl looked confused, then she smiled and said, "Tapes aren't any use in court."

"Some are."

"But not this one. You've been holding a gun on us for the last fifteen minutes. The tape doesn't show that. If we didn't cooperate with your silly nonsense, you'd shoot us. The tape doesn't show that. The tape doesn't show anything that's really important, does it?"

"You're very clever," Trace said, looking down at his empty, gunless hands.

"Thank you. That's a step up. Fifteen minutes ago you were saying we were stupid. Now why don't you put the gun away and leave us alone? We've had enough of your fantasies."

Before Trace could answer, there was a flicker of light on the wall. A ghostly white image began to take shape. And then it came clear. It was Porky Pig, and as Muffy looked first at the image, then toward the window, a voice resounded through the room.

"Th-th-th-th-that's all, folks."

"Chico," Trace yelled.

"And friends," she yelled back.

A moment later, Chico came bounding into the room. Right behind her were Lt. Wilcox and his wife. Mrs. Carey followed them.

"What are you doing here?" Trace asked.

"When you told me to leave with Mrs. Carey, I thought it might be time to call the cops. The lieutenant and his wife came back with us."

"Did you have to do Porky Pig? Come on."

"Best I could do. I wanted to let you know we were here

260

before you started to tangle with that big dude," she said.

Trace turned to Wilcox. "Did you hear enough, Lieutenant?"

"Enough to hold them. Let the county prosecutor figure out what to charge them with."

"Think about attempted murder. I saw Petey with the oxygen turned off at Mr. Carey's bedside."

"By the way, I'm getting tired of telling you to come into the office and make a statement," Wilcox said. "Do I have to book you too?"

"No. This statement I'll give gladly."

"Don't be too sure. I just may book you anyway."

"Why?"

"Why the hell didn't you give me that apple you found for evidence?"

"Wait until tomorrow and I'll think of an excuse," Trace said.

Wilcox turned away toward Muffy and her brother. "Okay, you two, let's get moving."

As he led them toward the door, Trace suddenly called out, "Hey, Muffy, wait."

She turned and Trace tossed her the crystal ball from the mantel.

"Here, look in that. And if it doesn't tell you the future, I will."

Chico had taken Mrs. Carey to stay with neighbors, and Trace sat alone, inside the study, thinking. Something was wrong; the whole package just didn't tie together the way it should have.

He heard a sound at the front door and he called out, "Chico?"

"Yeah." She came into the study, plopped herself down in the sofa facing Trace, and put her feet up on the coffee table. "It doesn't hang, does it?" she said.

He shook his head. "Something's wrong. How do two kids put together a double-murder plot? And what for? Muffy could have lived here with Mrs. Carey forever. You don't need money if you've got the use of money, and she'd have the use of plenty of it."

"I know," Chico said. "There's another screw that needs a quarter-turn to tighten this whole thing up."

They sat in silence for a few moments until Chico got up and walked quickly from the room.

"Be right back."

She left Trace thinking about money and who needed it, and he went to the telephone and called police headquarters. He was talking to Lt. Wilcox when Chico came back into the room, smiling, holding the copy of Muffy's book on drawing wills over her head.

"Thanks, Lieutenant," Trace said. "See you tomorrow." He hung up the phone, and Chico said, "Did you look at this book?"

"No, I didn't have time."

"Well, look at this. She had this page dog-eared." Chico began to read: 'A simple will, bequeathing a wife's estate to her husband or a husband's to his wife, can be drafted by anyone who will follow the forms in this book. However, complicated estates, involving large holdings or bequests to persons who are not immediate relatives, should always be drawn in consultation with a qualified attorney.' "

Trace nodded and Chico smiled. "That's not all. She's got a note in the book."

"You're going to tease me and not tell me what it is, aren't you?"

"When did the Plesser thing first get in the papers?"

"I don't know. Two or three weeks ago, I guess," Trace said. "What's on that note?"

"Her appointment. Two months ago to see your favorite trombonist."

"I knew it," Trace said. "Yule. Yule's involved."

"Yeah, you knew it," she scoffed. "How'd you know it?"

"I just called police headquarters and Muffy tried to call Yule to represent her. She told Wilcox that he was her lawyer. And she told me she never met him."

Trace went back to the telephone, dialed Las Vegas direct, and asked to be put through to the shift boss on the Araby Casino floor.

When the man came on the phone, he said, "Listen, this is Trace. Something you've got to do for me right away. Okay. Check with the central bureau while I hang on. Find out what kind of rating a Nicholas Yule has. He's a lawyer in New Jersey. I'll wait. It's important."

He drummed his fingers on the tabletop while he waited. Chico was reading through the book on wills. Then the shift boss at the casino was back on the line.

"Yeah," Trace said, then listened. "Thanks, Carlo. That's a big one I owe you. Yeah, Chico and I'll be back soon."

He hung up the phone and said, "Yule's credit is cut off all over Vegas. The word is that he's in hock to the loan sharks."

"Bingo. Motive," Chico said.

Trace nodded and grabbed her arm. "Come on," he said.

"Where we going?"

"To a dance."

The band was playing "The Alleycat," and Chico asked Trace to dance.

"The Widow's Waltz?" he said. "No, thanks, I'll pass."

They stood at the rear of the American Legion hall watching Nick Yule lead his band through its final number. He was dressed in a red-white-and-blue-plaid suit. As Yule marched along the bandstand, pumping away on his trombone, his long thin hair flew around his head.

"You hadn't told me what a great beauty he was," Chico said. "With those eyeglasses and that electric suit, he looks like something you'd see in an outpatient clinic."

"Give a kid a trombone and you lead him to ruin," Trace said.

Yule's band finished and the hundred people clustered on the dance floor and at tables around it broke into applause.

"Remember, folks," Yule shouted into the microphone. "I'm Nick Yule, your musical barrister, and we play at parties, dances, and weddings. The number's in the book. Have a nice night and God bless each and every one of you."

"Go slide down a barrister," Chico mumbled.

When she and Trace reached the bandstand, Yule was putting his trombone into its case. He looked at Trace, recognized him, and nodded. When he saw Chico, he asked, "She a singer?"

"No," Trace said. "We've got two singers already."

"Huh?"

"Muffy and her brother," Trace said. "They're down at police headquarters right now, singing away. Don't you think you ought to be there to lead the band?"

"Are you trying to connect me with something?" Yule snapped. "Impugn my integrity? Is that what you're trying to do?"

"Something like that," Trace said.

"I'm warning you. You'd better be careful. This state has tough laws against slander."

"Against murder too, as I recollect," Trace said. "Suppose we move it right along."

"I didn't do anything, you know. Nothing except draw a will," Yule said.

"Well, we'll let you and Muffy and Petey sort all that out for the cops. Anyway, look at the bright side," Trace said.

"What's the bright side?" Yule asked.

"You're not going to have to worry about a booking for the next twenty years or so."

30

Trace left Chico in the car when he parked a half-block away from the Plessers' house.

After doing what he had come to do, he rang the front-door bell. Mrs. Plesser materialized on the porch, inside the screen door.

"Mr. Marks, right?"

"Right. I want to talk to Calvin."

"Err, he's not home."

"His truck's here, he's home. Send him out. Or do I call the cops?"

She thought about it for a moment, then went back inside the house, and Calvin appeared. He held a handkerchief in front of his face and was coughing.

"Sorry. I got a cold."

"No, you don't," Trace said. "What you've got is a broken nose where I popped you the other night when you and your friend jumped me."

"What are you talking about?"

"What I'm talking about is that I think you don't really want to sue anybody, 'cause if you do, all of you might go to jail for assault. That's what I'm talking about."

He turned and started away.

"By the way," he called back, "I let the air out of your tires just now. We're even."

*　　*　　*

Trace drove to police headquarters. He asked Chico, "How'd you figure it out?"

"Well, the guy who hit the lawyer, he grunted, that made karate a pretty easy bet, especially when you had on your tapes that the nurse was reading a karate magazine. But the big guy that hit you didn't grunt. So it sounded like another guy. And leaving that sanatorium billhead by the car, well, that was just stupid. And when you're talking about stupid, who else but the Plessers?"

"I thought Yule might have put them up to it," Trace said.

"I did too, at first. But not when we figured out he was involved in some murder scheme. He wouldn't want you hanging around town. That's why he called you. First, he wouldn't deal with Jeannie Callahan, and then he found out you were nosing around and that Mr. Carey had talked to you, then he wanted you out of town fast. That's why he offered to make you the same deal he turned down from that Callahan woman the day before. He wanted you gone. No, it was the Plessers' brainstorm, all by themselves, to pop you. And they left the billhead by the car so you'd take a run at Meadow Vista, thinking the hospital was behind getting you slugged."

Trace nodded and parked outside police headquarters. "Wait here. I won't be long."

When Trace came back out, Chico was eating three hot dogs from a cardboard box she held on her lap, and he stared at her.

"Hey, cut me a break," she said. "You were gone a half-hour. A girl's gotta eat, doesn't she? What'd you do? Bop that lady cop again?"

"Shhhh. You'll get us shot," Trace said. "I just gave them a statement and most of my tapes. Let them sort them out. But everybody's singing, Muffy and Petey and Yule, so we're pretty well finished with it. Wilcox told me

I might have to come back if the grand jury wants to hear from me.''

He started the car's engine. ''Christ, I'll be glad to get out of this town. Do you realize I've been here a week and I haven't met one person that I'd call really sane?''

''Good. So now we're going home?''

''One more stop,'' Trace said.

When he pulled up outside the apartment building, Chico asked, ''Who lives here?''

''The lawyer,'' Trace said. ''I'll be right down.''

''It's Trace.''

''You can't come in. I look worse than yesterday.''

''I just wanted to say good-bye. I'm leaving.''

He was answered by silence, and then the door opened slightly. Jeannie Callahan stood behind it, peering out with just one eye, hiding one side of her face.

''You heard?'' Trace said.

She nodded. ''I talked to George this morning. He told me.''

''I didn't want to leave without saying so long,'' he said.

''Yeah.''

''You know, Mrs. Carey's going to be alone for a while,'' Trace said. ''You might think about staying with her for a few days. Might do both of you some good.''

''I'll think about it,'' she said.

He hesitated. ''Well, so long, then,'' he said.

''So long,'' she said. ''Thanks for making this a one-lawyer town again.''

He started away, but she reached out a hand to stop him.

''Trace?''

''What?'' he said as he turned.

''Could we stop drinking?'' she asked.

''Could you?''

268

"I don't think so."

"I don't either," Trace said.

"We came close, didn't we?" she said.

"Close but no cigar."

"If I visit Las Vegas, will you buy me a drink?"

"As many as it takes to drag you into bed," he said.

"One'll do it. Kiss me good-bye."

He took her in his arms and kissed her hard.

"Now get out of here," she said, "Before I make you change your mind."

They were halfway to Newark Airport before Chico broke the silence.

"How come so quiet?" she said.

"Just thinking."

Five miles more, and she said, "Trace, with us, it's never going to be like it was, is it?"

Five miles more and he said, "Maybe it never was."

31

Two weeks later, Trace got a call at his Las Vegas condominium.

"This is Mitchell Carey." The voice was gravelly and labored, as if produced only by great exertion and willpower.

"How are you feeling?" Trace asked.

"Matteson says I'm getting better, but I still feel like crap. I just called to thank you."

"Do what the doctor says," Trace said. "Tell me, did you know what was going on when you were kind of out of it?"

"Sometimes I did. I could hear things and sometimes I could concentrate. Like I knew that Muffy was using Amanda. I spotted that in the hospital, but then I got worse and I couldn't do anything about it."

"Do you remember, in the sanatorium, you told me that somebody was trying to kill you?"

"I kind of remember that," Carey said.

"You were counting," Trace said. "A hundred, a hundred hundred, do you remember? Do you know what that was about?"

"I was thinking about my brain cells dying. Maybe I was counting them off," Carey said.

"Yeah. I thought that's what it was," Trace said. "So get well."

"I'm working on it. And thanks."

* * *

A week after the phone call, Trace was summoned to appear before a New Jersey grand jury. The jury subsequently indicted Muffy, her brother, and Yule for attempted murder.

Trace got in, testified, and left the same day. His ex-wife and children never knew he was in the state until it was too late for them to do anything about it.

Three months later, he received in the mail an invitation to the wedding of Jeannie Callahan and Dr. George Matteson. He saw the marriage would take place in New Jersey, so he threw the invitation away. No point in pressing his luck.

About the Author

Warren Murphy is the author of more than sixty novels and screenplays, including the satiric adventure series *The Destroyer*, with more than 25 million copies in print. He is a former newspaperman and political-campaign consultant whose hobbies are chess, mathematics, and martial arts. He lives in Teaneck, New Jersey.